ASTRA

Mahatmas and Monsters: Book II

Kim Idynne

for Sensei Robert Fusaro, with gratitude

1

Elias joined the line of bogus monsters and waited his turn. Cheap-looking capes, gowns, and wigs adorned the patrons in front of him. Most of the women wore short-skirted "sexy monster" costumes and shivered in the cold night air, but one had deviated from the trend with a Cookie Monster onesie. They waited outside of Bull's-Eye night club, chatting on the sidewalk while the doorman made a painfully slow process of checking each ID and collecting small wads of cash. Elias watched the crowd impatiently and wondered, once again, why people found it "fun" to dress as monsters. He supposed it made them feel powerful, or simply safe—like those who dressed as ghouls on All Hallows' Eve to fool the dead and the demonic. *Don't prey on me. I'm one of you.*

Elias had no interest in the night's event. He had only come to look for Leitha, his roommate. She had been spending nights away from home and returning in the early morning hours, reeking of tobacco and booze. Elias had caught her chatter every now and then, as she made plans over the phone; she had been frequenting the bars and clubs in this area, later and later into the night, until one morning she didn't come home at all.

Yet, Elias knew she was alive and unharmed. The previous night he had found her here at Bull's-Eye, at a 21-plus event dubbed "Forbidden Friday." Many in that crowd were costumed in ways that perfectly illustrated the theme: a lot of tight-fitting faux leather, and even more exposed flesh.

Though he had put his vampire ways behind him, Elias maintained a degree of stealth. He was only nineteen, but he had gained entry to the event by slipping into line behind another young, pale blond and nabbing the ID from his pocket. While the perplexed young man strode away to look for the missing card, Elias proceeded past the doorman to the main room and took a moment to adjust to the darkness—a darkness interrupted by roving multi-colored lights and blasting sound. A strobe in the center of the dance floor revealed erratic glimpses of writhing figures, clad mostly in black, some in masquerade masks. Elias restrained an irritated sigh as he scanned the floor for Leitha's figure.

On the far side of the floor, a small crowd had gathered around a fire-dancing duo. Elias searched there; no Leitha. He was about to head to the balcony when he spotted her in one of the dancing cages, gyrating and twerking within the metal bars—or trying to, anyway, in tight vinyl pants that didn't allow for much movement.

Without thinking, Elias had stormed up the spiral staircase and yanked on the cage door—but not before Leitha spotted him. She shrieked and grabbed the bars from inside. In the midst of their tug-of-war, a few of the other patrons rushed to Leitha's aid. They dragged Elias down the steps while he tried to shout over the blaring techno track that he was not attacking her, that she was his little sister, that she was underage. His pleas were unconvincing. A bouncer caught hold of him and threw him out, warning him to *Stay away unless you want my boot up your butt* before slamming the door.

Tonight's event seemed less risqué. Beside the door, the brick wall was plastered with posters advertising *Saturday Night Monster Madness. Cover charge $7, or $3 for those in costume. Cash only.*

Elias fished in his pockets. He had forgotten about the cover fee. "Of course the tackiest club in the city requires cash," he muttered, and fell silent as a hulking figure filled the doorway. A woman had stepped from the shadows, standing tall in a pair of platform boots. Her height and bulk made for an intimidating specter, but tonight she was especially foreboding in a wild silver-and-black wig, heavy eyeliner, and black lipstick. Elias recognized her as the bouncer from the previous night—the one who had easily lifted him off the floor and sent him sprawling onto the sidewalk.

She peered down at Elias with disdain, and he caught a glimpse of plastic fangs between the shiny black lips. "Hey, you," she said. "Not another step. You think I don't recognize you?"

"I'm not going in," Elias said. "I just . . . wanted to return this." He held up the stolen ID. "Someone dropped it in the club last night."

The bouncer's dark eyes narrowed as she peered at the card. "Oh, he dropped it, did he?" She snatched the ID from his grasp.

"I don't suppose you've seen my sister," Elias said. "You know . . . the woman I supposedly 'assaulted' last night."

"Oh, Leitha is your *sister*. Yes, I can see the resemblance."

Elias understood her sarcasm. Leitha was dark-skinned, while Elias was pale as a cave dweller, his hair such a light blond that it turned white in midsummer's sun. Despite the bouncer's disbelief, Elias felt a glimmer of hope. *She knows Leitha. This is the place to find her.* "We're not biologically related," he replied.

"Right." She jerked a thumb toward the sidewalk. "Get out of here if you don't want any more trouble."

"I'm going," Elias replied, and paused to cast a pleading glance at the colossal woman. "But if you see her, please do me a favor and tell her that her brother misses her."

He was halfway down the block when he spotted her in the glow of the streetlight: Leitha, dressed in a sparkly tank top and white bolero, and denim shorts much too skimpy for an early spring night. She was flanked by two men who stood much taller than she. One, a burly figure in a flannel shirt, wore a fur-covered, pointy-eared hood, and his face had been

3

painted to look like that of a gray wolf. The other, a pale, thin figure in a long black coat, wore his hair slicked back from his face.

The black-clad figure locked eyes with Elias, and Elias froze. His senses shifted, becoming keener and taking in more detail, as though time had suddenly slowed. The hair on his arms stood on the end of goosebumps. This happened sometimes—those times when he encountered actual monsters. He recognized the eyes of a vampire.

Leitha's high, enthusiastic voice reached his ears: "You should have *told* me it was monster night!" She smiled up at the werewolf, then at the vampire. Seeing that the latter was fixated on something, she followed his gaze.

She jarred to a halt. "What the . . . ." Leitha's voice softened. "He's *here* again."

"Who?" the werewolf asked.

She sighed—or hissed, perhaps. "My roommate. Thinks he's my damn dad."

"Where? This fellow?" The werewolf gestured to Elias. "The square-looking one, who looks like he's boring himself to death?"

"Yeah, that's him."

Elias spoke up: "Thank you, Leitha. I appreciate that."

She made another irritated noise and linked arms with the werewolf. "Keep between me and him, will you? He'll try to grab me, and he'll treat me like a four-year-old in front of everyone."

As Leitha and the wolf walked on, the black-clad man kept in step with them, his eyes never straying from Elias.

Elias waited until they were about to pass. He stepped quickly in front of Leitha, but he made no move to grab her. "Leitha," he said imploringly, "please talk to me."

"Did that already," she replied shortly. She held a hand palm-out at him. "I'm on my own time now. Quit trying to be my dad—and quit telling people I'm 'underage' when you know damned well I'm an adult."

4

"I . . . ." Elias fumbled for words as the trio pushed past him. He turned and started after them. "I meant that you're too young to be at a twenty-one-plus—"

The werewolf spun around. "She told you to get lost. Quit creeping."

Elias tried to go around him, but the burly man grabbed his shoulder and shoved it, nearly knocking him down.

"Leitha," Elias pleaded, "they're monsters."

A light sneer touched the werewolf's lips. "What was that?"

Elias ignored him. "We made a pact. Remember?"

The werewolf pushed him again, harder this time. "Who's a monster? Me? Seems like there's only one sicko here."

Elias kept his balance, but the next shove sent him sprawling. His already-scraped palms stung as they skidded against the pavement. Yet he persisted: "Leitha . . . please come home. I know you're bored, but at least there, you have someone who cares about you. These jerks don't. You know they don't."

She turned suddenly and came to stand at the werewolf's side. "Oh, yes, I know. You love me like a *sister*. That's grand, Elias, but not very exciting."

Leitha started away, and as Elias got to his feet, the werewolf sent him down again. Elias looked up at the man's self-satisfied smirk and felt the beginnings of rage coursing through him. He was weak, he realized. He wanted to lash out, to rise up in anger and tear the werewolf to shreds, but his new manner forbade it. The rage that he had lived with for so many years, that he had used as his fuel, had dissipated; it no longer tormented him, and it no longer served him.

The werewolf chuckled. "Stay down, mate. A skinny, stuffy weakling like you shouldn't be creeping after someone like Leitha. She has friends to protect her." He grinned and added in a low voice: "We have *plans* for her." He kicked Elias in the ribs before striding away.

Elias lay open-mouthed on the concrete. That kick had hurt. He groaned, struggled to sit up, and watched as the trio disappeared into the club. The bouncer seemed to know them; she let them in without checking IDs or collecting money. Her eyes, though, stayed on Elias, and her look was one of troubled concern. When the three had gone inside, the hulking woman started to call out to Elias, but he heaved himself up from the ground and stalked away, one hand lightly bracing his bruised ribs.

New plans formed in his mind as he headed back to his car. The walk was a long one; the city blocks were jammed with vehicles, with hardly a parking space to be found, so Elias had stowed his car in the free lot across the river. He had checked out Leitha's favorite haunts on his way to the club, and there were plenty: a sprawl of bars and cafes, and nearer to the bridge, a small park that had become a hotspot for late-night trysts. He passed the courtyard surrounded by stone pergolas, which offered shade by day and a place to hide by night. The park had looked much different on the way in; the setting sun had exposed a large playground beyond the court, cast in bright colors, the picture of innocent play. Now, shadowy figures crept into the court, moving beneath the stone canopies of the pergolas, whispering and caressing as they disappeared into darkness.

Elias wondered about them. He wondered which were lovers, and which were monsters.

His mind turned again to the two men he'd seen with Leitha. It would be easy, he thought, to get rid of them . . . with the right weapon. Elias had defeated beasts much more sinister, and with only a small, dull blade—one so dull it couldn't even cut flesh. The astra had been crafted to pierce more ethereal things; it had been crafted to pierce the soul.

The next morning, Elias drove to Achiravati Abbey, the Buddhist monastery where he had first held the astra. Back then, a bhikshuni—a Buddhist nun—had given it to him freely; she had encouraged him to use it. Elias assumed it would be the same this time. He parked in the abbey's small front lot and strode toward the dormitory, past the cheap fiberglass statue of Buddha that sat in meditative pose at the edge of a small stone court. He found Lamia, the bhikshuni, in the gardens behind the dorms. She knelt on the earth in her crimson robe, planting new seeds, though the spring was still in its early phase; she was planting the hardy seeds that would survive the chilly nights.

"Here to lend a hand?" she asked, lifting her weathered face and shrewd eyes toward Elias.

"No," he replied.

He hardly needed to say more. Lamia was already standing, beckoning him to follow, as he added: "Can I talk to you in private? I need some help."

Lamia led him to the "gathering hall"—the cabin opposite the dorms, where visitors attended classes and rituals. They strode through the small lobby and into the prayer room, and the bhikshuni gestured for Elias to sit across from her on the floor, on the deep red oriental rug that ran between the doorway and the table laden with bells and candles. As usual, Elias felt a strange mixture of peace and anxiety, as though he was suddenly split in two: one half of him sanguine and comforted, the other half afraid of whatever challenging self-analysis he might be forced to endure. In this room, Elias had experienced deeper hope and love, and pain and sadness, than he'd been capable of experiencing anywhere else. Lamia had been a part of it. Aarya, too. Elias still keenly felt the sensation of Aarya's hand on his back, directly behind his heart, as he wept with years' worth of unacknowledged grief. The memory made him shiver as he sat at the edge of the rug.

Lamia listened quietly as he entreated her: "Leitha left home. She has at least two monsters hanging around her. One of them, a werewolf, told me that I had better stay away because they have 'plans' for her. So . . . I need to borrow the astra again."

7

Lamia was silent for a moment. Then she replied calmly, "No, you may not."

Elias had braced himself for such an answer, yet he fell into a surprised silence. He waited for an explanation, but none came. "Why?" he asked.

"I was careless with the astra last time," Lamia said, "and I received a lot of grief for it."

"Careless, how?" he asked, with an edge in his voice. "Was rescuing Luka careless?"

"I know that you saved a little boy," she said. "I'm glad you saved him, and honestly, I wouldn't change my decision if I could. But Leitha is a grown woman, capable of walking away from harm."

"Hardly."

Lamia started to speak, but she hesitated, seeming to choose her words carefully. "You said 'at least two monsters.' A werewolf, and who else?"

"A vampire."

She nodded. "Are they holding her against her will?"

Elias hesitated. "No, but . . . ."

"The astra killed two people," Lamia reminded him. "And it crippled several others—for the time being. It isn't meant to be used on people who aren't ready for it."

"Then what is it meant for?"

"For those who want it, and who are ready."

"Really. I would love to hear an example of someone who felt 'ready' to tear their soul open with a metaphysical blade."

"You are an example," she said evenly. "You used it on yourself first, remember? And it has helped you, whether you realize it or not. I've seen you become calmer, kinder, more open. And through your openness you've helped others, including me. I've lived here for seven years, and I've hardly moved beyond becoming an anagarika. But—"

"I don't know Buddhist talk," Elias cut in. "What's an ana-whatever?"

8

"It means . . . someone who has been trying out monastic life for a long time, without fully committing to it. I follow the necessary precepts, but I haven't followed through with ordination. Now, though, I'm feeling ready to take the next step."

Elias peered at her curiously. He had assumed that all of the bhikshunis were "real" nuns—especially Lamia, since she appeared the oldest of the group. "Are you not ordained?"

"Not fully," she replied. "I received a novice ordination here, but the full ritual takes place in Taiwan." She paused, giving Elias a probing look. "You've helped me with that, to some degree. After talking with you . . . I feel ready to let go of being Lamia."

Elias started to ask what she meant, but Lamia continued: "Those types of changes take time. I've been a siksamana, a trainee, for much longer than is required. I've had chances to go overseas, but I found reasons to stay behind and look after the monastery. They were legitimate reasons, but they weren't the core concern. There is . . . self-doubt at the core of my reasoning. There's guilt. It's mostly personal guilt, but there are also political controversies about women becoming fully ordained—shaming and admonishments that made me worry about over-stepping. It shows in little things, like the fact that I still introduce myself with my novice name, not my dharma name. If I had been ordained even a month ago, I wouldn't have truly been ready for it. Tell me this, Elias: If you had been forced open by the astra first, instead of spending time with Aarya and experiencing all of those weeks of self-reflection, and struggle, and step-by-step transformation—do you think it would have had the same effect?"

Elias looked at her with grudging silence.

"People with deep wounds are meant to heal slowly," Lamia said. "The astra can help those who seek healing; it can cut away the last layers of residue we've become trapped in. For the two people you killed, it was such a shock that their souls fled to the afterlife. I knew it could happen, but I

9

made an excuse—because the astra is meant as a tool of healing."

"*I* didn't kill them," Elias protested. "The astra did it—and it was self-defense, in a life-and-death situation. Luka would have died. Aarya died." His voice began to break.

"Yes, and again, I wouldn't change my decision," Lamia assured him. "Nevertheless, I broke my commitment to refrain from causing harm. And I can't give you the astra so that you can swing it at every monster who gets under your skin. Leitha must come around on her own."

"She won't, though. She needs help." Elias searched Lamia's deep brown eyes for some sign of concern, but her calm remained unbroken. Something about her gaze had changed in recent months; the harsh, wily look had been replaced by a stubborn placidity.

"And what if she isn't ready to accept help?" Lamia asked.

"Yes, what if? Do I just shrug her off?"

"Sometimes you have to acknowledge that you can't control others, and that they need to decide for themselves. You're putting yourself in danger to save someone who does not want to be saved. The result won't be good for either of you."

Elias left the building with a vague feeling of defeat. Though part of him saw the logic in Lamia's argument, another part refused to accept the idea of leaving Leitha at the mercy of monsters. In the parking lot, he stopped beside his car, gazing at the two buildings that made up the monastery. Lamia had returned to the gardens, out of sight. No one else was visible on the property. The other bhikshunis were probably working, engrossed in whatever they were doing.

Elias strode back toward the gathering hall. He hadn't noticed anyone else inside, but he paused and listened at the entrance, just to make sure.

He went to the prayer room, to the table at the far end, and lifted the drapery that hung there. A few boxes were stacked behind it. Elias immediately saw the one he was looking for:

a small box of polished wood. He pulled it out and set it on the floor. Inside, wrapped in a thick red cloth, was the astra. Elias removed the knife and held it up for a moment, studying the silver blade. Though the light in the room wasn't particularly bright, the blade seemed to deeply capture and reflect that light, so that it glowed brilliantly.

They probably won't even know it's gone, Elias assured himself as he slipped the knife into his jacket. The blade wasn't sharp; nevertheless, the sensation of the astra close to his body made him nervous.

Elias put the case back where he had found it. He slipped quietly from the hall, casually glancing around to see if anyone was watching, but saw no one as he hurried back to his car.

His cell phone rang as he started the engine. Elias felt a pang of alarm as he checked the caller ID; he thought it might be Lamia, or one of the other bhikshunis, asking what he'd been doing alone in the hall.

But it was just Wen, an eighteen-year-old who took qigong classes at the monastery. Elias had tentatively started to spend time with him, mostly due to the bhikshunis' insistence that he needed to make friends.

With some reluctance, Elias answered the call. "Hello?"

"Come over for dinner," Wen said, without greeting him. "My sister's gone for the month, and I've got the place to myself."

Again, Elias hesitated.

"We can eat skewers and go look for Leitha," Wen continued. "She still hasn't come home, has she?"

"No, and she's not likely to—not on her own." Elias explained his latest adventure in the party district, finishing with the part about being shoved down by the burly werewolf.

"Wow," Wen said. "Didn't you get beat up the last time you went there, too? By a girl?"

"That was no 'girl,'" Elias replied dryly. "That was a woman in the direct lineage of the Amazons—and yes, I got roughed up. But I'm going back. I have an advantage this time."

"What advantage?"

Elias sighed. He didn't want Wen to know he'd stolen something from the monastery—no, not stolen, but *borrowed* without asking. On the other hand, it might be unwise to go to the club alone. Wen was skinny, but he was a martial arts pro, a much better fighter than Elias. "I'll tell you when I get there," Elias said.

"So you're coming?"

"Sure. What time?"

"Whenever," Wen said. "You won't be interrupting anything."

Wen lived a few blocks away from the free lot where Elias parked during his searches for Leitha. Wen's apartment (or rather, his sister's apartment) overlooked the river, and from the living room window Elias could see the beginning of the route he'd walked: the brew house just across the bridge and the run-down bowling alley beside it. After that was the park known for licentious meetings and petty crime, and then an upscale cocktail lounge, and a string of bars and cafes—and, finally, the peculiar club where he had last spotted Leitha.

Elias ate dinner quickly and urged Wen to hurry. "We should leave before it gets dark," he insisted. "It's a long walk."

"Then, let's drive."

"And park where? It's probably full by now."

Wen was frowning at him. "What's with your ribs? You keep sticking your hand in your jacket, like your ribs hurt."

"Oh . . . ." Elias reached inside his jacket again. "They do hurt, but it isn't that." He withdrew the astra. "It's this."

Wen's concern turned to puzzlement. "What is it?"

"It's called an astra. It's . . . ." Elias trailed off, not knowing how to explain.

12

"That's an astra blade?" Wen leaned forward, studying the small blade. "A real one?"

"You know about it?" Elias asked.

"Well, just in theory. It's kind of a legend in qigong—like an astral dragon or a tethered eye. Where'd you get it?"

"I borrowed it from the monastery." Elias hesitated and added, "I sort of borrowed it without asking, but they let me use it before, and this is an emergency. Like I said . . . ."

"Yeah, some creeps have got hold of Leitha. You think this will work on them?"

"Yeah, it'll work. It's not the first time I used it. In fact, it won't be the first time I've used it to protect Leitha."

As Wen gazed at the astra, Elias gave him a quick once-over, studying his lean and muscular frame. True, Wen was small and skinny—but during his tai chi competitions, his usual goofy demeanor dissipated, and his jovial eyes became intensely focused. With the astra and Wen's fighting skills, the two of them were likely to stay safe—even if they failed to drag Leitha away from whatever toxic situation she'd gotten herself into.

"Well," Wen said, "let's get going, then. Leitha's probably wondering why it's taking so long for you to crash her party."

As they walked across the bridge, Elias kept his eyes on the sprawl of buildings beyond the riverbank, half expecting to spot Leitha or her companions among them. "Let's go straight to Bull's-Eye," he suggested. "We can visit the other places on our way back, if we need to." Elias glanced down at the astra. The setting sun should have cast it in an orange glow, but the metal seemed to glow with its own blue-tinted light. He felt a bit of hope as he looked at it—as though he could see its power in that glow. "Even if we run into a dozen werewolves and vampires, this thing can take them down easily."

"Where exactly is this club?" Wen asked.

"It's about ten blocks that way," Elias said, gesturing with the astra toward the city skyline. He opened his mouth to say

13

more, but the words died as he realized that the astra had slipped from his grasp. Elias looked at his hand in disbelief. It was still suspended in mid-air, hovering over the guard rail, the fingers now clasped around empty space. The archaic dagger had sailed over the rail, into the deep waters below.

Wen swore as he leaned against the railing. He craned his neck to look into the river and swore again. Then he cast Elias a remorseful look. "Well, that's a goner. Was that the only one?"

2

Elias returned to Achiravati Abbey with every intention of confessing to Lamia. He knew full well that keeping such a secret from her would only make things worse—but when he saw her kneeling in the garden, her weathered face set in a look of grim determination, he was overcome by a strange chill. His jaw clenched, as if to stop him from greeting her, and his feet led him back the way he had come.

He found reasons to justify being a coward. Of all the bhikshunis, Lamia was the one Elias did not want to cross. He had often detected a darkness behind her gaze—though perhaps she simply reminded him of his own dark side.

Elias skulked around the gathering hall, hoping to find one of the other nuns. He'd made a point of showing up during the bhikshunis' work time. Lamia generally preferred working outdoors, while Vela, one of the gentler women, could usually be found at the weaving loom. Elias found her in a back room, where she sat weaving a small tapestry. Elias hesitated in the doorway, reluctant to start a conversation about his misdeed. He also didn't quite know how to greet Vela. Everyone at the abbey called her by a long title that Elias could never remember—something like Venerable Thumb Tongue George.

She wore her bhikshuni robes, crimson with a bit of yellow peeking from underneath. She didn't look up, but continued to work, drawing a wooden skewer between a spread of fine threads, working so slowly that Elias felt a pang of impatience as he watched. Vela was a beginner, he decided. She was working with only three colors, blue and gold and violet, and creating simple shapes: Vs and diamonds, a single pagoda, and something that looked like a crude winged dragon. Her work was unimpressive compared to the elaborate tapestries that adorned the prayer room.

Finally, she glanced up at him. "You look anxious, Elias," she said, and resumed weaving. "I heard that Leitha ran off. Are you worried about her?"

"Ah . . . I am. But . . . that's not why I'm here."

Vela didn't respond, so Elias took a deep breath and continued. "I had a bit of an incident with the astra," he admitted.

Vela's hands stopped moving. Her eyes fixed on him. "What kind of incident?"

"I . . . dropped it." He paused. "In the Mississippi River."

The bhikshuni didn't react the way he'd anticipated. She went back to maneuvering the wooden skewer and emitted a quiet sigh.

"By accident," Elias added.

"Yes, I assumed as much."

"Can we get another one?" he asked. "I kind of need it."

"I see. And what do you 'kind of' need the astra for?"

"Same thing as last time. Too many monsters lurking around."

"There are always too many monsters," Vela replied. "A single astra can't cure all of them." She lowered her hands and placed them in her lap. "It's probably for the best that the astra is out of reach. We will procure another one when it's needed."

"I need it *now*, to save Leitha," Elias insisted.

"Is that so?"

"Yes, you know it's so. I met the people she's been hanging around with, and they're about as seedy as you can get. A brute werewolf, a sleazy vampire, and who knows what else. They hang around a smutty club in—"

"Is she being held against her will?" Vela interrupted.

Elias suppressed a groan. "Not you, too. Does it really matter?"

"A social worker came to our seminar last night," she replied. "A corrections social worker, someone I met through our prison outreach program. I talked to him afterward, and we had a discussion about how hard it is to not be able to save people from their own decisions. He advised me that we should focus on helping those who want to be helped. People have the right to make bad decisions, despite your love and advice. Leitha isn't being held prisoner. She's living the life she chose. If she has a change of mind, you can decide whether you want to help her, but the burden is on her now."

Elias realized he'd been gritting his teeth. He unclenched them and said, "You didn't answer my question. Is there another astra?"

Surprisingly, Vela smiled—a thin, tight smile, as though she was trying to hide her amusement. "Probably, but I don't know where. If you want another astra blade, you'll have to make one."

"And how can I do that?"

She shrugged. "Train yourself in the ways. Fix yourself first before you consider how to fix the world around you. To create an astra, you have to decide how to make yourself, and how to mold your own power, and how to traverse dimensions. Only then can you mold and secure an inter-dimensional instrument of power."

"Right. In other words, it can't be done."

"It can—but not now, not by you. If you want to make an astra, you have to apprentice yourself first."

"Apprentice myself to what? Are you trying to convert me?"

Again, the bhikshuni gave a slight shrug of her shoulders. "A good start, for you, would be to become mindful of your energy. You should start attending our qigong sessions. I know you can afford them."

Elias restrained a sigh.

He had, in fact, attended the abbey's qigong sessions, which had lately been hosted by a guest teacher. He found them unbearably slow and boring, a spectacle of sweatpants-clad people who were either too old or too lazy for real exercise.

"I know you didn't love qigong," Vela continued, "but we have another guest teacher who's holding classes for the next two weeks. You might enjoy learning from him. He's a little more . . . interesting." Vela glanced at Elias. Her gaze drifted downward. "Did you get into a fight? Your hands are scratched."

"It wasn't a fight. I got knocked around when I was trying to talk to Leitha." Elias turned his hands palms-up and scrutinized the scab-crusted flesh. "I miss the old days, when a scratch disappeared in a minute or two. These cuts still sting. They hardly look any different from yesterday."

"That's good," Vela replied gently. "The kind of rapid healing you had before—that wasn't the healthy kind. It wasn't *any* kind. It was caused by outrage at being wounded, and a refusal to endure a slow healing process. That process takes the wound from the body and hides it in the astral body—in the spirit plane, where it can't be found and truly resolved. It leaves you without any time to consider your wounds."

"My scraped hands don't give me much to consider."

"Don't they?" Again, Vela looked impassively at Elias' injured hands. "You should appreciate the fact that your wounds are healing normally. It's a good sign. But if you want to become even more grounded, and more powerful—*truly* powerful—you should take the next step. You can start by disciplining yourself with qigong and tai chi."

"Which you offer here, for a fee," he replied dryly.

"We offer them for a good reason. I would let you attend them in exchange for volunteer work, but there is already the matter of the theft you committed. What will you do to pay off the cost of the astra, and of your own transgression?"

18

Elias raised his eyebrows. "The cost of the astra? How much did it cost?"

A dry chuckle escaped Vela's lips. "I'll let you figure that out."

"I really didn't plan to steal it," Elias insisted. "I borrowed it. It was just sitting there, in—"

"Elias," she said in a warning tone. Her eyes flashed with a stern look—not anger, but disappointment.

"Sorry," he said.

"Elias, do you even know what we used the astra for?"

He hesitated. "Is it not for stabbing monsters?"

"I brought the astra here," Vela said. "It was given to me as a gift by another qigong master. I used it to open the ethereal parts of people that were clenched, blocked, and traumatized—from a distance, without direct physical contact. The astra isn't meant to be used in the way that you used it. When you have a better understanding of qigong, you will better understand the astra." She turned away, giving Elias a dismissive wave of her hand. "There's an open house on Friday afternoon, and another on Sunday. Our new teacher, Shi Miao Xing, will give a demonstration and a short lesson—free of charge. There's nothing to stop you from leaving if you don't like it."

Elias finally released the sigh he'd been withholding. "Thanks anyway," he said, taking care to sound disappointed.

With the qigong session, too, Elias anticipated a letdown. The day was cloudy and gloomy—not ideal for an outdoor class. He picked up Wen and arrived late on purpose, hoping to avoid the banal small talk and cheery smiles that preceded activities at the monastery. Wen gave him an earful about his tardiness: "I really wanted to listen to Shi Miao Xing's introduction. We'll have to stick around afterwards and try to talk to him. From what I've heard, this guy is no joke. He's a genuine practitioner of Shaolin qigong."

Elias chuckled. "Shaolin, huh? Then he's a phony for sure."

Wen gave him a puzzled glance. "Why do you say that?"

"Shaolin is a fictional martial arts group."

"Um, it is not. Shaolin is one of the oldest types of kung fu. It was developed at the Shaolin temple in China."

"It's fictional," Elias insisted.

"Just because you've seen it in movies, that doesn't mean it's fake. The temple was built at Mount Song more than fifteen hundred years ago. The first monk who—"

"Fine, fine. Shows how much I know. The only thing I'm certain of is that it's going to be another half hour of me trying to attribute meaning to a lot of silly and painfully slow gestures."

Wen settled back into the passenger seat and stared ahead. "You're always such a downer," he muttered.

At the monastery, they found the attendees spread out just beyond the small courtyard, on the grass that sloped gently upward toward the buildings. A young monk— Shi Miao Xing, presumably—stood on the upper part of the slope, where he could be easily seen by the crowd. Elias stood at the back of the group, ignoring Wen's whispered pleas to move closer.

The group was silent, fixated on the monk as he progressed through a series of fluid, sweeping motions. Shi Miao Xing hadn't donned a gaudy sweatsuit for the demonstration, as other guest teachers were prone to do. He was dressed in a dark, layered robe that tapered out at the bottom and at the end of the sleeves, giving a flowing and graceful quality to his movements. Elias soon became captivated by the man's seeming power and grace. His movements were familiar: initially natural and powerful, as though the monk was channeling a strain of beautiful unseen energy—but, while Elias had quickly become bored with previous routines, he remained intrigued by Shi Miao Xing. The monk's movements would suddenly slow down at times,

20

usually when he drew his hands back toward his body—a gesture that added sensuality to his movements. And his fingers, rather than flailing stupidly in the air, seemed to play the invisible strings of the cosmos. He could have been the star of a fine arts performance—a skilled dancer rather than a monk.

Elias began to feel something moving within him, an energy awakening. After just a few minutes of the simple, stunning display, he once again started to believe in qi.

Yet, when the monk asked the audience to follow his movements, Elias felt overcome with the usual self-consciousness. Wen moved to the edge of the crowd and crept closer to the front, wanting a better view, but Elias remained in the back, where no one would watch him.

The participants had enough space between them to allow a good view of the man at the front. Elias followed along, awkwardly at first, then with more ease as the monk went into a series of repeated movements: one hand up, one sweeping down to "gather energy into a ball" near his solar plexus. Elias followed him into the next step, his right hand moving gracefully upward while his left moved down. Elias started to transition out of the position, but he stopped when he realized that Shi Miao Xing wasn't moving. The monk remained motionless for several seconds, looking out at the group, until his gaze fell on Elias. In that moment the clouds broke, allowing a beam of sunlight to pass through and douse the monk in sudden illumination. Shi Miao Xing seemed to glow, and as Elias stood there wondering why that position seemed so familiar, and why it affected him with sudden emotion, he realized: That was the position Aarya had died in. The *bhūmisparśa* pose—that was what the bhikshunis called it.

Perhaps it was the bald head that reflected the sunlight so strongly. That strange, intense glow, and the sudden blur of Elias' tears, created some sort of momentary illusion. In the deep brown of Shi Miao Xing's eyes, Elias suddenly saw Aarya's eyes looking back at him: that same shade of brown,

21

that same calmness, that same subtle power. And love—he saw love there, too, gentle and undemanding.

The monk was moving again. Elias' arms trembled as he tried to follow along. The cycle of repeated gestures came to a close, and the monk ended the session, inviting the participants to come to him with questions.

A little old woman in front of Elias turned around and smiled at him. She, too, had tears in her eyes. Before he could react, she came to him and clasped his hand, speaking to him in what sounded like Mandarin. The man next to her also looked up at Elias; he smiled and chuckled softly as the woman squeezed his hand, patted it, and released it.

"What was that about?" Wen asked as the couple ambled away.

"I have no idea," Elias replied.

Wen's eyes narrowed. He scrutinized Elias' face. "Dude, were you crying?"

"No," Elias replied sharply. "My eyes are just watering." He put a sleeve to his eyes, trying to hide the evidence. "It's the sunlight—it got intense all of a sudden."

Wen nodded slowly. "Yeah . . . yeah, it did. But you're totally crying."

Elias tried to scowl, but he didn't succeed. He wasn't in a scowling kind of mood.

"No judgment," Wen added. "I'm just saying, you cried during qigong." He smiled. "Maybe it's a good fit for you after all. I'm going to talk to Shi Miao Xing, okay? I'll just be a few minutes."

Elias waited much longer than a few minutes. Wen delved into a cheerful, animated conversation with the monk and another practitioner, and he was still grinning on the drive back.

"You're going to the next class, right?" he prodded Elias. "Even though he's teaching beginner-level stuff, I'll still go just to watch Shi Miao Xing."

"He did impress me," Elias admitted.

22

"Oh, yeah, I noticed." Wen flashed a sly smile, using his fingertips to trace invisible tear streaks down his cheeks.

"Knock it off," Elias said.

"He impressed me, too. I'll try not to let my crush show when I'm at his sessions, but I'm not making any promises."

"By all means, if you want to make a fool of yourself."

"We hit it off, though, didn't you think so?" Wen asked. "Afterwards?"

Elias gave him a look of disbelief. "He's a monk."

"I'm not trying to get anything from him. I just think he's amazing, and I'm happy just thinking he's amazing." Wen shifted in his seat, putting his hands behind his head. "Don't you feel much more at peace after that session? I just feel . . . *good.*"

Elias didn't respond, though the session had indeed left him with a sense of calm. That feeling vanished, though, the moment he arrived home and turned the key in his front door.

The lock gave no resistance. It had been left unlocked— something Elias never did.

He opened the door and called out tentatively: "Leitha?"

No answer came. He hadn't really expected one. The townhouse opened to a small entryway, and beyond that a sitting room—and there, in the middle of the coffee table, was Leitha's key. No note, no explanation, but Elias got the message. Quietly, he went to Leitha's bedroom and peeked inside. The closet door had been left open, revealing mostly empty space, except for a few unwanted garments that had been discarded on the floor. The photos had been removed from the wall, the small electronics were gone, and the vanity was no longer strewn with cosmetics.

"Damn it," Elias whispered. "Leitha, you damned fool."

She was gone—really gone this time.

After a fitful night, Elias resolved himself to a different strategy. If he couldn't persuade Leitha, he had to at least know where she was living, and who with, and under what conditions. He would make a more discreet attempt—not with an astra blade, but with a cheap party costume.

The vampire cape and plastic fangs had been a gift from Leitha. At the time, she'd had her mind set on going to a Halloween bonfire, and she thought it would be amusing if Elias came along dressed as a vampire, and she as a succubus: the monster forms they had once embodied. For herself, she had purchased a skimpy black girdle with fishnet tights and a pair of curved horns. Elias humored her and tagged along. Leitha, determined to party and meet people, instead spent much of the night trying to keep the over-sized horns from sliding off her head.

Elias used a tub of braiding gel that Leitha had left behind to slick back his hair. He slipped the plastic fangs onto his teeth. Elias gazed at his reflection; then he opened a vanity drawer and pulled out a stub of Leitha's black eyeliner. After lining his eyes, he reddened his lips with a bit of lipstick.

"That's more like it," he whispered, and bared the plastic fangs at himself. A brief pang of guilt passed through him. He closed his mouth, donned the cape over his black clothes, and headed for the door.

Wen greeted him at the free lot. He, too, had dressed up—in a full-body hot dog costume, hooded at the top to make his head look like the rounded tip. A strip of yellow mustard meandered up to his chin, and a thick fabric bun encased his slender figure.

Elias stared in dismay. "This isn't Halloween," he said crisply. "It's monster madness." He enunciated slowly: "*Monster.*"

"This is the only costume I have," Wen replied.

"You know you'll have to walk all the way through downtown in that, right?"

"This is actually pretty easy to walk in." Wen demonstrated, taking a few steps and swinging his arms. "It's fine."

"It's really not. Take it off."

24

Wen's shoulders must have sagged; the fabric bun dipped slightly. "What am I gonna wear? There aren't any costumes on sale this time of year."

"I didn't expect you to buy a costume. I brought this." Elias held up a plastic package, waving it in front of Wen. The label read: *Pro FX Zombie Makeup*. "Take that thing off. I'll throw it in my car, and we can—"

"No, I have to go back up. I'm, uh, not wearing a lot of clothes under this thing."

Contrary to Wen's claim, the giant hot dog was not easy to walk in—not in narrow stairwells and doorways. Elias helped Wen free himself when the fabric bun caught on a door handle and got walloped by the bun seconds later. "Maybe don't walk next to me," Wen advised.

Elias waited for him to dress, and then he used the makeup kit and Leitha's red lipstick to create a guise of open wounds and rotting flesh. When Wen looked sufficiently repugnant, the two began the long trek to Bull's-Eye.

The sun set well before they arrived. The light above the entry door shone on tonight's bouncer: a man in a Victorian-style vampire costume, with a velvet, gold-buttoned vest over a puffy-sleeved white shirt, and a thick cape hanging heavy at his sides. Not a real vampire, and not the giant female bouncer who would likely throw Elias across the walkway. He let out a quiet sigh of relief.

They found the club already packed. A long, careful search of painted faces and masked figures turned up no sign of Leitha or her new companions.

"Could that be her?" Wen pointed to a short figure in a Grover costume; the wearer's face was hidden by a full-head plush mask.

"Absolutely not. Sexy costumes only. Leitha wouldn't be caught dead in Sesame Street." Elias gave a frustrated glance around the room and covered his ears. "Let's call this a fail. If I have to listen to this godawful techno music for . . . ."

He trailed off as a familiar face caught his eye—not Leitha's, but that of the werewolf he'd found in her company the week before. He was dressed much the same way, in jeans and a flannel shirt, minus the costume paint and hood. He was moving toward the back of the club, past the dance floor and cocktail tables.

Elias nudged Wen. "Look. That's one of the guys Leitha was with. The big guy in the flannel shirt."

Wen turned, spotting the werewolf just before he disappeared through a stage-side door. "Is that the one who beat you up?"

"He pushed me." Elias looked around again, saw no one else of note. "Let's go."

"We're leaving?"

"We're following him."

"Uh . . . ."

"Don't worry. If anyone stops us, we'll say we were looking for the bathroom."

Elias started for the back before Wen could argue. He peeked behind the metal door and found an empty hall. Wen followed him into it reluctantly.

Inside, another door opened to a storage space cluttered with electronics and janitorial supplies. The next led to a small, dank restroom. Elias placed his hand on the knob of a third door and hesitated. A strange sensation passed through him—a warning, a pang of dread and certainty, as though he could sense the presence of supernatural predators nearby. He looked at Wen, whose makeup suddenly looked too real in the low light: dark circles around his nervous eyes, the rest of his face pale and streaked with rotting wounds and congealed blood. Elias resisted a shudder. He steeled himself and quietly opened the door.

Inside was Leitha's new vampire companion. He sat on a plush three-section couch at the back of the small lounge, dressed stylishly in a white shirt and black suit jacket, flanked by a small, brown-haired woman in a cocktail dress and a dazed-looking young man with bloodshot eyes. In front of them was a long table scattered with half-finished glasses of red wine and small plates of hors d'oeuvres—fruit, jams, and something that looked like raw beef.

Elias hardly glanced at the other figures. His gaze was locked on the vampire. The whites of the creature's eyes seemed almost luminescent, his gaze so intense that it took Elias some time to notice another figure that seemed eerily out of place: a child, a boy of about seven or eight, sitting alone on the right-hand side of the sectional. He stared vacantly up at Elias.

"Well, well," the vampire said. "What a surprise."

Elias' gaze moved back to those penetrating eyes. He found himself unable to speak, or even to think of something to say. He hadn't planned this carefully enough, he realized. The idea had been to learn more about Leitha's new companions, but now that he was face to face with the vampire, he was overcome with a certainty that he did not want to know this creature.

The werewolf turned. He made a sudden sound of disbelief, then swore under his breath and started toward Elias.

"Just a moment." The vampire held up a hand. "Stand down. Elias, come inside." He tilted his head slightly, looking past Elias. "Bring your friend. You are both welcome here. I think we should clear up the little misunderstanding we had on our last meeting. Lovely costumes, by the way. I especially like your friend's visage of living death—and you, Elias, you wear the vampire well."

Still, Elias didn't react. The vampire beckoned him impatiently. "Come in, make yourself comfortable. Leitha isn't here—but you know, that's probably for the best. She wouldn't be in a welcoming mood." The vampire smiled—a small, cryptic smile. Beside him, the woman also curved her lips into a grin, and her eyes shone with mockery. "She is good company, though, to those who appreciate her," the vampire continued. "Very sweet. Sometimes too sweet, I think, when it comes to men, but I've always found it a bit supercilious to meddle in the affairs of consenting adults. Don't you agree?"

Move, Elias prodded himself. *This is what you wanted, so act on it. Don't let him dominate you.*

Slowly, Elias went into the room. He moved toward the little boy—presumably the safest of the group—but remained standing. "I'm glad to hear that last week was a misunderstanding," he said, as Wen silently joined him. "What exactly is it that you misunderstood?"

"Oh, here we go again—another misinterpretation. I believe *you* were the one who misunderstood." The vampire paused, eyeing Elias steadily, and added: "You called me an uncaring jerk, though you didn't know me. You called me a monster. I wasn't in costume, so naturally, I was perplexed. What was it about me that you found so monstrous?" He paused again but received no answer. "Leitha suggested that perhaps you saw me as somewhat similar to yourself. A monster is always best at identifying another one; we both know that the true self can be completely opposite from what's on the surface."

Elias struggled to find his voice. "You have some insight into that, do you?" Before the vampire could answer, Elias added: "This is a nice little space you have back here. Is this the VIP lounge?"

The vampire laughed. "No. Plenty of people show up here who have no importance at all—but some of them prove to be useful. Some can even be fun. Take Leitha, for instance. She's both. In fact, she's making herself very useful as we speak."

Elias' teeth clenched. The edges of the plastic fangs pressed into his gums. "How so?"

"Well, she's entitled to discretion, and I respect her privacy—and she *is* doing something rather private. Private, but profitable."

Wen, leaning back against the wall, made a sound of disgust and stood up straight. "What a scum," he whispered. He moved close to Elias and tugged on the black cape. "Let's go."

The vampire's gaze flicked to Wen. "No, no, please stay," he said with a lingering smile. "Now that I've gotten that bit of hard honesty out of the way, we can chat about something that's more agreeable to everyone. You must tell me who did your makeup." His eyes brightened as he looked back at Elias. "Was it you? You do have a knack for turning people into living corpses." The smile widened into a cruel curve. "Like I said, it's very convincing; I would mistake you for the undead, if you didn't have so much anxious life in your eyes. The undead don't get nervous. They have no passion."

Wen replied dryly: "Neither does a pathetic, passive-aggressive shell of a man."

The vampire's mocking smile vanished.

The exchange brought Elias to his senses. He felt a flash of envy toward Wen. Usually, Elias was the one to come up with scathing comments, while Wen was more amiable. *Get it together*, he admonished himself—but before he could act, the werewolf made a grab for Wen, who easily twisted out of his grasp. "Don't get so familiar," Wen said. "I don't even know you."

The vampire agreed: "There's no need, Latham. Petty jabs only offend the thin-skinned."

Elias countered: "Yes, and claims of being thick-skinned are only necessary for people who aren't." His mind raced; he tried to think of a way to nudge the vampire into giving up something about Leitha. "Private, but profitable," he repeated. "Sounds like the sort of 'private' that's illegal here, no matter how consensual."

"I wouldn't dare. My club gets enough flak for its bondage nights and risqué dancers."

"*Your* club," Elias said. "You're the owner?"

29

The vampire hesitated. For a moment, Elias felt like he was gaining ground. He gestured to the boy who sat silently in front of him. "Do you also get flak for bringing children to your adults-only events?"

"Close-knit families like us support one another however we can—whether it's child care, emotional support . . . ." The vampire continued with emphasis: "*Financial* support, or whatever the need may be. And Leitha is, I assure you, a member of *our* family, by her own choosing. She may have chosen you before you started mingling with self-righteous old ladies, but chopping vegetables and pulling weeds with a bunch of drab nuns never suited Leitha. Neither did living with a bore who gave up his power because of a naïve weakling—a weakling whose over-confidence cost her her life." Again, the vampire held up a hand—at Elias this time. "Don't look so outraged just yet. Tell me this: if I was truly 'thin-skinned' enough to take offense to you, do you really think you would have the power to leave this room unharmed? Your body is weak now. Your whole being is weak . . . ." His gaze fell to Elias' cape. "And you don't seem to have your pretty little knife."

The vampire looked penetratingly at Elias, saw the look of realization on his face. "Yes, Leitha told me. She told me plenty about you, even when she knew it might put you in danger. You and your friend are free to leave now, and when you do, know that you are leaving because your existence is of absolutely no consequence to me—or to Leitha."

Wen was tugging at Elias again, more insistently this time. "Elias. Let's go."

They left quietly, under the unbroken stares and triumphant smiles of their hosts. In the hall, Elias charged toward the door to the dance floor, rushing to leave behind the monster in the lounge—him, and everything he'd said.

"What now?" Wen asked as they stepped onto the front sidewalk. "I don't know if I believe what he implied about

Leitha. It might be true, but he might have just said it to get under your skin."

"Well, he definitely *did* get—" Elias' words slurred, mangled by the plastic fangs, which were slipping from his teeth. He stopped next to a trash can and reached into his mouth, yanking the plastic strips away. "Damn things. They're . . . ." He trailed off, staring at the fangs in his palm. He lifted his other hand and examined it.

"What's wrong?" Wen asked.

Elias dropped the plastic strips into the trash. He held his hands palms-up in the light of the streetlamp. "Look," he said quietly.

"I'm looking. What is it?"

"My scrapes are gone."

"Well . . . they healed, right? You got them a week ago."

"The scabs fell off, but I still had red marks when we went into the club. They're completely gone."

They checked again, scrutinizing Elias' palms for even the slightest mark, but found none. Elias lifted a hand to his mouth again, gingerly pressing a fingertip against one canine tooth, then another.

"What is it?" Wen pressed him.

Elias didn't answer. On his own teeth, his real ones, he could feel the beginning growth of fangs.

31

3

On the front lawn of Achiravati Abbey, Elias and Wen sat beneath a shady tree, waiting for the day's tai chi session to begin. Elias had a new purpose, now, in pursuing such arts: he was chasing peace, trying to ward off the new sense of fear and anger that had triggered the regrowth of his fangs. The vampire's words had, indeed, gotten under his skin. They had crept unbidden into his psyche and snaked into his physical form.

"I don't get it," Wen told him. His thoughts were on Elias, but his eyes scanned the grounds for Shi Miao Xing, who would be demonstrating along with a guest teacher. "If you really were a vampire before, and you recovered from it, or whatever—how can you start turning into a vampire again? No one bit you."

"It's still in me," Elias admitted. "I don't think it ever really goes away. Once it's in you, it just becomes a choice of whether to manifest it or not." He paused. "I think it'll be a part of me for the rest of my life."

Wen still didn't look at him, but Elias saw a troubled expression in his eyes. "Are you sure your hands weren't already healed? I didn't see any scratches on your hands last night."

"Did you look at my palms before we went into the lounge?"

"Well, no."

"I'm certain of it. That crappy sidewalk did a number on my hands, but now there's nothing. My rapid healing came back, and even my fangs started to come back, when that creep made all those digs about Aarya—and about how I'm a boring idiot who gave up my power. It got to me, so much that my vampirism started to surge up again. I . . . wanted to use it to tear him apart." Elias saw a sudden distracted look on Wen's face. He turned and saw Shi Miao Xing approaching from the parking lot, dressed in his long gray and black robes, striding up the hill beside a frumpy-looking man in sweats. Elias got to his feet. "Here comes your crush. Let's find a good spot."

Elias really did want to do well at tai chi, to patiently develop a new type of strength, but he felt his patience ebbing as the guest teacher droned on about the importance of the bow stance: the angles of the stance, the metaphor of the bow and arrow, how much to bend the knee, how easily one could shift from one bow step to another, and blah, blah, blah. After the first fifteen minutes, during which the attendees learned a few standing positions and how to make a simple fist, Elias leaned close to Wen and whispered: "What's with all the boring monologues?"

Wen shushed him, but Elias persisted: "I don't even need to use martial arts. I can just talk about it for half an hour, and my opponents will be bored to death."

The second half of the session was more active, though the movements proceeded at a frustratingly slow pace. Elias took deep breaths as he moved, reminding himself to focus—but a tiny, nagging voice in his head warned him that this was all *too* slow, too weak, and useless when it came to fighting monsters.

As if Shi Miao Xing could read his thoughts, he added a fitting piece of advice as the session closed: "If the pace of tai chi makes you feel impatient, remember that if you wish to conquer the negativity around you, you must first conquer yourself. The Buddha taught that it is better to conquer yourself than to win a thousand battles; then, the victory is yours. Once it is truly yours, it cannot be taken away from you, not by angels or demons, by heaven or hell." The monk's gaze rested on Elias as he spoke; his eyes shone with a gentle compassion.

Once again, Elias felt a surge of emotion as he looked back at Shi Miao Xing—a mix of feelings in which grief was the strongest. He blinked as tears welled in his eyes.

As the group dispersed, Wen turned to Elias and made a small sound of surprise. "You're crying again."

"Fine," Elias conceded. "I admit it. It was that thing Shi Miao Xing just said. I took it personally."

"The thing about conquering yourself? Was that sad?" Wen turned, squinting at the few stragglers that had crowded around the monk and the guest teacher. "You should talk to him. Or, at least, to one of the nuns. You're going to tell them what happened, right?"

Elias hesitated.

"Elias, you have to. They can help you."

"I know they can. But they're also going to tell me to stop chasing after Leitha."

"Well . . . ."

"And maybe they're right, for the time being, but what if she really gets into trouble, and there's no one to help her? Those people—those *scum* . . . they're really dangerous. I just want to be there for Leitha when she changes her mind."

Wen sighed. "Talk to *someone*, though, okay? I feel like I'm not much help." He gestured to the monk, who was saying a cheerful goodbye to the last of the attendees. "Look, he's free. And he's looking at you. Let's go talk to him. You don't have to tell him everything, but at least tell him about the struggles you're having. Maybe he'll help."

Elias looked hesitantly at the monk. Shi Miao Xing was alone now, watching him, his eyes curious and welcoming.

"Look," Elias said to Wen, "I know you jump on every opportunity to talk to Shi Miao Xing, but . . . this time, let me talk to him alone."

"Sure. I'll wait up there, in the meeting hall."

Elias watched him go. The monk continued to wait expectantly, likely knowing that Elias needed help. Shi Miao Xing had that air about him, a gentle intuition that saw the pain and fear in other people's souls and was ready with wise words and a kind, assuring disposition. Elias took a few steps toward him, but he came to a dead stop as tears filled his eyes.

Shi Miao Xing approached, still smiling gently, the robes swishing around his ankles. Elias couldn't stop the tears; they spilled onto his cheeks, and his breath became shallow and ragged. He quickly wiped his eyes as Shi Miao Xing came face to face with him.

"Give me your hand," the monk said.

Elias wiped his hand on his jeans and extended it. Shi Miao Xing clasped it in both of his hands. After a pause, he reached up and placed one palm on top of Elias' head.

"Sorry," Elias sniffled, though he knew he didn't need to apologize. "I don't know why I'm crying."

"You've been hurt," the monk replied.

The words opened a vault of grief buried deep in Elias' soul. He shook with quiet sobs; his vision became obscured by a flood of tears. Shi Miao Xing continued to hold Elias' hand, and the crown of his head, as he wept.

"Tai chi moves and opens things inside of you," Shi Miao Xing said. He spoke clearly, though with a distinct Chinese

35

accent. He added: "A lot of people don't let themselves weep, and it comes out during practice. Do you see it as a weakness?"

Elias didn't know how to answer. After a moment, though, he simply whispered: "Yes."

The monk was quiet for a while. Suddenly, he asked: "Do you have a place to live?"

The question confused Elias. The monk clarified: "Some people who come here are homeless."

"Oh," Elias said. "Yes. I have a home."

"You have an internet connection?"

"Uh . . . yes."

"You can find tai chi and qigong videos on YouTube. Use those to practice. Do at least an hour every day: tai chi, qigong, guided meditation—all of these things will help you, but you have to slow down. Think about the energy of the practice, not the goal of becoming powerful. Every day. Okay?"

Elias nodded.

The monk squeezed his hand; he withdrew his own hands and made a slight bow. "Let's talk again next time. Don't forget: at least an hour every day." Shi Miao Xing looked into Elias' eyes, and his smile deepened, all peace and tranquil power.

Elias decided that he had been wrong. That vampire, the creep at the club— Shi Miao Xing could blow him away.

He watched as the monk retreated to the lot, where the sweats-clad teacher waited with a car. Alone and still weeping, Elias felt his face flush with sudden embarrassment. He began to pace the gently sloping hill, waiting for the tears to subside.

As he walked, he remained fixated on Shi Miao Xing's kind but powerful presence. Elias asked himself: *Can I really become that?* The bhikshunis insisted that anyone could achieve such peace, but it seemed a long and doubtful journey for Elias. *That isn't me. I don't have it in me. Or do I?*

He promised himself, then, that he would heed Shi Miao Xing's advice. He would seek peace on YouTube.

When he had stopped sniffling and his eyes had dried, Elias headed for the gathering hall. The front door opened to a small lobby with a new loveseat and a couple of plush chairs set up in the corner. Wen lounged on one of the chairs, and on the loveseat was Ana, a young volunteer who was fairly new to the scene—a seventeen- or eighteen-year-old, still in high school, with long, dark hair and warm eyes.

Elias immediately tensed. He disliked Ana—not because she wasn't an agreeable person, but because she was too agreeable. She had a habit of looking at Elias with a too-eager smile, a too-interested brightness in her eyes, a look that screamed "I am interested in you, and I need you to know it." Ana had acted that way from the first glance, as though she'd liked his looks and instantly become smitten.

That wide smile spread across her face when she saw him. Her eyes lit up with exaggerated delight. "Elias! Come and join us."

"I'll pass."

"No, come on. We're playing a really interesting game. Well, it's not a game—it's a question set. Supposedly, if you sit and talk with someone about these questions—they're all really personal—and then you stare into each other's eyes for four minutes, you fall in love." Her smile took on a sudden slyness.

"Wen likes guys, and I'm not interested, so you're wasting your time," Elias replied. He tapped a finger against his wrist, as if gesturing to an invisible wristwatch. "We really should go."

"Why not?" Wen chided him. "Afraid you'll fall in love?"

Elias' eyes narrowed.

"Just answer one," Wen insisted. Before Elias could respond, Wen prodded Ana: "What's the next question?

"Um . . . ." Ana brushed a fingertip against the screen of her cell phone and read aloud: "How do you feel about your relationship with your mother?" She bristled. "I don't want to talk about my mother."

"My mom ran away," Wen said. "She told me and my sister that raising kids was too hard and she wished she never gave birth to us."

Ana looked back at Elias. "We don't want to talk about our mothers. What about you?"

Elias replied tonelessly: "She died when I was little. I barely remember her."

"Okay, scratch that question. Let's try another one. Let's see . . . what is your most horrible memory?"

Elias scoffed and turned away. "I'm going. If you want a ride . . . ."

"All right, I'm coming." Wen stood and started for the door. "On the way back, can we—"

"Don't go out there," Elias snapped.

Wen stopped in surprise. "What?"

Elias didn't respond. Behind the chairs, a window looked out onto the wide front lawn. The hill sloped gently enough that Elias had a full view of the grounds. One of the bhikshunis was leading a visitor toward the community hall.

Abruptly, Elias turned to Ana. "What did you volunteer for today?"

"I . . . ." She faltered. "Picking and chopping vegetables. They're making snacks for the che . . . I don't know how to pronounce it. It's a workshop on non-retaliation."

"Elias, what's up?" Wen asked.

Elias pointed to the window. "Look who's coming."

Wen stood beside him and followed his gaze. "Venerable Nyima? She's . . . ." He stepped closer to the glass. Elias saw a sudden tension in his shoulders. "No way. What the hell is *he* doing here?"

Leitha's vampire friend was walking beside the nun. They were close now, and the vampire's gaze was fixed on the window, his mouth set in a smile. Elias tried to brace himself for a confrontation, but he felt frozen, as if a heavy block of ice had formed in his stomach and immobilized him with its weight.

The bhikshuni, Ven. Nyima, led the vampire inside. She smiled brightly at the trio in the lobby. "Oh, Elias! I didn't know you were here."

A few more guests trailed quietly inside. Elias recognized two of them from the private lounge at Bull's-Eye: the dazed-looking guy and the petite woman with cold, wily eyes. She, too, recognized Elias, and gave him such a chilling smile that he shuddered.

The bhikshuni turned to the vampire, who was dressed inconspicuously in black slacks and a light jacket. "This is Andrei, and Maria, and . . . ." She hesitated uncertainly.

"Akari," Andrei spoke up, gesturing to a listless woman in a drab gray dress, "and Sanjay."

Neither Akari nor Sanjay spoke up. The young man stood gazing at the floor, while the woman looked aside and scratched the back of her head.

Ven. Nyima didn't let it faze her. "And these are a few of our volunteers," she said. "That's Elias, this is Wen, and that's Ana. You might know Elias already. He's Leitha's roommate."

"We've met," Andrei replied. Without missing a beat, he addressed Elias: "Leitha encouraged me to come here. I should have guessed I would run into you."

Elias struggled to speak. "Come here for what?"

"Today, it's for the Chenrezig workshop. You must be here for the same reason—to practice standing down."

Andrei's smile didn't waver. Nor did the barely veiled mockery in his eyes.

Ana was moving toward him, grinning cluelessly, extending a hand. "Hi. It's nice to—"

"We were just about to leave," Elias said, grabbing Ana's wrist. He forced her hand back down and didn't release it. "Wen has to work, so we need to get going."

Ana gaped at him. "But—"

"Let's not make him late," Elias insisted. He let go of her just long enough to put his arm around her shoulder and push her toward the door.

She complied, but she didn't hide her astonishment. When the trio was a few paces from the building, and the door had closed behind them, Ana asked in a low voice: "What was that about?"

Elias released her. "Keep walking." He glanced back, saw no one watching through the window. "Don't let that scumbag touch you," he advised Ana. "He's a predator. He has Leitha somewhere, earning money for him, and he won't tell me where she is."

"Well . . . Wen said that Leitha doesn't want to talk to you."

"It's because of *him*."

"How so?"

Elias found himself unable to explain. Wen, too, was at a loss. "It's not even about Leitha," Wen said at last. "That guy is a phony, passive-aggressive jerk."

"He's much worse than that," Elias cut in.

Wen continued: "That comment he made about standing down—that was a jab at Elias. Last night, that guy, Andrei, threatened us, and he called Elias a weakling who can't stand up for himself. Then he said that Leitha was of no real importance to him, but she's—where are you going?"

Elias had veered aside, toward the opposite building, where the bhikshunis resided. "I'm going to tell the other nuns what's happening."

"You can't just burst in there," Wen warned, hurrying to catch up with him.

"I can. They're starting the medicine meal. It's not like they're in the middle of a prayer."

Elias had visited the abbey's kitchen several times before; it was a place that Aarya had spent a lot of time in before she died, and Elias liked to think that it still held a trace of her presence. He found Lamia and Vela there, chatting and smiling as they prepared dumpling wrappers and tofu pockets.

"Vela," he cried as he burst into the kitchen.

"Venerable Dorje," she corrected him.

"There's a vampire in the gathering hall, and three other monsters with him. It's the vampire who's been keeping Leitha away from me. He says he's here for the workshop, but . . . ."

Lamia and Vela became suddenly serious. They exchanged knowing glances, as though they were not surprised by the news. "A vampire?" Vela repeated.

"Yes, the vampire from Bull's-Eye. His name is Andrei."

"Well," Vela said slowly, "unless he commits an act of aggression, he's welcome here. He might benefit from attending the workshop."

Elias stared at her. "Are you serious?"

"Nevertheless," she continued, still casting pensive looks at Lamia, "it wouldn't hurt if we had some extra supervision." She set down her rolling pin and rinsed her hands. "Maybe you three can help Lamia finish up while I head over there."

"I have to go to work," Wen replied. He gave Elias an imploring look. "I need to leave soon, or I'll be late."

Elias turned to Ana. "Do you have a car?"

She shook her head. "I take the bus."

"Do you know how to drive?"

She hesitated. "Yes."

Elias fished his keys out of his pocket and thrust them at her. "Take him to work. Please. I need to stay."

Ana gazed doubtfully at the keys in Elias' hand. "I don't want to drive your car. If something happens to it, I'll—"

"Doesn't matter. Just go, please." Elias felt a pressure in his throat as he added: "Finding Leitha is more important to me than my car. Can you stay for a few minutes to help Lamia? I want to go back to the hall."

Lamia waved dismissively at him. "Never mind. The other bhikshunis can help. You three go and do whatever you need to do." She gave Elias a stern look and added: "As long as you don't overreact. Let us handle it."

Elias arrived at the hall before Vela, having gone at a more hurried pace. He found Andrei's crew already in the meeting room at the rear of the building; they sat near the back, in the cushioned folding chairs that had been placed out for the guests. Elias slipped quietly inside, staying close to the doorway, his back against the wall.

Vela also entered silently. She chose a seat close behind the guests. Andrei noticed her presence right away; he turned and greeted her with a smile and a nod.

A few more visitors filtered in, with Ven. Nyima greeting each one, and several stopping to exchange cheerful banter with Vela. For a few minutes, everything began to seem placid and unthreatening. The room was filled with peaceful energy, its walls hung with images of bodhisattvas and symbols of compassion and power; that energy overshadowed those few ill-intentioned guests.

Ven. Nyima began the session with a guided meditation. She invited everyone to silence (during which the gray-clad woman loudly scratched her head), and then to self-reflection. "Our motives and beliefs determine our actions," she said, smiling gently at her listeners. "Therefore, we must learn to perform a serious and ongoing self-analysis, a deep self-reflection. Do our actions come from a deep sense of wanting to help others? Do you know that feeling of limitless compassion? Take this time to connect with that feeling inside of you, that genuine wish for the best for all of creation. We must find this aspect of ourselves, and nurture it, before it can begin to influence our behavior . . . ."

Andrei's peers began to fidget. Sanjay, the dazed-looking one, groaned and covered his eyes; he leaned forward in his seat, clutching his head in his hands. Maria, the cold-eyed one, matched Andrei's sense of composure; she wore a clean white dress and had her hair partially tied back with a barrette, and she sat up straight and attentive. Suddenly, though, she turned around. Her gaze fixed on Elias, and she smiled.

Thought he did not want to, Elias lowered his eyes. The woman's gaze was so chilling that it hurt to look back at her.

It was during Ven. Nyima's dissertation on Chenrezig that the trouble started. She gestured to a tapestry on the side wall, a large piece mostly done in bold shades of red, black, and gold. "This is our bodhisattva, the four-armed Chenrezig, with each arm representing how he has become one with his commitment to compassion. The two hands in the center hold a sky-blue crystal in front of the heart. This is our altruistic love, our commitment to compassion for all sentient beings."

Sanjay, still with his head in his hands, snickered. Then he raised his head and belched loudly.

Ven. Nyima faltered; her eyes riveted on Sanjay. The man's restless fidgeting and quiet disturbances, punctuated by occasional burps, persisted as she discussed Chenrezig's symbolism. Other guests began to glance uneasily at Sanjay, and Elias could hear a note of uncertainty in Ven. Nyima's voice. "The lotus also reminds us that our ultimate goal is to release all of creation from suffering, and to practice conflict resolution rather than aggression," she finished. "Today's guided meditation focused on deep self-analysis. When we contemplate the bodhisattva Chenrezig, we also consider the way of non-retaliation. When someone strikes us, or demeans us, we can respond from a place of compassion instead of feeding into that anger. Deep self-analysis can help us to slow down, to react with intentional compassion rather than a habitual reflex. This doesn't mean we simply let the other person beat us up. It means that we can become more powerful in our ways of responding; we can change the dialogue, change the flow of energy."

Sanjay emitted a sudden burst of sound—a wet sound, as though he had emitted snot or a mouthful of spit into his hands.

Beside him, Akari finally roused herself. She looked at Sanjay and gasped. "Eww!" she cried.

44

Maria cackled and covered her mouth.

In front of them, other audience members turned around, staring as Sanjay began to shake with laughter. Akari continued her moans of disgust as he wiped his soiled hands on his pants.

Suddenly, the young man raised his head. "Idiots," he hissed.

A murmur went through the audience. Elias sprung to action, hurrying toward Andrei's crew, leaning past Akari and whispering sharply to Sanjay: "You need to leave."

Sanjay's lips and chin gleamed with snot, and his pants were streaked with globs of mucus. His eyes had become even more bloodshot, yet he finally seemed focused. He glared at Elias and whispered back: "Pathetic twit."

Elias reached out to take the man's arm, but he recoiled as Sanjay lifted a snot-streaked hand to slap him away—and then Vela was there, standing just behind Sanjay, her hand lingering gently on his shoulder. The young man turned toward her with a scowl, but as she leaned over and spoke quietly in his ear, his face relaxed; the angry spark faded from his eyes.

Vela drew back, gently coaxing him. "Come on."

Andrei began to stand, but Vela held up a hand and gave him a reassuring smile. "It's all right. We'll wait for you in the lobby."

Elias withdrew. He watched as Vela led the unruly guest away, and then he resumed his post against the back wall.

Andrei seemed relaxed enough, though he did turn a few times to look at the doorway. When the session finished, Ven. Nyima led a Q&A session, and then she invited the guests to help themselves to snacks in the lobby.

Elias trailed behind Andrei's group and found Vela alone at the front. She flashed another welcoming smile at Andrei.

"Your friend wanted some fresh air, so we took a tour of the abbey," she explained. "He's waiting for you in the courtyard."

She raised her voice and addressed the other guests: "We have tea and water at the far table, and we also have a sampling of spring rolls, vegetable dumplings, and stuffed tofu. Please help yourself if you're hungry. This evening is also our open house. Venerable Thubten Tseten will lead a guided tour around the abbey, but you can also take one of our brochures and do a self-guided tour. We ask that all visitors help maintain the quiet and reverential atmosphere at Achiravati Abbey."

Andrei replied apologetically: "I should check on our friend. My apologies for what happened; he's been having a tough time. I thought the meditation would be good for him."

"It was," Vela replied softly.

Andrei's false smile wavered.

"Feel free to bring him back any time," Vela continued.

"Actually, I have some other acquaintances I would like to bring," Andrei replied crisply. "Young people. Children. I have two young acquaintances who are *very* interested in this place, and I promised them a visit."

"Everyone is welcome," Vela said.

They exchanged a few more words, but Elias didn't hear them. He was standing once again with his back against the wall, intently surveying Andrei's group. Maria stayed close to the vampire, while Akari stood awkwardly beside the appetizer table; she faced away from it, motionless, her hands clasped tightly in front of her. She didn't move as the other guests reached around her to sample the dumplings.

At least, her body didn't move. A lock of Akari's long hair slowly curved toward the table, gliding onto the surface as if it had a life of its own. It snaked toward the nearest platter, and in a flash, it curled around a dumpling and snatched it away beneath the cover of dark hair.

Elias watched as another dumpling vanished, and then another—until, between Akari and a few other guests, the entire platter had been cleared. He could see some other movement, now, at the back of Akari's head. Elias pressed into the back corner, trying to get a better glimpse, but couldn't quite make out what was happening—until Akari turned to look at Andrei, and Elias had a clear view of the back of her head.

Three locks of hair were raised up like skinny tentacles, one clutching a steamed dumpling, the other two parting Akari's hair—and there was exposed, on the back of her head, a small, thin-lipped mouth, complete with a set of white teeth and a tongue that gleamed with saliva. Elias stared in horror as the dumpling bulged against the little mouth; the tentacles gave it a frantic shove, and it disappeared inside. The act took only a moment, and then the hair dropped and resumed the guise of normalcy.

Elias' heart was still pounding after the guests had left and he was left alone with Vela.

"What's wrong, Elias?" the bhikshuni prodded him. "You look like you saw a ghost."

"That woman," he said, "has a mouth in the back of her head."

"What woman?"

"Akari." Elias raised his hands, saw them trembling. "That was so disturbing. I've seen some weird things, but . . . ."

"The next time someone disrupts one of our sessions, don't try to interfere," Vela said. "Remember, we want to approach people with compassion. A disruption isn't a big deal."

47

Elias let his hands drop. "So, what—people get to sit there and laugh at you? You film those sessions. That's going to be on—"

"That man wasn't laughing," Vela interrupted. "He was purging. I brought him to the lobby and talked to him for a while. He did laugh and lash out a few times, but he mostly cried."

"Okay, but . . . that woman had *a mouth in the back of her head.*"

Vela released a small sigh. "A mouth," she mused.

"Yes, a mouth."

"Are you really that shocked? I've seen some strange things too, believe it or not. Akari has some kind of monsterization—some kind of mutation—"

"You don't say," Elias replied dryly.

"—but I don't think she came here with any intent of harm," Vela finished. "I can't say the same for the other two, but it isn't your concern."

"It involves Leitha. It is my concern."

Vela looked at him contemplatively. "Speaking of Leitha . . . did you tell her about Lamia?"

"Why?"

"I'm just wondering how Andrei knows about Lamia's past."

"Lamia? What do you mean?"

"I guess you didn't hear it. Andrei said he wanted to bring some kids here—two kids who are really interested in this place. Then he mentioned Lamia's special affinity for children."

Elias felt a sudden sense of dread. He thought back, recalling late-night conversations with his former roommate. "I did," he said reluctantly. "I was trying to convince Leitha

48

that people can change, no matter what they might have done in the past." He paused. "I'm sorry."

"It's all right. From now on, though, please try not to dwell on someone else's past, unless they give you permission to talk about it." Vela gestured to the table. "Help me carry these back."

Ana returned after they had brought the dishes back to the kitchen and put the tables away. She found the two of them washing dishes; she inserted herself between them and helped them finish. Elias braced himself for more of her flirtations, but Ana mostly talked to the bhikshunis and hardly looked at him. Perhaps she had finally lost interest.

"Thanks," Elias said as Ana handed him his keys. He paused, and then added reluctantly: "Do you need a ride?"

"Not really, but I would appreciate one. The bus doesn't come for a while, and then I have a transfer."

"Let me take you home, then."

She smiled.

Elias was quiet on the drive, but after several minutes, Ana began to pester him with questions. "Don't you have to work, too?" she asked. "Wen told me you had an evening shift."

"I'm a freelancer," Elias replied. "I choose my hours."

"A freelancer at what?"

"Computer stuff."

"Oh, computer stuff," Ana said. "That's really specific."

"I write computer programs and design web sites."

"Okay," she shifted in her seat, turning towards him. "Slightly more interesting. What kinds of programs, and what web sites?"

"Right now I'm developing a series of programs for a manufacturing company. It's mostly so they can automate things that most other companies are already automating." Elias glanced at her. "It's not that interesting."

49

"I'm fascinated. I think this is the first time you've said more than ten words to me. You could talk about the lamest subject on Earth, and I would still be amazed, just because you're saying words."

"Just tell me where to drive," he replied crisply.

She directed him to a small house in the middle of a sprawling suburban neighborhood. A woman stood in the open garage, getting ready to pull the trash bin outside. She stopped and stared at Elias eased the car onto the driveway. Her brow wrinkled in puzzlement, and Elias saw a confused gaze behind her large eyeglasses—but she saw Ana and smiled. She was small, smaller than Ana, with wispy brown hair and a skinny frame.

"Is that your mom?" he asked.

She gave him a vaguely astonished look. "I don't live with my mom. This is a foster home."

"Oh," he replied.

"I assumed Wen told you."

"He didn't."

Ana paused as she reached for the door handle. "Aren't you going to ask about my parents?"

"Um . . . no. That seems kind of rude. It's the kind of thing people tell you about when they're ready." He gestured ahead. "She's waiting for you."

Ana gazed at him, again with a slightly mystified expression. "You know," she said, "I know that you like to seem unsympathetic and off-putting, but you're a good person."

Elias bristled. "I'm really not. Just go."

Later, in the dead of night, the image of the little mouth crept into Elias' dreams. He was back at the office complex where he used to live, out in the parking lot, where gleaming

50

white teeth flashed somewhere in the dark. Elias found himself drawn closer, though he didn't mean to approach. The mouth floated nearby, with no face to hold it; there was only a mass of slithering hair, its movements sounding like a multitude of soft whispers. The lips widened in a sudden smile, and the teeth began to stretch into long, pointed sabers. The hair receded, while the mouth grew and grew, until it reached such a massive size that it became inescapable. A void of stinking breath and merciless teeth threatened to draw Elias in—and then he saw her, trapped behind the long teeth and clutching them like prison bars.

Aarya was there, crying out in silent desperation.

Elias awoke with a groan. The image of Aarya's tormented face lingered in his mind, but his memories of her quickly replaced it; her strength, her persistence, rose in his thoughts with a reassuring presence and a seemingly audible whisper: *Just a dream, Elias. It's not real.*

Elias opened his eyes, but he quickly closed them again, not wanting to wake from the warm sensation of Aarya's companionship. He basked in it until it faded completely, and then he was left with the cool solitude of his empty home.

He tried to let the words reassure him: *It's not real.*

It had been real, though. Aarya had been devoured—or killed, at least—by a wendigo.

His fault. He had brought Aarya into the company of monsters. The bhikshunis always reassured him that Aarya had died at peace, that her life was a triumph, and that the wendigo had not touched her soul.

The nightmare was nothing new. He'd moaned and cried in his sleep for months. At those times, Elias would get out of bed and seek Leitha—and if she was asleep, he would make noise in the kitchen until she came out to ask him what the hell he was doing. Elias didn't confess his nightmares, but

Leitha probably guessed. She could be naïve and self-destructive, but she was surprisingly kind to people she cared about. She knew how to comfort others. When she sat and talked to him on those mournful nights, exchanging stories and little encouragements, Elias no longer felt like the elder person; Leitha became a big sister who offered solace and relief.

Now, though, when Elias went into the kitchen to make a cup of coffee, it was the only warmth and noise he would find. Leitha and Aarya were gone, and he was alone.

4

Elias crossed the river bridge and the downtown walkways with determination in his step. The day was drawing to a close, and that meant the patrons at Bull's-Eye were celebrating in bizarre "Monday Madness" costumes, but Elias wasn't there for frivolity. He paid the seven-dollar cover charge and entered as himself.

He'd found it difficult to regard the attempts at qigong and tai chi as nothing more than lessons in futility: waving his arms in slow motion, swaying in the safety of his living room. He couldn't help feeling that he was flailing uselessly when he should have been looking for Leitha. Elias was keenly aware of what might be happening to her at any given time, and instead of relaxing, his body tensed with frustration at the slow pace and his own clumsiness—and Andrei's words nagged at him. *You must be here for the same reason—to practice standing down.*

Elias knew that Andrei was trying to get under his skin, and he dutifully followed Shi Miao Xing's direction. He even took the bhikshunis' advice to heart, because he knew from experience that they were right.

It was in this spirit of humble but uncertain persistence that he returned to Bull's-Eye. In the intermittent lights penetrating the dark, in the swirl of frenetic energy, he saw her. Leitha was recognizable at once in denim cut-offs and a pink halter top, with matching pink devil horns fixed to a headband. Her small but full figure was dwarfed by a tall middle-aged man in an expensive-looking satyr costume complete with boots custom-made to look like hooves. Leitha always knew how to spot the ones with money. Elias had a brief glimpse of her smile as she planted herself in front of the satyr; she undulated and snaked her arms toward him in a brazen invitation. The satyr stared for a moment, and then he turned and moved away.

Elias couldn't see Leitha's expression, but he knew she felt dejected. Even strangers—including the ones Leitha had flirted with just so she could pickpocket them—could easily hurt her. Leitha wanted to feel loved. She sought it without knowing what it was.

Elias hung back for a minute, not wanting her to know that he had seen the rejection. It would only intensify her anger.

When he did approach, Leitha was dancing alone. Her face was turned down, her body moving in jerky, desperate movements, as though she was trying to shake something off.

"Leitha," he said.

Her eyes fixed on him, and Elias saw the sudden gleam of spite in her brown eyes.

"Don't glare at me," he said, leaning close so she could hear him over the noise. "I'm not here to scold you. I just came to apologize, and to tell you that I'm not going to bother you anymore."

The flash of anger dissipated. Leitha regarded Elias with silent caution.

"I'm . . . going to respect your choices," he continued—and those words pained him, because Elias did not respect Leitha's choices. He loathed them. "But if you ever want to hang out, or if you ever need a friend . . . ." He choked on the words and took a few moments to compose himself. "I'm always there. I'll be there any time of day or night, if you need someone to talk to."

Leitha's uncertainty changed back into a scathing look. "Right," she said bitterly. "You're there any time of day or night, because I clearly need your help."

"That's not what I mean, Leitha," he said. "I just miss you. I need friends, too."

Elias watched as Leitha tried to maintain a look of coolness, of distrust, but he saw the threat of tears in her eyes. "Do you?" she asked. "So, what? You suddenly respect me now?"

"You're not the one I don't respect," Elias replied. He hesitated, not wanting to irritate her. Leitha was looking at him without that now-familiar resentment, but her eyes still bore a hint of sadness.

"Good luck," Elias said, struggling to hide the tremor that he felt. "And thanks."

"For what?" she asked, her voice subtly cracking.

"For before. For all of it." Elias wanted to say more, but his mind went blank; he was only aware of his own grief. He walked away.

Before he was even halfway across the club, Elias began to have doubts. He wished that he'd said more, that he'd been more specific in his expressions of gratitude. *Thanks, Leitha, for staying awake and chatting with me after all of my stupid nightmares. Thanks for always smiling at me and making me feel like I was capable of being a decent person. Thanks for the little bit of fun and friendship I finally got to have.* How could she not miss it? She said computer programming was tedious, that working long hours in front of a screen was boring, but how could this life be better—these nights of broken and desperate people, of insincerity and emptiness?

His thoughts were interrupted by a sudden bulk that blocked his path. Elias raised his eyes and saw, at first, a worn-out flannel shirt—and above it, the bearded visage of Latham, Andrei's werewolf companion. The strobe flashed in the werewolf's icy blue eyes; it glinted off his teeth as he sneered at Elias. "Back for more, are you?" Latham shouted over the music.

"I'm leaving," Elias shouted back.

"Oh, you're leaving? Let me help you out."

As the werewolf's fingers dug into the collar of Elias' jacket, he fully expected to be dragged out of the club in humiliation—but Latham gave a swift kick to the back of Elias' legs, and he found himself hurled to the ground instead. Latham leaned over, raising his hand for another blow.

Elias didn't mind being hit this time, not really. The physical pain took his focus off the heartbreak that was building steadily inside of him. *I just said goodbye to Leitha. I invited her home, but I said goodbye, too—and I will never see her again.*

Latham didn't strike again. Someone stepped between him and Elias—another tall figure, extending a thick arm toward Latham's chest, planting a hand firmly on the red flannel. In the erratic flash of light, Elias recognized the bouncer. She wore the same vampire costume from the week before—the same cheap silver-and-black wig and heavy makeup, the cheap plastic fangs that flashed between her lips when she spoke. The bouncer glanced at Elias with brief but intense scrutiny, and then she turned to face Latham. Elias didn't catch what she said, but the werewolf scowled in reply.

The bouncer continued in a louder tone: "He didn't harass anyone. And he's leaving now." She gave Elias a pointed look. "Right?"

Elias nodded and pushed himself up from the floor. Instinctively, he started to look back at Leitha—but he stopped, instead steadying himself and resuming his trek toward the exit. His mind raced with things he should have said instead. If he had just yelled at Leitha differently, if he'd shaken her while shouting sense into her: *Andrei thinks you're silly. Latham thinks you're silly. They use you because they think you're a moron, but I know you; I know that you're more than a leech who seduces men to pick their pockets. You're kind. You're fun. You're insightful. You're beautiful. Do you really want to keep living like this, like a pathetic little idiot?* Of course, he had tried such arguments, and they only outraged Leitha and drove her farther away. Elias had an unnerving idea that this short but painful journey out of Bull's-Eye was like Orpheus exiting Hades—that if he looked back in pleading uncertainty, Leitha might really disappear forever.

On the sidewalk, Elias heard the clunk of heeled boots close behind him. The bouncer had followed him outside. The streetlamps were just beginning to spark to life along the street, illuminating the black-lipped face heavily lined eyes that looked down at Elias with concern.

"Hey," she said, in a softer tone than he'd thought her capable of. "Are you hurt?"

Elias lowered his gaze. He steadied his voice. "I'm fine. He didn't hurt me."

The woman gave him a knowing look. "Who did, then? Leitha?"

Elias returned her probing gaze. "Do you still think I'm stalking her? Why not let Latham beat me up, then? Or are you starting to realize what kind of people you're working for?"

She didn't respond, but Elias saw the answer in her troubled expression.

He chose his next words carefully, not knowing how much she understood. "Andrei is a blood-sucking leech. You know that, right?"

The hulking woman glanced briefly toward the club, where the doorman was checking the IDs of a mad scientist and Frankenstein's bride. She looked at Elias, sizing him up. "Is Leitha really your sister?"

"Sort of," he said. "We're . . . orphans. She doesn't have anyone else." Elias paused, his throat constricting with sudden emotion. "Could you keep an eye out for her? I can't do anything for her now, but if she's in trouble, and there's anything you can do . . . ."

The bouncer nodded. "I'll keep an eye out. And yeah, I know there's a leech or two around here. I'm starting to see that."

Elias lowered his head and tried to say "Thanks," but he found himself unable to speak. His throat wouldn't loosen, and tears began to well in his eyes.

"Hey." The bouncer gently slapped his shoulder, as if admonishing him for crying. "I mean it: I'll keep an eye out. Jerks who prey on women are my pet peeve. If they mess with her . . . ." She made a fist and slammed it into her palm.

Elias didn't reply. Andrei was already messing with Leitha, but he had her consent. The bouncer's fist was powerless against that.

He faced that same sense of weakness only two days later. Elias sat at his computer, immersed in his work and mostly ignoring his phone. Programming helped him stay calm and confident; it was a skill he had mastered, and it was engaging enough to take his mind off his worries.

He didn't notice the initial pinging of the text alert, but after he got three calls in a row, Elias finally muttered to himself and checked the phone.

Wen had sent a short text: *Andre and Leetha are here.*

Elias stood. He grabbed his car keys and hurried out the door while texting back: *Where?*

He asked even though he knew.

As he pulled into the parking lot at Achiravati Abbey, he spotted a figure in the nearby courtyard. Elias recognized Andrei at once: simply but stylishly dressed, his dark hair falling in a neat wave to his shoulders. The vampire stood facing away, gazing up at the twin buildings that loomed at the top of the grassy slope. Elias slowed his pace when he realized that Andrei was not alone.

Two children were perched on the low stone wall, on either side of the Buddha statue. A girl, perhaps six years old, sat looking at Elias, her eyes somber and dull. Her long, dark hair had a faded and brittle quality, and her frock was just as drab. Elias recognized the boy at once; he had seen the same vacant-eyed child in the back room of Bull's-Eye, a handsome but zombie-like thing with large, dark eyes and tousled hair.

It was only when Elias came close that Andrei finally turned to face him. The vampire smiled—not the mocking smile that Elias had become accustomed to, but one that seemed to express genuine pleasure, as though Andrei had just spotted a good friend.

"Elias," he said.

Elias suddenly realized how he had rushed into the situation. He'd had the entire drive to consider how to confront Andrei, but he had only thought of seeing Leitha. Now he stood like a fool, not knowing what to say.

"You snuck up on me," Andrei continued warmly, still smiling. "I suppose I should use more caution, considering that stunt you pulled with your little knife—the astra, or whatever you call it. I heard it can do some damage to fellows like me."

Elias kept his voice cool. "The astra isn't a threat to you. I very clumsily dropped it in the Mississippi River—and I decided that I need to drop Leitha, too, unless she wants to come home on her own. There's not much chance of me getting either of them back, so you can relax. Don't you agree?"

A perverse delight seemed to glint in Andrei's eyes—a sinister, not-so-subtle glee—but he quickly suppressed it. "In the *river*. How unfortunate."

"Yes, it's gone. And Leitha's gone. So, there's no reason for you to keep coming here."

"I think you mistake my purpose," Andrei said, his voice suddenly gentle and entreating. "There are other things here that I . . . *want*."

He didn't elaborate, but stood silently. Elias tried to guess the meaning behind Andrei's words. What other use could a vampire have for an abbey full of feel-good lectures, vegetables, and bald-headed bhikshunis? None of it catered to his style or ambitions.

An answer snaked its way through Elias' mind—a soft echo of Andrei's words, a hint planting itself in Elias' mind. Elias was suddenly struck by the tone of Andrei's words: soothing, but subtly compelling in their message of desire.

"Is something wrong?" Andrei asked softly. Elias found himself unable to look away from the vampire's eyes. They were changing somehow. The pupils dilated, but the gaze also seemed to deepen, like mystical pools that widened around Elias' awareness, preventing his escape—and when the vampire spoke, Elias heard the voice as if it was speaking in his own mind.

"Or rather, is something *right*," Andrei said. "Perhaps you sense it now—how being a vampire could have been powerful and right, instead of pathetic and weak. I gathered from Leitha that you never finished becoming the master you could have been. And you—your demeanor says a lot about what you lacked as a vampire, about the things you didn't know. For instance, it seems that you never learned about calling the blood."

Elias tried to rouse himself from the seeming trance. He had a vague awareness of Andrei mocking him again. He tried not to look clueless, though he didn't have the faintest idea what Andrei meant—but in the next moment, he *knew*. He knew what it meant to "call the blood" because he felt it: Andrei's presence inside of him, moving in his bloodstream, permeating his body and being. The sensation sparked a sudden alarm, but it quickly faded. That presence gave Elias a contrasting sense of excitement and comfort—a deep, warm feeling, like the warm brown hues of Andrei's eyes. Elias seemed to have fallen into those eyes. He found Andrei's essence soothing, promising; it flowed with the blood like an endless stream of whispered promises, offering solace, safety, and pleasure . . . a river of dark peace.

Elias hadn't noticed the vampire moving closer, but he felt Andrei's breath on his neck. That, too, impressed him with a comforting warmth. He stood still and basked in it. The idea of Andrei penetrating his veins, and relishing the blood that flowed there, didn't disturb him. Instead, a part of him desired it.

The breath stopped, and in the absence of it, Elias felt a prickle of impatience—and then Andrei whispered: "I could teach it to you. You would like that, wouldn't you?"

"Elias," a voice shouted.

Elias felt a strange jolt in his brain. He closed his eyes for a moment, grimacing as he put a hand to his head.

Andrei glanced back. The spell broke; Elias shook himself out of it, heard the shuddering of his own breath as he took an unsteady step backwards.

The vampire turned to him again with a small, knowing smile, his pupils still a pair of wide pools. "Maybe another time."

Elias managed to look past him, and his attention became consumed by what he saw. Vela was coming down the hill— and beside her was Leitha, dressed more conservatively than usual in a baggy jacket and ripped jeans. Elias tried to meet her eye, but Leitha stared at the ground as she ambled toward him.

Vela addressed Andrei: "We're finished. Leitha had a productive session, and you're both welcome to come back any time. If you'll excuse me, I have some business with Elias before we start the evening meditation."

Andrei maintained his confident tone. "Of course. I'm glad things went well. Leitha, let's leave them to their business."

Finally, Leitha looked up. She met Andrei's eyes and smiled—a grateful and captivated smile, a reaction to that same treacherous warmth that Elias had just experienced.

In that moment, Elias wished that Leitha would glare at him again, or that she would express any kind of connection or feeling for him at all.

Andrei beckoned to the children. In their silence, Elias had forgotten about them. Now they roused themselves, moving to stand at either side of the vampire. Remembering Leitha's fondness for children, Elias expected her to greet them—but they all remained as they were, three dazed-looking people not looking at one another.

Only Andrei remained keenly alert. He coaxed Leitha and the children back to his car, and they followed noiselessly.

Elias turned to Vela. "What's going on?" he whispered.

"It's okay," the bhikshuni replied quietly. "Let them go. We can talk inside."

He managed to wait until they were in the lobby of the gathering hall. As soon as the door closed behind them, he blurted: "What's with Leitha? What did she say?"

Vela went to sit on one of the plush chairs. "Well," she replied, "She didn't say much. She's a little out of it, as you saw."

"Do you think he drugged her?"

"No. Something else was wrong."

Elias waited, impatiently, for an explanation.

"There's some kind of entity inside her," Vela said.

"An entity? You mean . . . like she's possessed?"

"No, not possessed. Not really." The bhikshuni paused. "I think it was just using her as a vehicle—to get to me. I started a qigong session with Leitha, and the entity tried to transfer itself into me. I had to stop the session."

"Why? Why would it want to get to *you*?"

Vela seemed to ponder that. She didn't answer.

"You got there just in time," Elias said, with relief in his voice. "He was going to bite me, and . . . I was going to let him do it."

"Yes, I saw that."

"It was like he put me in some kind of trance." Elias thought back to the sensation of Andrei's presence within him. The memory of his own desire made him shudder. Grudgingly, he added: "It was like . . . he was in my mind, and in my *blood*. I don't know how to describe it, but it was like . . . even though I knew it was dangerous, it kind of felt . . . good. A part of me even wanted him to bite me."

The bhikshuni nodded, unruffled as usual. "Elias, this is another reason you should train yourself in the energy arts. Vampires don't fight with their fists. They fight with energy. If you learn to master your own qi, Andrei can't manipulate you."

"I'll keep training," Elias promised. "Even though . . . ."

She raised her eyebrows, waiting.

"I don't believe in qi," he finished.

"You will. Anyway, you believe in the power of a vampire's energy. Why can't you believe in your own?" Vela didn't wait for an answer, but continued: "I haven't had much time to process what happened, so let's try to work it out together. Tell me everything that happened between you and Andrei before I came out with Leitha."

Elias described the brief exchange between himself and Andrei. "He made it sound like Leitha talked about me," he added. "And the rest of what he said . . . ." He trailed off. "He's trying to get under my skin and make me feel weak."

"And to tempt you," Vela said. "Don't you think so?"

"I guess so. Every time he talks to me, he tries to convince me that I'm pathetic—and now, he's implying that he could help me become more powerful as a vampire." Elias paused, remembering the strange and sudden warmth of Andrei's presence—or rather, he felt it surging gently inside of him again, as though Andrei had left a trace of it behind. "He was showing me the power I could have," he said. "Like, this ability he had—'calling the blood'—is some sort of great thing that I missed out on, because I didn't finish becoming a real vampire. I *did* have that kind of ability before, but . . . not like Andrei has it. It didn't work on most people, and I wasn't in control of it."

Vela was nodding again, distant and contemplative.

"He knows about the astra," Elias added. "Actually, that was the first thing he said to me. I told him that it isn't here."

Vela was roused from her thoughts. Her gaze slowly rose to meet his, and Elias saw a glint of tension there. "What exactly does he know?"

"He knows I used it on other monsters. He mentioned it before—but this time, I told him that I dropped it in the Mississippi River."

The bhikshuni's demeanor seemed to shift. Her voice reflected the change, taking on a cool, strained tone. "Why do you think you told him that?"

Elias hesitated. Something about Vela's stare was disconcerting. "Well . . . I didn't want him targeting the abbey. He seemed threatened by the astra, and I figured that if we're not a threat to him, he won't keep coming here."

A heavy silence ensued. Elias tolerated it, worried that he had done something terribly wrong.

"Andrei does have a reason to corrupt my energy," Vela said at last. "His . . . former lover, Lucian, is in prison, and for some time now he's been involved in our prison outreach program. I'm his mentor. Andrei wants him back, and he has been trying to visit him, but Lucian won't allow it."

Elias took some time to let the words sink in. He stared at Vela with astonishment. "*Your* prison outreach program? But . . . wait a minute. When did you find out that this guy was involved with Andrei?"

"We've known for some time."

"Some time, like . . . a few days ago, when he showed up at the abbey?"

"No, Elias. Longer than that. We suspect that Andrei used Leitha to get information about the abbey. He may be trying to use you as well."

65

Elias felt his astonishment giving way to anger. "So . . . you already knew about him. The whole time—the very first time I mentioned Andrei—you knew everything. You didn't think I should know, too?"

"No, we didn't," Vela replied matter-of-factly. "You're impulsive, Elias; you don't think things through before you act. You lost the astra, and now you've told Andrei where it is. You were getting into useless fights, and your vampire impulses were coming back. We thought it best to wait until you had some time to cool down and self-reflect."

Her words stirred Elias' resentment. "Yes," he seethed, "I fought. I was desperate because I was facing him on my own—but 'We thought it best'? This whole time, you and the other nuns have been talking about me behind my back, and leaving me in the dark? Has it occurred to you that I wouldn't have told Andrei about the astra if I had known not to?"

Vela's eyes widened in sudden surprise. "Elias," she said.

He turned and stalked out of the hall. As he began to descend the hill, he caught sight of Wen hurrying toward him from the other building.

"Elias!" Wen called breathlessly, as Elias showed no sign of slowing. "Where's Venerable Dorje?"

Elias came to a sudden halt. "Your supposedly venerable doorjamb is back there," he said, jabbing his thumb in the direction of the hall.

"Wait, what's wrong? Did you see Leitha?"

"Yes, and it did no good, and I'm about done with this place and its hypocrisy. The bhikshunis are always giving speeches about right intentions and truthful speech, but . . . what is it?"

Wen was staring at him with the same wide-eyed surprise that Elias had seen on Vela's face. "Your mouth," Wen said.

"What about it?"

And then he felt it: the extra expanse of teeth, the point of fangs. Elias lifted a hand to his mouth and gently touched one of the smooth curves.

"What the hell," Wen murmured.

Elias resumed walking, more slowly this time, and Wen followed uncertainly.

"Are you okay?" Wen asked. "I mean, do I need to be afraid, or . . . ."

"I'm fine," Elias snapped. There was some truth to his claim; he felt no urge to attack anyone, yet he had a vague awareness of a lingering desire—a yearning to feel that dark warmth and comfort again, to know what it meant to "call the blood." He wondered if Andrei felt that same pleasure when he called the blood of others.

"I would have stayed with Leitha," Wen said, "but Venerable Dorje said she wanted to be alone with her, and I wanted to make sure Lamia was all right. She was pretty rattled. I'm not sure what happened, but it had something to do with the kids Andrei brought with him."

Elias stopped again, staring down at the courtyard, remembering the dull eyes and vacant faced of those children. He thought of Leitha's bedazzled smile and her refusal to acknowledge him. Perhaps she hadn't even noticed his presence.

"Lamia told me . . . ." Wen hesitated. "Well, I'm not sure what she meant, but when I asked her who those kids were, she said that they're not kids."

"Tell me what happened," Elias replied, still gazing at the court. "Were you there when Lamia saw those children?"

"Yeah. Andrei brought them to the dormitory. I was helping Lamia and Venerable Tseten with the medicine meal, and he just walked in. Lamia went really pale, and while Vela was talking to Andrei and Leitha, she just left the room. I went with Venerable Tseten to check on her. Lamia hardly said anything; she just said that she recognized those two, and that they aren't kids."

Elias thought back to Andrei's first visit to the abbey. Vela had said that Andrei wanted to bring two children, and that he'd made a passing comment about Lamia's past—a past that presumably involved harming children, though Elias didn't know the details.

"He's trying to get under our skin," Elias said. "It's not just me; it's all of us. Vela told me that Andrei's ex-boyfriend joined the abbey's prison outreach program, and now he's refusing to see Andrei. Andrei probably blames the nuns."

"Her name isn't Vela," Wen corrected him. "It's Vener—"

"I'm done following the rules of this place," Elias snapped. "This whole time, *Vela* knew that Andrei was using Leitha to get to the abbey, and she knew it was because of Andrei's boyfriend, and she intentionally didn't tell me."

"Dude . . . your eyes." Wen's face betrayed a sudden anxiety. "Your pupils are totally dilated. Okay, I believe you about the vampire thing. Your face, and your fangs—I'm looking at a vampire right now."

"Maybe that's for the best," Elias replied tremulously. "I'm starting to think it's better than being in league with people who just sit around giving self-righteous speeches and doing absolutely nothing. These people never gave a damn about Leitha, or about me."

Wen had reason to be nervous; Elias could feel himself coming dangerously close to losing control of his anger, but Wen made a small sound of disbelief and chided him: "So, what are you going to do—bite Andrei's neck and drink his blood? Andrei and his friends would just beat the crap out of you. You haven't said much about your supposed experiences as a vampire, but it sounds like you just went around looking for sad young girls to lash out at."

Elias felt his shoulders tensing, his fangs pressing tight against his gums.

"And when you went up against monsters," Wen continued, "you couldn't do it on your own. You had to use the astra. Sorry, but I'm with the bhikshunis on this one."

"Of course you are," Elias muttered. He strode at a determined pace toward his car, and though Wen called after him, Elias ignored it. He threw himself heavily into the driver's seat and slammed the door. He made a show of accelerating noisily out of the lot, and he maintained a fast and reckless speed through town, until he heard sirens blaring behind him.

Elias hurriedly ducked his head and put on his sunglasses, hiding his dilated pupils. He mumbled apologies to the officer who pulled him over, trying to veil his still-protruding fangs. Vela's words stung him: *You're impulsive. You don't think things through. Your vampire impulses were coming back. We thought it best to wait until you had some time to cool down.*

She wasn't wrong. Elias knew that. His own anger, and the memory of what his anger had done to him in the past, gave him reason to pause. What disturbed him most, though, wasn't the rage that darkened his eyes and warped his teeth into dangerous points; it was this new desire that Andrei had planted in him. Elias wondered again if being a vampire could give him the power to create that calming and alluring sensation on his own. Elias needed calm; he suffered from anxiety, from nightmares, from inescapable despair. He wanted to be soothed, and it was tempting to accept any form of comfort, even one that came with an empty promise—or a fatal promise. He knew beyond the slightest doubt that Andrei could give him no comfort, that he would only create new nightmares.

Elias watched in the rearview mirror as the officer finished writing up the ticket. "They're right about me," he whispered.

By the time the cop returned, Elias' fangs had receded—and when he was politely asked to remove his sunglasses, he did so without any fear. "Thanks for stopping me," Elias said. "I was driving along like a jackass. I'll be more careful."

He hoped he would be able to keep his word.

5

Round two, Elias thought as he entered the gathering hall. He assured himself that this time, when he made his confession and apology, he would go straight to the recipient—but he paused on the way to the weaving room, where Vela likely sat making one of her dull tapestries. Venerable Nyima, the bhikshuni who had led the Chenrezig workshop, was vacuuming the meeting room, and Elias had a sudden urge to help her clean up.

Ven. Nyima switched off the vacuum. "I'm finished, but thanks," she said in reply to his offer. "I didn't expect to see you here. Are you volunteering?"

"I'm . . . looking for Vela," he said.

"Who? Oh, you mean Venerable Thubten Dorje. She's at the weaving loom. Do you know where to go?"

"Yeah," Elias replied uneasily. Of course, he knew where to go, but he was battling a sudden cowardice. He eased himself further into the room and glanced up at the wall, at the row of tapestries that had been rolled up and tied shut with colorful ribbons. "I was kind of looking forward to seeing Chenrezig again," he said. "Why do you keep his tapestry rolled up in between workshops? Is he sleeping or something?"

She smiled. "It's called a thangka, and no, he's not asleep. It's mostly to preserve the thangka for as long as possible, but it's also tradition. In the past, they had to be rolled up and transported from place to place—but these are going to stay

71

here." Ven. Nyima gave Elias a pointed look. "I don't know if anyone told you, but Andrei will be at tomorrow's workshop."

Elias felt his shoulders slumping. He'd hoped that Andrei was really just after the astra, but it seemed there was much more to Andrei's designs than he'd realized. "Fantastic."

Venerable Nyima shrugged. "Yes, that's how I'm choosing to think about it."

"Do you know about Andrei?" Elias prodded, searching her face for signs of understanding. "I mean, do you know what he is?"

"I've heard some things," she replied vaguely.

"He's a vampire. Take it literally or figuratively, but it's no exaggeration."

"So I've heard," Ven. Nyima replied softly. "I'm not familiar with . . . so-called monsters, but I did notice something off about Andrei and his friends."

"Well, that's an understatement."

"I'm surprised that Andrei didn't come with other vampires," the bhikshuni continued. "It seemed like he wanted to intimidate us, but he brought people who aren't intimidating. They just seem kind of lost."

"Most monsters don't congregate with their own kind," Elias replied. "It's like getting an unpleasant glimpse in the mirror—and they usually end up competing for power."

She gave him a mildly probing look. "And you know this from experience?"

Elias lowered his head. "Yeah. I've had experience."

She nodded. "I've always been in the opposite place. I always just wanted to be *good*, so I lived a pretty sheltered life."

"So did I," Elias replied, "at first—but it didn't last." He paused. "I don't think I could do what you do—being a monastic, I mean—just because of the burden of my own guilt."

She laughed. "It isn't easy for me, either. I believe in this way and I give it my all, but I have outsider syndrome—or imposter syndrome, or whatever you want to call it. I'm always worried that people will catch on to the fact that I'm a phony."

"There's nothing phony about you."

"My confidence is phony," she continued. "I try to think positive thoughts, but I always have this uneasy feeling that things will naturally fall apart for me. I was rattled during the Chenrezig workshop. I felt like Andrei and his friends knew my weaknesses and were laughing at them—but I remembered the other bhikshunis' advice, and I just started lecturing on the situation."

Elias looked from Ven. Nyima's anxious face to her hands, which she was wringing nervously, to the point that her skin had turned white where she was crushing it under straining fingers. It was unfortunate, Elias thought, that she had been the one hosting the workshop. All of the bhikshunis were "nice," but Ven. Nyima gave the impression of being easily cowed.

"I still feel a little bit nervous about it," she admitted, "but I think it turned out to be a good thing that they showed up when they did. Ultimately, it was a reminder that I just need to keep practicing my faith, and reflecting on it, and things will be okay." She gave Elias a warm smile. "Maybe it's the same for you. Sometimes, when people do things that make us uncomfortable, it's a chance for us to analyze ourselves and grow into something stronger."

Ironically, it was Venerable Nyima who made him uncomfortable at the moment; Elias felt unworthy of that smile. Yet, he was grateful for it. "I'll go and find Vela," he said.

She raised her eyebrows. "Venerable Thubten Dorje."

"Right. Thanks."

He found Vela in a back room, sitting at the loom with her wooden skewers in hand. She toiled away at the same tapestry he'd seen before—blue, gold, and violet, simple in design—and at the same pace, so slowly that Elias was struck by an impression of intolerable boredom.

"Oh, you're back," Vela said, looking up from the loom. "Good. I wanted to talk with you."

"About what?" he asked.

She beckoned him. "Don't just stand there. Come inside. Have a seat." She gestured to a chair near the doorway, but when Elias sat, she beckoned again. "Not way over there. Bring it closer."

Elias dragged the chair so that he sat a few feet away. Vela gently set the wooden poles down and turned to face him. Elias braced himself. Vela had a pale and aging face, with layers of eye bags and creases that gave an impression of weariness, but the eyes themselves betrayed a tireless discernment and vigilance—and the bhikshuni was never afraid to speak about what those eyes had discerned.

"I want to apologize," she said. "You were right: I should have told you about Andrei. I may have put you in danger by withholding what I knew. From now on, I'll be more forthcoming."

"That's funny," Elias replied dryly. "I also wanted to apologize. I was going to tell you that you were completely in the right—but when you say it that way, yeah, it really seems like you were wrong."

He was being facetious, but she ignored it, or missed it. "I think it's a good idea for you to become more involved with the abbey," she said. "What do you think about being part of our prison outreach program?"

The question caught Elias off guard. He stared at the bhikshuni, uncomprehending.

"I think it would be good if you and Lucian met," she said. "He's learning to trust us, but he's inhibited by guilt. If he meets others who are part of our community, and who have a similar past, it can help our situation."

"A similar past?" Elias repeated.

The bhikshuni clarified: "Remember, he used to belong to Andrei's crowd."

"Ah. I see." Elias nodded. "What exactly am I supposed to do—announce to him that I used to be a vampire?"

"Lucian is incredibly perceptive," Vela replied. "I think he'll know."

Elias folded his arms across his chest. "Is this why you apologized to me?" he asked coolly. "You wanted to make peace so you could use me to influence Lucian?"

"It's meant to help all of us," she answered, "including you."

Elias was silent.

"You don't have to answer now," she added. "Take your time."

"Do we have time?" he replied quietly.

Vela didn't answer the question, but gave him a look that exuded calm. "How is your qigong practice going?"

"Oh, it's going. I flap my hands in the air and wave my arms a few times a day. It's great, really. It's astonishingly simple."

"So is my latest project," she said. "What do you think of my work?"

"It's boring," Elias replied. "Sorry, but I got spoiled by all of the beautiful tapestries around the abbey."

Vela nodded. She gestured to the far side of the room, to a silk hanging that featured a phoenix and dragon, elaborately detailed with multi-colored wings, plumes of smoke, flower blossoms with pistils and stamens, streams and water droplets and complex rays of light. "That expression of yin and yang took four years to create," she said. "It's a particular type of silk brocade that not many people know how to make. A team of people created it, with two people working on it every single day, and with so much fine detail that they could only make a few centimeters each day. Can you guess how much it cost us to have that piece?"

"I don't know," Elias replied. "Several thousand? Tens of thousands?"

"It was donated," Vela replied, "as a celebratory gift for the opening of the abbey. We worked for four years to establish this abbey, and it took those people four years to finish their gift. It took a lot of time and effort, yet it was completed at just the right time."

"Then, why do you have it in here?" Elias asked. "Shouldn't you have it on display, where other people can see it?"

"Oh, it *was* on display," she replied, "and it will be again—but for the time being, it has a purpose in this room. It inspires me."

Elias' gaze fell to Vela's comparatively unimpressive work. "Yes, I can see the inspiration."

"My piece isn't quite finished," Vela said, "but it's far enough along that you can see the pattern. Do you know what it is?"

Elias inspected the weaving: Vs and diamonds connected by golden threads on a blue background; a winged dragon in the upper middle; a golden pagoda at the center. "No idea," he said.

"They're the major meridians—the channels through which our qi flows." Vela pointed to the figure of the dragon, tracing the pattern of its wings. "These lines are where the meridians lead into the arms and shoulders. The dragon's body forms the meridians that run along the spine—and down here, the pagoda is the Du Mai, the Governing Vessel."

"Okay," Elias said. "I'm sure that's fascinating to people who know what you're talking about."

"You'll know," she said, "if you continue to learn about qi." She picked up the skewers and resumed her work. "When I started this piece, I had the end in mind, but it took a long time before I could see it taking the shape I imagined. Making another astra, and securing it from another plane, is also a long and painstaking work, and you don't know its philosophy and patterns yet. If you work each day, though—even if it's just a few centimeters of progress a day—you'll eventually create something beautiful and powerful. You must think: what *can* you do each day? You can't make an astra in a day, but you can study qigong. You can't 'call the blood,' but you can heal your own blood by learning to manage qi. Eventually, if you reach qigong mastery, you might even can help to move other people's qi in beneficial ways, rather than exploitative ways. Andrei has been studying you to learn your weaknesses, and to move you for his own gain. Perhaps you should study him as well."

Elias sighed. "Vela."

"Venerable Thubten Dorje," she corrected him.

"I'm sorry I was a jerk earlier. I overreacted. I'm . . . in a dangerous spot, I think, and you *are* helping me, and I appreciate you." He paused. "But I can only take so much Buddhist talk at a time. I'm going to leave—and I will think about what you said, and I'll flail along with a few qigong and tai chi videos on YouTube, and I'll come back tomorrow

77

to keep an eye on Andrei and his goons. No—I'll *study* Andrei and his goons."

He stood and dragged the chair back to its place. Vela set her tools down just long enough to press her hands together; she made a slight bow of her head in Elias' direction and murmured: "Until tomorrow, then."

Elias left the building and headed toward the rear of the campus, to the vegetable gardens where Lamia was likely working. He guessed that she hadn't opened up to anyone about her encounter with Andrei. Elias, though, was someone she could confide in. He, like Lamia, had committed grave sins.

He found the bhikshuni among the cucumbers, diligently pulling weeds with a small, pronged hoe. She must have heard his approach, yet she didn't stop her work. Elias sat down on the earth beside her. "How are you?" he asked.

"I'm all right," Lamia replied.

He watched as she finished shaking the loose dirt from a clump of skinny roots. "Are you allowed to pull the weeds up like that? I thought Buddhists weren't allowed to kill plants."

"We don't consider plants to be sentient beings."

"But, isn't that why you don't eat onions and garlic—because you have to pull up the whole plant and kill it?"

"No," she said gruffly, as she shoved the hoe into the dirt. "It's because of the smell, and the way they can affect qi."

"Ah," Elias said. "Right. God forbid we eat anything that has flavor."

Lamia set the hoe down beside a half-uprooted weed. She turned to face Elias. "I supposed you're curious about what happened between me and Andrei."

"I'm curious about the kids," he replied.

The Bhikshuni lowered her gaze. "You mean, the doppelgängers. Andrei brought them for me—*made* them to show me."

"Made?" Elias repeated. "You mean, like, he made them recently, after meeting you? How does Andrei suddenly 'make' a pair of children?"

"It's possible," she replied vaguely. "He probably wanted to show me that he can get into my mind, and that he knows my weaknesses."

"Why?" Elias asked. "Why would you be of any significance to him? Is it just because he thinks you and the other nuns are trying to take his boyfriend away?"

She looked at him probingly. "You know about Lucian?"

"I do now. No thanks to you."

"Andrei has been exploring all of our weaknesses, including yours. You need to be cautious around him, Elias. He's trying to turn you." Lamia paused, letting the warning sink in. "I think he also wants us to know that he has has some kind of power in the astral realm. It probably sounds crazy, but those kids weren't real; they were astral projections. It's not really them, but more like the partial fabric of them."

Elias thought back to his brief encounter with the children, to their vacant but very tangible faces and the details of their scruffy clothes. That they were mere projections did sound crazy, but Elias urged Lamia on. "Projections of what?"

"My past. Andrei must have seen them when he got into my energy, and he somehow created an astral likeness of them."

"So, who are they?"

Lamia's gaze fell to the pile of uprooted weeds. Her fingers clenched, and she fidgeted as she spoke. "Well . . . when I was young, I kept having these particular recurring

79

nightmares, and they came with such a sense of guilt and grief. I couldn't figure out where it all came from, so I tried hypnosis and past-life regression, and meditative dream states . . . and other things. And I kept seeing this event from a past life, a tragedy that involved my village being attacked by another tribe, and my children being killed—and in this vision, I resolved that I was going to kill all of the other tribe's children as revenge. That's who those two kids are; they're from my vision, my own kids who were killed."

Elias stared at her. He could feel his face shifting into a dumbfounded expression. "Your vision," he said slowly. "Hold up. This horrible crime you claimed to have committed, that involved harming children . . . it was just in your mind?"

She let out a quiet sigh. "Is the astral plane also just in my mind?"

"No, don't go there," he said. "All this stuff you've been telling me about your past . . . you're saying you didn't actually do anything. It was all just your imagination."

"Not just mine," Lamia replied.

"Not just yours?" he asked in disbelief. "Whose, then? Your hypnotist's imagination?"

"You know that Buddhists believe in reincarnation, and in the evolution of souls," she said. "I've done some dark things in this life, too, because that compulsion has stayed with me. When I was a teenager, I almost killed a boy, and I wasn't sure why I did it. I was just . . . angry, and he was weaker than me, and no one was looking. I pushed him into a pit at a construction site and left him there. A house was being built in kind of a remote area near my neighborhood, but construction was shut down for a while because of money, and I figured no one would find that kid—but he managed to climb out. I got hell for what I did, but the idea of that boy getting hurt didn't even bother me. What bothered me was that I didn't know the *why* of it. I felt giddy about the idea of harming someone's child—like I was getting some sort of unremembered revenge. That's when I started to seek answers."

"And your answers are all made up," Elias said flatly. "You didn't have any, so you created them."

"And being a vampire—was that made up, too?" Lamia asked. "Don't be so quick to dismiss the supernatural."

"What about the astra?"

"What about it?"

"Is it real? I mean, I know the one we had was real, but is it true that I can somehow access another dimension, and make another one there, and bring it back?"

"It's not the sort of thing I would lie about," she said.

Elias could feel his gaze darkening as he stared at the bhikshuni. "Maybe you would just convince yourself that it isn't a lie."

She looked at him with wordless resignation.

"You fed me this made-up story about how you've done worse things than me," Elias continued, "and how you were still able to become a better person, and therefore, *I* can become a better person—and it's all fake. It's just like all this qigong nonsense that Vela has been spewing at me: It hasn't done a damn thing except waste my time. It's . . . a *fantasy*. You know, I *am* trying really hard to be a better person, and I've been relying on you and the other bhikshunis for help with that—but since I came here, I've heard nothing but long-winded fantastical b.s."

To his surprise, Lamia chuckled. "Qigong nonsense? Elias, I haven't seen you practicing qigong. I *have* seen you posing and swinging your arms. I've seen you arguing and whining, and running around in a panic, just to get yourself beat up. I've seen your ego and your tantrums, but I haven't seen you learning to manage your qi. One good thing that came from your behavior is that Andrei thinks you're a fool—but are you going to continue being a fool?"

Anger flared in Elias' chest. He felt his face getting warm. The fangs would surely come next.

Elias turned and left, hurrying back toward the lot at the edge of the grounds. Once again, he made a show of speeding out of the parking lot, but he slowed his speed as he approached town, his eyes darting back and forth in search of patrol cars.

He drove to Cinnabar Park, where he often went when he felt lost and upset. Elias shoved his earbuds into his ears and picked out a playlist on Aarya's old MP3 player—the "Moody," playlist, in keeping with his feelings and the suddenly overcast weather. He walked the park trails, meandering slowly toward the bridge with the chain-link fences, finally stopping at the love lock he shared with Aarya. It hung among an eclectic collection of padlocks ranging from plain to elaborately ornate, some engraved with messages of lasting devotion, some with names scribbled in permanent marker. Aarya had promised Elias, back when they'd hung their own lock, that the two of them would be together even if it took more than a lifetime—even if that time was as far away as nirvana.

At the moment, it seemed another fantastical fib.

Elias crossed the bridge and went to the large, flat rock where he and Aarya had shared deep conversations and silent reflections. He spread himself flat on the surface, trying to soak up the last of its ebbing warmth, the same way he always tried to absorb the last traces of Aarya's presence from the abbey and other places they'd visited together. Through the earbuds came a gospel rendition of "Sometimes

I Feel Like a Motherless Child," and that was how Elias felt at the moment: alone and uprooted, like the weed that Lamia had so callously pulled from the thriving garden. The slow, moody song seeped into his soul, and then there were tears running down his face, mingling with the sudden spattering of light rain.

Elias often got more comfort out of this visit, this lying on Aarya's rock and listening to her specially selected songs, than he did from the abbey. This time, though, he simply felt loss. His attempt at feeling Aarya's warmth was subverted by his seething—not at Lamia, but at himself for being so easily swayed by his own temper. At the moment he was merely annoyed at the bhikshuni, mostly because of her insight rather than her reincarnation fantasy: *I've seen your ego and your temper tantrums, but I haven't seen you learning to manage your qi.*

Elias turned his head, making a quick survey of the area to make sure he was alone. "What should I do, Aarya?" he asked quietly. He supposed he knew what Aarya would say if she was there. *So what if Lamia's story sounds crazy? You have plenty of crazy things to talk about, too. You should have at least listened to her.*

The playlist had moved on to the next song. Elias homed in on its pleading confession: *I'm sorry* and blah blah blah, sorry for blaming and hurting you, I did it because I'm broken inside, and so on.

Elias let out a hissing sound as he pressed the "skip" button. He wasn't in the mood for apology songs. Perhaps it was his own desperate fantasy, but Elias often thought that Aarya was whispering to him through these songs, pushing him to action just as she had done during the last days of her life. She had chosen each track carefully, and especially for him, to help him through tough times and hard decisions—

but Elias didn't want to hear about apologies. He had tired of his habit of lashing out at the bhikshunis, storming off, and then returning to apologize.

As he mused over his next steps, though, he realized that the playlist's theme hadn't changed. Elton John was singing much the same message: *I'm sorry* is hard to say, and everything's sad, and blah blah.

"Fine," Elias muttered. "I get it. I'll go back and apologize. *Again*." He pushed himself up from the rock. "And I'll go and watch more YouTube, and I'll try to focus more on my qi—and I'll listen to Lamia, even though she's as nutty as a squirrel turd."

His next visit to the abbey didn't provide a chance for private apology. Elias found Vela and Lamia together in the kitchen, preparing snacks for the evening's workshop. Elias stood awkwardly apart from the bhikshunis, trying to figure out what to say, but he was quickly distracted by the slimy gray slab that Vela was cutting with slow precision.

"Good God!" Elias exclaimed. "What is that?"

"Konjac steak," Vela replied, "made from yam."

"It looks like a block of speckled slime."

"It's quite good, especially when it's fried with soy sauce and sesame oil." Vela didn't look up, but gestured to a large, blossomed lotus, its damp petals spread in perfect geometry around its central fruit. "You can make yourself useful and julienne the bell peppers, or slice those mushrooms. We're preparing a lotus meal for our special guests."

"What special guests?" Elias asked.

"Andrei and his friends."

He stared at her, then at the flower. "What's special about the lotus? It is poisoned?"

84

A vague smile played on the bhikshuni's lips as she tossed the gray cubes into a frying pan. "It's healthy and delicious, and it's symbolic. The bloomed lotus looks beautiful and pure, but it grows out of the mud. It represents that we all have beautiful souls, and on our journey, we—"

"Yes, yes, I know," Elias interrupted. "We have to grow through the mud, and the fully bloomed lotus represents enlightenment, and all that. So I've heard."

"This meal takes a long time to prepare," Vela continued. "The seeds have to be peeled and the sprouts removed, and the stem chopped and fried—and the other vegetables must be prepared and cooked well. It's a meal you make for a special event or a special person."

"Arsenic is symbolic, too," Elias said. "It grows among sulfur, and it kills pests. It's a good meal to serve to someone who's trying to destroy you." He looked at the flower with open contempt. "Do you have any idea how hard Andrei would laugh if he knew you were making this for him? He's not the kind of person who gives a damn."

"Oh, I know. He has made that very clear."

"Then, why bother?"

Vela placed a knife and a red bell pepper on the cutting board in front of Elias. Quietly, she replied: "It's a reminder. And it's not just for him. Wash your hands, please, and slice this pepper julienne style."

Elias withheld further comment as he worked, except to ask for direction. He and Lamia sliced and fried the rest of the vegetables and, when the food had cooled, arranged it neatly on the petals.

The evening's workshop was another meditation on Chenrezig, led this time by Vela. Elias positioned himself a few rows behind Andrei, who had arrived with Maria and Akari. That Sanjay was absent, Elias thought, was a good sign. Perhaps Andrei feared the effect that the abbey was having on him.

Vela finished the meditation—the same one she'd led at the prison—and transitioned into her lecture. "When injustices happen, and when people slight us, people often ask us: 'Why aren't you outraged? Don't you know how wrong this is?'" The bhikshuni's gaze, as she spoke, was riveted on Elias. "Rage doesn't have to be a prerequisite for justice. Of course, we know that there are injustices in the world, and we spend a great deal of time learning and practicing how to act in such cases—but we have also chosen to move beyond samsara, the cycle of incarnation and accumulated karma, so that when we move in the world, no matter what we're facing, we can observe such events as a Buddha."

Elias resisted the urge to roll his eyes. His attention drifted to the trio in front of him. Andrei and Maria sat up straight and unmoving, while Akari drooped, her head hanging forward as though she had fallen asleep. The only sign of wakefulness was the occasional snaking of her hand up to the back of her head, where she rubbed at some invisible irritant. The trio's behavior during the lecture was so unremarkable that Elias began to let his guard down—and then the lecture concluded, and the special meal began.

In the lobby, the snack table had been moved to the middle of the room, where the small crowd could gather around it. The lotus plate sat between platters of rice balls and konjac, its petals laden with strips of salted and fried vegetables. Lamia and Ven. Nyima served small plates of morsels to the visitors, who *ooh*ed and *aah*ed over the colorful arrangement.

Akari stared at the spread with hungry eyes. She wore a pale yellow dress with white flowers; the fabric was thin enough that Elias could see how skinny the woman really was, could even make out the outline of her ribs and the concave slope of her belly. One thin hand reached up again to scratch the back of her head, where the little mouth was probably salivating, waiting to be fed.

Vela wrapped a few strips of fried squash in a lotus petal and offered it to the petite woman. Akari took a step back; the hungry look vanished from her face.

"Akari is dieting," Maria explained, flashing her chilly smile. Her voice, Elias thought, sounded like needles.

"No pressure," Vela replied, "but you can all be assured that this is an extremely low-calorie food—and the konjac as well."

"I'll try it." Andrei's tall figure loomed over the bhikshuni as he reached for the wrap and popped it into his mouth. His eyebrows went up in feigned delight. "Mmm." The vampire swallowed and added: "Very delicate. I like it."

The door to the prayer room opened. Ana and Ven. Tseten emerged, wearing twin expressions of bewilderment. Ana caught sight of Elias and made her way over to the corner, where he kept watch over the room.

"What's up?" he asked.

Ana leaned close, replying in a low voice: "We had an intruder."

"What?"

"There's a mess in the prayer room. Someone tore through all the boxes under the table."

Elias' gaze shifted back to Andrei, who now hovered over the food, enjoying another sample from the special meal that the bhikshunis had prepared for him. Maria stood at his side, and Akari at the other—surely about to let her snake-like tendrils of hair grab at the remaining cubes of konjac. "Did they take anything?" Elias asked.

"No. Venerable Tseten said nothing is missing."

He's looking for the astra, Elias thought. Sanjay, or one of Andrei's other goons, had likely searched the room after the workshop began.

Elias debated where to move next. It seemed best for him to make a search of the abbey; Andrei's presence was likely a distraction from the intruder, who might still be prowling the grounds.

He was about to leave when he spotted a sudden, strange movement from Maria. At first, it looked like she spat something onto the table—but he quickly realized that the ejection was a long, thin tongue, now slithering across the table toward a pregnant woman on the other side. The woman chatted away with another guest, smiling and oblivious, as the sharply forked tongue slid past the plates and toward the curve of her belly.

Elias moved without thinking. He picked up one of the ceramic platters and dropped heavily it on the tongue. Maria gasped; the freakish tongue retracted, shooting back up into her open mouth.

"Oops," Elias said. He had dropped the platter with such force that it broke in two; the smaller fragment bounced and fell to the carpeted floor.

Andrei bent to pick it up. As he leaned over, Elias caught sight of a necklace that had been hidden in the vampire's shirt; it swung forward, revealing a shiny black stone flecked with gold specks, encircled by a silver ring.

Maria hurried out of the lobby, holding a hand over her mouth as she fled through the front doors.

"She's fine," Andrei assured the other guests, standing and placing the broken ceramic on the table. He quickly tucked the black stone beneath his shirt. "She burned her tongue earlier. It probably still hurts—but the food looks so good, she couldn't resist." As the other guests left the now-empty table, the vampire smiled broadly and addressed Elias. "Aren't you eating?"

Elias ignored the question. Andrei grinned at him and tried again. "Have you ever devoured a lotus? A beautiful, soft, and frail flower, just bloomed? I'm sure you have. Exquisite, isn't it?" He shoved the last of the lotus petals into his mouth and chewed slowly, making a show of savoring it.

"Sorry Leitha couldn't make it," the vampire added, when he had swallowed the wrap. "She's resting after a bit of a wild night. Nothing new, I'm sure." Andrei licked his fingers. "She has a delicious vitality—for now, anyway."

Anger writhed in Elias' muscles; he thought he felt the first push of his canines, but he remembered Vela's words and calmed himself. *You're pathetic*, he thought, *and I don't want your disgusting false comfort*. He heard the anger in those words and checked himself. *I have no need of a false comfort.*

He asked Andrei softly: "What are you trying so hard to get?"

His calm demeanor had no effect on the vampire. Confidence shone in Andrei's eyes. "Sometimes I'm not sure," the vampire said. "At first, I suppose I was interested in the legend of the astra—an instrument supposedly drawn from another plane of existence, with unusual and unique powers. Lately, though, I've learned to access other planes in ways more suited to me—and for more interesting purposes." Andrei smiled coldly. "Maybe I'm just trying to get beyond the 'cycle of incarnation,' as your bhikshuni calls it. Rebirth seems so tiring, and death is unpleasant too—but you know all about that. Leitha told me about your mother, and about poor Aarya, your true love. It must be difficult to observe those things as the Buddha."

Elias gritted his teeth, but he strove for calm. He held in his mind the image of Shi Miao Xing performing qigong, ever peaceful and powerful.

"But I'm sure that coming here is a big help," Andrei continued. "There aren't many places willing to help people like us. In fact, forgiveness is such a rare thing that there are all kinds of people wanting to come here to heal from the things they've done. Your stepfather, for instance. What was his name? Gorensen? He perhaps needs this place more than anyone. Shouldn't we invite him?"

The image of Shi Miao Xing was shattered. Elias felt his breath coming ragged and shallow. His nostrils seemed to fill with the sour smell of sweat—the stench of his stepfather.

"Is that too uncomfortable an encounter? I guess it's a drawback of helping damaged souls, but someone has to take the risk." Andrei smiled again, his eyes hard and cold as ice.

Elias heard himself beginning to wheeze. He turned and left the building—not to search, as he had planned, but to escape. He went at first toward the parking lot, but he realized that Maria was probably there, and Andrei would soon head in that same direction—and Elias wasn't in any state to drive. His mind raced; his body began to hunch forward, stooping in a strange manner as he tried to determine the safest place to flee. He tried the restrooms first, but he found them locked, with "restroom closed" signs taped to the doors.

Elias ended up in the kitchen, a place where Andrei surely would not intrude. Vela found him there when she and Lamia returned with the empty dishes.

Neither of the bhikshunis commented on the way he stood: slouched in a corner, facing the entrance. When he looked up, though, he saw Lamia gazing at him with quiet sympathy.

Before she could say anything, Elias diverted: "Did you find the intruder?"

"Not yet," Lamia replied. "We're not especially concerned. They made a mess in the yard and in a few of the rooms, but no real damage was done."

"And they didn't take anything?" Elias pressed. "Are you sure?"

"Cucumbers."

Elias raised his eyebrows questioningly.

"They ate the cucumbers," Lamia said, "in the garden."

"That's all? They took the cucumbers?"

"They didn't just *take* them. They left teeth marks. The intruder was chomping down right there in the garden."

It seemed an important detail, merely because of its peculiarity. "Don't you think it was a monster?" Elias mused. "Monsters have particular tastes, and they don't exert manners when they're hungry. Andrei likes blood, Maria seems to like unborn babies, Akari likes . . . anything, I guess, as long as she can eat it through the back of her head. Maybe there's a monster that likes cucumbers." Neither bhikshuni agreed or dissented, and he added ruefully: "I should have never taken the astra. Not just because it was wrong, but because if it was still there, Andrei might have accidentally touched it. He'd be toast by now."

"It wasn't Andrei," Lamia replied. "It happened during the Chenrezig meditation."

Vela, who had been rinsing dishes, turned off the faucet. She finally spoke up, her voice calm, but with a hint of an edge. "You know, Elias," she said, "when you're here, you're rather private. I had no idea you had such a big mouth. Did you also tell Leitha where we kept the astra?"

Elias felt himself flushing. "I wasn't that specific." He tried to check through his memories, to ensure that his claim

91

was accurate. "At least, I don't *think* I was that specific. Is that what they were looking for?"

"Andrei may have been making sure you lost the astra," Vela replied. "Now, he'll probably be checking the river."

"He'll never find it," Elias insisted.

"Let's hope not."

"What could he possibly do with it? Destroy other monsters? He's trying to build them up, not break them down."

Vela exchanged a brief look with Lamia—a look of exaggerated, grim silence, the look of a shared secret. "We're not certain, yet, about his intentions," Vela said.

Elias' voice conveyed a jaded impatience: "What are you not telling me?"

They shared the look again, though he saw it plainly.

"Does it have something to do with Lucian?" Elias pressed. "Why is Andrei so hell-bent on getting him back that he'd terrorize you for it?"

Lamia spoke without looking at Elias. "Monsters hate seeing other monsters break free. They will do what they can to claw you back down into the cesspool, so that they don't have to look miserable and weak in comparison."

"Is it that simple?" Elias asked. "There must be more."

She shrugged. "Andrei seems to manage a lot of people. He has plans for his business, and our movement is getting in his way. He knows the same people in prison that we know. He may be fighting to keep them under his thumb."

"Maybe, but there's something else you're not telling me. I can tell by the way you're refusing to look me in the eye."

The bhikshuni turned to face Elias and spoke calmly: "Andrei was wearing a black tourmaline stone. Venerable Thubten Dorje noticed it when he leaned over."

"Yes, I saw it."

"Do you know much about tourmaline?"

Elias scoffed. "Do you think I've ever heard of it?"

"It's a special gem that absorbs dreams and residue from other people, especially when they speak," Lamia explained. "Their auras are carried in their vibration, and they permeate the stone. That may be how Andrei knew about me. Some people use black tourmaline to absorb negative energy and transmute it, but others use it to capture people's nightmares and examine their deepest fears."

"I'm sure Andrei does the latter," Elias replied. He continued hesitantly: "Andrei mentioned my stepdad. Leitha doesn't know his full name, but she knows that I changed my surname from Göransson to Hellström because I didn't want to share that slimeball's name. Andrei threatened to bring him here. He might be looking for him."

Lamia's lips pressed together, as if she had a thought in her mind but hesitated to say it. "You know . . . you can always report your stepdad and press charges," she said after a moment. "That would ensure that he stays away from you."

"No, I can't. Call me a coward, but I'm not putting myself in that position, even if it means protecting other kids. Nothing will happen to him. He'll start following me around just to show me how powerless I am, and he'll pass it off as a coincidence. He'll put on his show of good-hearted bewilderment, and no one will believe me, and I'll get cast as a mentally troubled liar—and *everyone* will find out. And every time they look at me, I'll see that discomfort in their eyes, and . . . I'll be *reminded*."

"That might happen sometimes, especially at first," she replied, "but people don't think about your issues as much as you imagine. They're wrapped up in their own business."

"I know what people are like. This isn't something you can lecture me on. It's out of your realm."

"So you assume. But, Elias, you're not the only person in this community who has been preyed on and traumatized. Unfortunately, it's not that uncommon." Lamia's eyes conveyed genuine, gentle sympathy. "You could try talking to someone else who has been through the process of reporting an abusive parent. Ana has done it. She's open about it."

"Is she?" Elias asked, thinking back to Ana's question game. "She didn't seem eager to talk about it when she had the opportunity."

Lamia ignored the comment. "Exposing what happened is a personal choice," she said. "You don't owe anyone the truth. Only the perpetrator owes that—but I think your biggest fear is that your stepdad is still out there, behaving like a monster and hurting others."

"My biggest fear," Elias said, "is being targeted by him."

"But you faced him with bravery when you left."

"That wasn't bravery." Elias' voice was thick with a growing bitterness. "It was survival—and I didn't face him. It's true that I warned him to stay away from me, but I left him a note."

"Nevertheless, he has no real power over you now. Is the idea of facing him really what's bothering you?"

Elias made an effort to stay calm. He thought of Shi Miao Xing, of his YouTube meditations, but Lamia's audacious assumptions chased the words from his mind and pushed his helpless rage to the surface.

"Facing *you*, and listening to your clueless presumptions, is what's bothering me," he spat. "He hurt *me*, he was a monster to *me*, and I don't have room in my being to care about what he's doing to other people—and I can't convince anyone, anyway. You ask about what's 'bothering' me like we're discussing a disappointing meal or a bad movie. That scumbag doesn't 'bother' me. You don't know how terrifying and . . . pointless it would be to face him again. He always had all of the power. Even when people could *see* that I needed help, they just smiled and believed the charming show that he put on—and he *knows* that." Elias was trembling, his vision marred by tears, so that Lamia and Vela became twin blurs. "He knows that people will always choose his great show over my pathetic little cry for help. They always choose the charming aggressor over the loser. That's how people are, and that's why I chose to be a monster. People are weak, and hypocritical, and selfish. As a vampire, at least, I wasn't putting on a show of decency." He sniffled, heard his voice beginning to break, but pushed on: "I hurt people, I drained and broke them, but at least I didn't pretend that I wasn't a monster. I didn't pretend to be good. That was all I . . . ."

His voice gave out. Elias tried to control his sudden shaking, but it wracked his body so that he began to sink to the floor, slowly, helplessly. He grasped the counter to keep from falling. Try as he might, Elias couldn't stand; fear and grief overcame him, made him weak. *Just like it would if I ever faced that scumbag again.*

A firm pair of arms grasped him, keeping him upright and diminishing his trembling. Bhikshunis, he knew, were not allowed to hug men; nevertheless, Lamia held him while he wept into her shoulder.

They huddled like that for some time, silent except for Elias' shuddering gasps. When he withdrew, he saw the crimson of Lamia's robe stained with his tears and snot; he jerked back, wiping at his nose in embarrassment.

"You're okay, Elias," Lamia assured him. "You're safe here. We believe you, and if Andrei ever does bring him here, we'll protect you."

Those words caused the tears to surge again. Elias shook his head. "Thanks, but stop talking about it, okay? I just . . . I need to use the bathroom. Can I use the one in here?"

Vela responded sharply: "The bathrooms are closed."

He looked up, blinking to clear his vision. "The ones in here are closed, too? Why are they all closed?"

"Use one of the bathrooms in town. Go to the gas station or the grocery store."

Lamia protested: "Let him use it. I'll check it first, just in case."

Elias got to his feet, still wiping at his face. "No, I'll get going."

"All right." Lamia stood up with a soft grunt. Elias watched her push herself up with her hands on her knees; he heard the crack of her ankles, and he noted the dark circles and deep lines that had appeared under her eyes. The bhikshuni seemed suddenly old and frail.

"This business has made me uneasy," Lamia said wearily. "I'm going to meditate and pray on it tonight."

"You do that," Elias said. He sniffed again and steadied his voice. "I'm going to pay a visit to the monster district. I'll see what I can learn about Andrei."

"Be careful, Elias."

"Don't worry. I'll keep to the shadows this time."

Andrei and his creepy friends seemed to have gone. On the grounds, near the parking lot, there was only Wen, friendly and harmless. He didn't fail to notice that Elias had been crying as he moved closer; Elias saw his expression change from one of eager welcome to genuine concern.

"What's wrong?" Wen asked.

"Never mind. What are you doing here?"

"I wanted to go to the meditation, but I suppose it's over. I left work late, so I missed the bus. How was it? Did it affect you that much?"

"It's not a good time, Wen. Just let me drive you home."

In the car, Elias tried to think of a way to bring up Ana's past. Trying for his most casual tone, he said: "Wen . . . how much do you know about Ana?"

Wen gave him a perplexed look. "Why? I thought you weren't interested in her."

"I'm not. But I was talking with the nuns, and . . . they mentioned that Ana had some trouble with one of her parents. I'm guessing it was her mom."

"Oh, that. Yeah, Ana's mom is a piece of work. She has raging temper tantrums, and one day she beat Ana half to death. She smashed her up with a metal pot, threw her in the shower, and sprayed her with hot water."

For a moment, Elias' breath stopped. He felt a sudden, faint pang—a rare moment of sympathy.

"Ana finally reported her while she was recovering in the hospital, but her mom got her friends to testify that she was such a great mom, and she said that Ana was a mentally unstable, attention-starved liar, and—"

"Wait a minute. Ana's own friends testified against her?"

"No, no. Her mom's friends. Her mom's best friend, and one of her co-workers. She got them to testify against Ana, and she said that Ana caused the injuries herself to get attention—but Ana's teachers and her friends' parents stuck up for her, and they managed to point to enough evidence that Ana's mom received a prison sentence."

For some reason, the tail end of Wen's story brought tears to Elias' eyes. He turned his head slightly aside to hide his feelings, watching the road from the corner of his eye. "That must be nice," he mused.

Wen scoffed. "Uh . . . I'm not sure how being beaten half to death by your mother is 'nice.'"

"Not that," Elias said. "I mean, having people protect you and stick up for you." He tilted his head, trying to distribute the tears over the surface of his eyes so that they didn't spill over and expose the fresh wave of grief. "I wish I'd had that. Or, that I'd had enough of it that it made a difference."

Wen didn't respond for a while. Then he said, "Elias, I know you're still crying. You're being so obvious. Just look forward and face the road."

Elias grudgingly turned his head. The pressure of his tears receded.

"What happened to you?" Wen asked.

"Never mind."

"Okay. But if you ever want to talk about it, you know I'll be discreet, and I'm not going to be a jerk."

Elias reached out and turned on the stereo.

That night, his visit to Bull's-Eye's "Forbidden Friday" gave him no new insights; he prowled quietly outside, saw no signs of Andrei or his companions—just lonely, scantily clad strangers eager to drink and dance in the dark. Random spying felt suddenly useless; Elias had not the patience to lurk in such a place night after night, for hours on end. He would have to enlist some help.

Back at the abbey, Ana was the first possibility he encountered. He knew that if he asked for help, she would readily accept, but he hesitated. She would surely take it the wrong way and shower him with unwanted flirtations.

He found her in the gathering hall, coming out from the back rooms. When she smiled at him, there seemed to be a new slyness in the expression, as though some secret thought delighted and amused her. Elias stiffened at the sight—and then he remembered Wen's story. He thought of Ana's pleasant face being smashed with a metal pot, and his grudging resistance faded.

"Hi, Ana," he said.

"Hey. Who are you looking for?"

"Um . . . Lamia, I guess."

She raised her eyebrows. "You guess?"

"I need her help with something."

"She's not here. She went to a conference with Ven Thubten Dorje and Thubten Tseten.

"Oh," Elias said, hearing the disappointment in his own voice. He hesitated, considering the alternative. If he asked Wen and Ana for help . . . .

"You're very polite today," Ana said, the hint of wiliness still showing on her face. "You're saying words again, and you even called me by my name."

Elias was silent, still locked in an internal debate.

She flashed a friendly smile. "I know that you asked Wen about me," she said, "and that Wen told you about my mom. Is that why you're being nice to me now?"

"Am I? It wasn't intentional."

"You know you are. Is it because you feel sorry for me?"

"Why should I?" he asked.

She paused for a long time. Her lips pressed together into a thin line—something she did, Elias had noticed, when she was deep in thought.

Suddenly, the smile reappeared. "Do you feel sorry enough to do the thirty-six questions game?"

Elias felt tension creeping into his muscles. "You mean, the game that includes questions such as 'What's your most horrible memory' and 'How do you feel about your mother'?"

"Yes. That one. And the four-minute stare."

99

Elias suppressed a sigh.

"Or just the four-minute stare," Ana suggested. "The questions are kind of lame anyway."

He walked away, headed back toward the doors. He had made it all the way outside when something stopped him— some strange reaction to Ana's smile, to her naïve advances. *You're a good person,* she had said, and for a moment Elias resented her for being so clueless—for unintentionally shoving his depraved flaws in his face.

He went back inside. Ana still stood where he had left her, but the wily look had vanished.

"Four minutes," he said.

"What?"

He went to one of the chairs and moved it so that it faced the other chair. "The four-minute stare." He opened the clock app on his phone, adjusting the timer and letting his thumb hover over the start button. "If you still want to do it, we're doing it now. I don't have time to waste." He sat down and looked up at her, his gaze stark and unfeeling.

Slowly, she sat down across from him. She had pretty eyes; Elias knew that, though he had no interest in them. Their warmth, their essence of hope, repelled him.

"I'm starting the timer," he said.

He set the phone on the table beside him, and he and Ana stared at each other in the silent room. Ven. Nyima came by at one point and greeted them, but they ignored her; the exchange remained unbroken, and the bhikshuni got the point and left them alone.

This time, Ana didn't laugh. In the third minute, she opened her mouth as if to speak, but the lips barely parted before closing again. A sad gravity filled her eyes, the weight of something mournful; the guise of flighty immaturity vanished, and for the first time, Elias saw in Ana's eyes that

100

she had been through difficult things, had been stomped on and shattered, that her lighthearted warmth was her way of putting herself together again. As the fourth minute approached, her pupils suddenly dilated. Her eyes became red, and the beginning of tears gleamed there. Elias wondered if she was crying because of what she saw in his eyes, or because of what Elias was seeing in hers.

The timer sounded, gentle and rhythmic. Elias broke his gaze away and turned it off. "Well?" he said dryly. "Did you fall in love?"

"No," Ana replied, averting her eyes. She stood up and left without saying anything else.

6

On the drive home, Elias found himself indisposed to anything emotional. He avoided music and switched the stereo to the local news. Not more than a minute had passed when the mention of Cinnabar Park caught his attention: *A council spokesperson stated that the walking bridge at Cinnabar Park has been compromised by age, rust, and the added weight of hundreds of padlocks. This week, the process of tearing down the bridge will begin. The wire gates will be replaced by metal panels. Any remaining locks will be recycled. . . .*

Elias glanced in the rearview mirror. He slammed on the brakes and made a U-turn in the middle of the street.

As he drove, his gaze shifted to his keychain. Next to the keys for his townhouse, car, and mailbox was an ornate, ancient-looking brass key with green patina—one of two keys that opened the "love lock" he shared with Aarya. He carried it with him as a reminder; the other key remained in his desk for safekeeping.

The lot at the park was empty. Elias parked haphazardly and jogged down the path to the bridge. He found the chain-link gating still studded with padlocks. Elias easily spotted the large brass padlock heavily stained with green patina, now further weathered by the elements. He unlocked it and stood for a while, feeling its weight in his hand and thinking about the vows he had made while standing in this same spot. He remembered the sensation of Aarya's fingertip poking firmly into his chest, the intensity in her eyes as she demanded: *Don't harm others. Perpetuate kindness instead.*

Elias laughed softly at the memory. "Perpetuate kindness," he whispered, and added: "I don't know how. You were supposed to show me."

He studied the figures on the lock's surface. Elias had meant to find a Buddhist-themed padlock, but he had mistakenly bought one that featured the Hindu deities Ganesh and Vishnu. Aarya had found it appropriate. Vishnu represented dharma, the path of righteousness, she said, and Ganesh was a symbol of new beginnings—of clearing away obstacles to ensure success, of destroying demons that might plague the attempt.

Elias put the padlock in his jacket pocket and headed back across the bridge.

At home, he found that his zeal for spying on Andrei had vanished. He decided to finish his latest website commission instead. Elias sat at his computer with a cup of coffee, his hands poised beside the keyboard. Minutes passed, and he sat staring at the screen, muttering to himself—not about his work, but about Lamia's presumptuous directives and Aarya's self-satisfied speeches about redemption and forgiveness. "That disgusting psycho would never redeem himself," Elias whispered. "Screw you guys. Why even make me think about that scumbag?"

It wasn't a fair accusation. Andrei had brought up his stepfather first, and then Elias himself had mentioned it to Lamia. Still, her assumptions and suggestions irked him; he ruminated on those rather than Andrei's threat. *I think your biggest fear is that your stepdad is still out there, behaving like a monster and hurting others.*

There had been many times when Elias had been on the verge of looking for his stepfather online. The man was outgoing, friendly, the type who went to church and volunteered at charity events, the type who would maintain a social media account to show everyone how wonderful and harmless he was.

At home, though, in private, he was controlling, intimidating, and cruel. Manipulation lived on his breath.

Elias' fingers hovered above the keypad. *I could just look. I don't have to report him. I can just check to see if he's doing what I think he's doing: using social media to make more friends, show everyone how great he is, and have more people who believe in him. The more people he has on his side, the harder it is to speak up about him.*

Elias lowered his hands into his lap.

After a few minutes, he opened a search engine and typed: *how do I report someone who committed an assault years ago?*

The search led him to a website called No More Excuses. Elias read every word on the page, his attention completely consumed. The site's authors acknowledged that many people privately lived with the aftermath of abuse, and that *if you want to talk about what happened to you, we will listen, and we will believe you.*

As Elias read those last words, emotion welled up in him, deep and unstoppable. His breath shuddered as he began to weep.

He simply sat and cried for a while, until his tears subsided enough that he could continue reading. He thought of Lamia's words of comfort: *You're safe here. We believe you, and if Andrei ever does bring him here, we'll protect you.* She was probably repeating what she'd heard from organizations like this one, from people who were familiar with the fears of the victims: of not being believed, of being cast as a troubled liar, of aggravating and bolstering the monster.

The next section was about reporting abuse: *It's never too late to talk to the police.* The words brought a sense of relief, but Elias knew he couldn't do it. The mere thought made him sick. He was already grinding his teeth, and he knew what would come next: sleepless nights, hours of gnashing teeth and a racing mind, muscles and nerves racked by stress and fear.

Yet he read on, soaking up relevant details. *People who get away with sexual violence often continue to commit similar crimes. Your report may help to prevent further abuse.* The website claimed that even if the victim of such crimes was an adult, and even if the case was tried in court, the victim's identity would be protected—but Elias knew from experience that this promise was meaningless. "Protecting the identity" simply meant concealing a name. The news media were prone to revealing details about the victims, and they would surely mention in this case that the victim was the perp's stepson. Everyone would know it was Elias. Andrei would torment him with that knowledge.

Elias bookmarked the website and closed the browser.

He abandoned his work and tried to do a short qigong routine, but his focus strayed. His gaze shifted to the bookshelf, where a copy of *The Art of War* stood out among the other books, its blood-red spine stamped with gold and black print. Supposedly, the book had been written by Sun Tzu, an ancient Chinese military strategist and philosopher. Elias had only skimmed through it, and now it held his attention. He was at war, after all. The book might provide a more effective distraction and give him new ideas about how to fight against Andrei—and against his other problems. The thought of fighting back, instead of anticipating victimization, might help him overcome his fears.

Elias pored over the book for the next hour, making a mental note of the takeaways that stood out to him: *You cannot win unless you know yourself.* The passage listed the traits of a weak leader: recklessness, a quick temper, cowardice, anxiety, ego. Elias sighed and whispered to himself: "That's, like, my whole personality."

Know your enemy; take advantage of their weaknesses; do not attack their strengths. Use spies. Warfare is based on deception; convince the enemy that your strengths are your weaknesses. Know the terrain and use it to your advantage.

Elias grabbed a pen and paper and wrote down a few ideas, and then a few more, until the paper was cluttered with notes.

By the time he went to bed, his mind was no longer plagued by fear, and his teeth had stopped gnashing.

"Know yourself" meant more than knowing his own strengths and weaknesses, Elias realized. Andrei had targeted him as part of a group, and the team of bhikshunis and volunteers was small enough that Andrei was examining them on an individual basis. He had been inside their heads. Elias decided to do the same.

On the day of the prison visit, he carefully timed his arrival at the monastery. Volunteers usually arrived by 8:30 a.m. and were led in a short prayer; Elias ventured into the campus at 8:40, ensuring that he missed the prayer but still had time to spend with the bhikshunis. He caught Venerable Thubten Sonam, the youngest of the nuns, on her way to the parking lot; he helped her pick up trash and sweep out the lot, and then he offered to sweep the small court nearby.

Elias made small talk as they worked, awkwardly at first, but his discomfort didn't last long. Ven. Sonam was bright-eyed and friendly, with a youthful and perpetually oily face that made her seem more like a teen than a woman in her late twenties. While Elias swept the court, she cleaned the small fiberglass Buddha statue and brushed dirt from the stone wall, and then she sat down and waited for Elias to finish. "How do you feel about going to the prison?" she asked. "Are you nervous?"

"No," Elias replied. "It sounds pretty boring, actually. Have you been there?"

"To the men's prison? No."

Elias considered her reply. "What about the women's prison?"

"Ah . . . ." The bhikshuni laughed nervously, and Elias saw hesitance in her bright eyes. "Yeah, I've been there."

She was looking down now, staring at the stone floor, and Elias took the opportunity to quietly examine her. He saw a hint of shame in the young woman, of embarrassment stubbornly residing in the joyful demeanor. He guessed at the source of her shame: "Were you there as an inmate?"

"Yeah," she admitted. "I was in for eight months. That's actually how I found out about Achiravati Abbey: I was one of the inmates who joined their outreach program."

"And now you're ordained," Elias said.

"Yeah. This place is . . . everything I looked for in life, but never had. It took prison in order for me to find it."

Elias carefully considered what to say next, how to get the bhikshuni to open up even more. "The nuns invited me to the prison thing because they want me to talk about my past," he said. "I was never in prison, but . . . I've done things. I just didn't get caught."

"Is that why you're here?" she asked.

Elias stopped sweeping. He rested his chin on the tip of the broom handle. "I don't know," he replied. "Did they ask you to participate in the outreach program, too? It seems like you would be a perfect candidate—someone who served time but became a nun."

"It's complicated for me," Ven. Sonam replied. "I went in for assault, but I'm actually a weakling. I don't like hitting people. When I got arrested, I was dating a guy who was kind of wild. We went out with one of his friends, and they got into an argument about money. My boyfriend beat him up and told me to take his wallet, and . . . ." Shame glinted again in her eyes. "I took the wallet. So, I ended up in prison, and one of the guards knew the victim. I had robbery and assault charges, and this guard would encourage other inmates to beat me up. So, it was a pretty terrible experience. And . . . ." The young bhikshuni peered up at Elias. "You know Ana, right? The girl who volunteers here?"

"Yeah, of course."

"How well do you know her? I mean, do you know much about her family?"

"Just that her mom is in prison."

Ven. Sonam nodded. "Well, in our state, there's only one women's prison—and it's pretty big, but I happened to be in the same behavior program as Ana's mom. Ana is really nice; we all love her, but her mom is another person I don't want to run into."

"Did she beat you up?" Elias asked.

"No. She was trying to convince everyone of her innocence, so she couldn't go around assaulting people—but she encouraged other people to beat me up. She said I was a monster who beat a skinny kid half to death, so I should be beaten the same way. The whole thing is just . . . a traumatic experience that I'm still learning to cope with." She folded her hands in her lap, relaxing her shoulders, as if she had suddenly noticed the tension building there. "Andrei has connections at that prison, too," she said.

"What kind of connections?"

"We have a couple of newbies in the women's prison program. They both worked at Andrei's club. They joined after he started targeting us, so we figure they're surveilling, or . . . getting close to us for some other reason."

Elias lowered the broom. He leaned it against the stone wall and sat beside the bhikshuni. "Has Andrei approached you?" he asked.

"Not yet, but I'm sure he will, when he gets the chance. From what I hear, he likes to use people's mistakes against them, and make them feel like they don't deserve forgiveness."

"Yeah. He did that to me, too. I've done things far worse than what you've done."

The bhikshuni raised her eyebrows. "Such as?"

Elias chose his words carefully. "I . . . attacked a girl who used to volunteer here."

"Attacked her, how?"

"I bit her."

"You bit her," Elieen repeated. Her tone betrayed disbelief, but Elias saw a sudden realization in her eyes. "Oh, that's right. I heard that you were . . . ." She trailed off.

"I bit her," Elias repeated, "and she committed suicide afterwards. Andrei wants me to remember that I'm a monster, and that I don't deserve to be forgiven—especially not by these people." He waved a hand in the direction of the monastery. "But I'm here, and the nuns want me here. I think I mostly come here to remind myself that I can be forgiven, even if I feel like I don't deserve it."

Ven. Sonam nodded but said nothing.

"Andrei is also trying to make monsterization seem really great," Elias continued. "Like, if you're a monster, you have supernatural power, but if you're human, you're just a pathetic weakling. He tries to scare us and make us doubt ourselves, and whatever else can weaken us. So, I've been thinking about how to fight back—as a human, not as a monster. Andrei is exploring our weaknesses. I think we should do the same—think about our weaknesses, I mean, so he can't use them against us."

"Well, I agree with that. We're already doing that. Lamia had an unsettling experience with him, and she basically said the same thing."

"But we should do it as a group, not just as individuals," Elias insisted. "If we team up, we can fight against him easily. The best way to fight is to know ourselves and the environment we're fighting in, and to be ready to change with the circumstances—and to be aware of our opponent's strategies, so we can redirect them."

She smiled, her pale green eyes full of amused warmth. "You must be practicing tai chi."

"No; I've been reading *The Art of War*." Elias turned around, looking toward the left-hand building that housed the dormitories. "I should let Vela know I'm here."

"She's called Venerable Thubten Dorje," Ven. Sonam said, standing up. "I can tell her. I have to put the supplies back. Thanks for your help."

Elias remained in the court, deep in thought. It sounded like the bhikshunis were coming around to the same idea he had: that they needed to better know their vulnerabilities. Ven. Sonam, even as an ordained bhikshuni who strengthened herself daily with meditations and philosophy, was clearly still plagued by guilt and self-doubt. It was the sort of thing Andrei would latch onto. In a group, though, where the members were aware of each other's shortcomings and willing to offer support, such weaknesses would be diminished.

The squeal of brakes sounded from the road; a city bus had pulled up near the lot. Elias hardly paid attention to it, but then the door opened, and Ana stepped into the street.

Elias watched her with grudging resignation. He had not wanted to face her again so soon, but he supposed it couldn't be helped—and though he hoped that she would walk past him, she was heading straight for him, deliberate and confident, her gaze fixed on him as she approached. "Hi, Elias," she said. "Are you meditating?"

"I'm waiting for Vela."

"Venerable Thubten Dorje," she corrected him.

"Right." Elias masked his dismay as Ana set her handbag down and sat beside him. "Why are you here?" he asked.

"Ven. Nyima is teaching me how to make temple food." Ana peered at Elias, and then perhaps decided to be less direct. She gazed at the stone floor, gently kicking her heel against it.

"You're going to wreck your shoe," Elias said.

"Wow, you're worried about my shoe? How considerate."

Elias' face flushed. He was about to ask Ana if she was offended by the cold four-minute stare he'd exchanged with her, but his thoughts returned to his intended task: learning about the strengths and weaknesses of those at the abbey. Ana might be one of Andrei's targets. She was a frequent presence at the monastery; she had made contact with Andrei and his monsters; she was "nice," the kind of person Andrei would think of as easy prey.

"Can I ask you something?" he said.

"What?"

Elias looked up and saw Ana regarding him with cautious inquisitiveness. Her soft brown eyes reaffirmed what Elias had already discerned: Ana was kind, well intentioned, forgiving and ready to help. Her eyes blatantly announced: *I don't care that you're cold. I like you. Let's be friends.*

"Your mom," Elias began.

"What about her?"

"Is it true that she tried to kill you?"

Ana didn't reply, but looked searchingly into Elias' eyes, and he quickly added: "I'm not just being nosy. I have a reason for asking."

"What reason?" Ana pressed him.

Elias tried to think of an explanation, but Ana answered while he was still struggling to speak. "Yeah, it's true," she said. "I don't think that was her intention; I think she was just lashing out. But yeah, she could have killed me."

"Did she do that more than once?" Elias asked.

"Yes."

"Did you ever try to run away?"

Again, Ana scrutinized him, wondering at his question. "Well . . . there were times when I stayed at a friend's house because my mom was having one of her episodes, but I didn't think about running away."

"Why? Were you afraid she'd find you?"

Ana laughed. "No. I didn't want to run away from my mom. She's my only family. Aside from her, I just have my grandma and my uncle, who live hundreds of miles away in California." She resumed kicking her heel against the stone and added: "I don't know who my dad is."

"You love your mom," Elias said—a statement rather than a question.

Ana looked at him with suspicion. "Why are you asking about her?"

"Andrei is going around and trying to find out about everyone's past traumas, so he can get under our skin and use them against us," Elias said. "He may not have done it to you yet, but . . . ."

"That's your reason?" Ana looked amused rather than concerned. "So, what? Are you trying to get me to think about my weaknesses, so I can defend myself against him?"

"Something like that," Elias said.

Ana smiled—a sad, wistful smile—and looked out across the lot. "Yeah, I loved my mom. She wasn't always mean. She was . . . energetic, always encouraging me to try new things. She was fun. When she had one of her tantrums, her eyes would just glaze over, and she was totally out of control. It was like she didn't even see me."

Or maybe that's just what you want to believe, Elias thought.

"My mom is a perfectionist," Ana continued. "Her moods usually started when something didn't turn out the way she wanted—like her makeup, her hair, or something she was making. Once she threw a cake knife at my head because she made a cheesecake that wasn't perfect—like, it was fine, but it didn't look like it belonged on the cover of a magazine. It dipped down in the middle, or something, and she blamed it on me; she said that she opened the oven too early because I distracted her by talking. I dodged the knife, and I was just standing there, kind of in shock, and . . . ." Ana pulled one of her sleeved up over her shoulder, turning away so that Elias could see the expanse of pink, rumpled skin where she had been burned. "She threw the cake at me."

"Jesus," Elias said.

Ana released her sleeve, smiling as she wagged a finger at him. "Uh-uh, Elias. We say 'Buddha' here."

Elias didn't smile back at her. "It isn't funny."

113

"Is anything funny to you?" Ana asked. "You must have your own trauma—something Andrei can use against you. Now you know about mine. Are you going to tell me yours?"

Elias winced. Something about the earnest look in Ana's eyes was suddenly repugnant.

"I'm not concerned about Andrei," Ana said. "I've dealt with worse things than a thirty-year-old bully."

"He's not just a bully."

"Oh, right. He's a monster."

Elias kicked his own heel against the court floor, suddenly awkward and fidgety. He realized he was imitating Ana and immediately stopped. "Do you hate your mom?" he asked.

"No. I feel sorry for her."

"But . . . didn't she lie about you? Didn't she say you were a crazy liar, and . . . ."

"Yeah. But that doesn't make me hate her. It just . . . hurts." Pain flashed in Ana's eyes, brief but torturous. "And it makes her seem even more pitiful."

Those words, too, filled Elias with repugnance. *That's your weakness*, he thought. *You humored a monster, and let her beat you up, because you cared and felt sorry for her.* "Weren't you ever afraid of her?" he asked.

"Sure. But she would slip out of her moods, and . . . she wouldn't really apologize, but she would make excuses for what she did. Like, she'd say 'I've been really stressed because of this thing at work,' and I would take that as an apology. Like, 'She didn't mean to hurt me; she just lashed out because things aren't going well for her.'"

Elias made a mental note. *Weakness number two: She makes excuses for her attacker.*

"I kept hoping things would get better," Ana continued, "but they got worse. She hated the fact that she was getting older. The day I ended up in the hospital, she was mad because her makeup didn't hide her age spots and eye bags. She spent the whole morning staring in the mirror and messing around with her makeup, saying 'I'm *old*! I look like a disgusting *hag*!'" Ana's voice, as she mimicked the words, hissed with resentment and rage, and her eyes shone with bitterness. After a moment, though, the angry guise vanished, and she gave Elias a clear-eyed and determined look. "When I get older, I'm going to do everything I can to embrace my cronehood."

"Good for you," Elias said, unnerved by her unexpected performance.

"I still hope that she'll get the right mental health support," Ana said, "and that she'll eventually admit what she did, instead of making me out to be a crazy liar. I don't think that will happen, though, because her perfectionism is more important to her than anything else. It's more important than the truth, and it's more important than me." Ana smiled, but Elias heard her voice beginning to break as she uttered those last words. He saw the tears in her eyes.

Elias stood up. "I'm going to find Vela," he said.

"Okay," Ana replied softly as he walked away.

As Elias approached the dormitories, he was relieved to see Vela and Lamia coming out of the building. He stopped and waited, and by the time they arrived, his relief had turned to irritation. "What took you so long?" he demanded.

Vela greeted him with a slight bow of her head. "Hello, Elias. We were making jam for today's lunch. It took longer than usual because there were worms in the berries."

"Right. And I suppose you couldn't just rinse them down the drain; you had to serve them a lotus meal, and meditate with them, and—"

"There's no need to be snarky, Elias," Lamia cut in.

"I'm not being snarky," Elias retorted mildly. "I just have a dry sense of humor."

"We still have plenty of time to get to the prison," Vela assured him. "We wanted to arrive early so we could have a talk before the session started, but there's not much to discuss. Today, you can just observe; you don't need to speak, or participate in any way, if you don't feel comfortable." She waved at Ana, who was headed for the building, and greeted her warmly. Elias avoided looking at her.

The monastery's van was in the parking lot, a rusted and ancient-looking vehicle that rattled on the drive to the prison. "Don't you guys get donations?" Elias asked as they drove through town. "Before you buy more tapestries, or whatever, you should consider getting a car that won't fall apart on a ten-minute drive."

Vela, her hands clutching the steering wheel, replied: "It's a half-hour drive to the prison."

"Yes, Vela, thank you for correcting me."

"Venerable Thubten Dorje."

"Thubten Georgia?"

"Dorje," she said. "You can call me Ven. Dorje, and no one will scold you for being ill-mannered."

A tiny smile played on Elias' lips. "Is that why the volunteers are always frowning at me? I'm ill-mannered?"

"You have a reputation for not practicing etiquette."

"Does it offend you?" he asked.

"No," Vela replied. "On the contrary: A lot of people treat monastics like demi-gods. Appreciating someone's knowledge and commitment is fine, but worshiping them is a setback. Rude people like you help keep me humble. If you weren't here to check my ego, my pride would be so inflated, I might float away."

116

Elias glanced at her, saw her face calm and serious. "Now who's being snarky?"

"I just have a dry sense of humor," she replied.

The prison was some distance down the freeway, in an empty stretch of land surrounded by fields. Vela parked and checked into the conference room, a longer process than usual because of Elias' presence. He had filled out some forms in advance, but he found himself pummeled with questions and subjected to a pat-down before he was allowed to follow the nuns.

The conference room was unimpressive, much as Elias had expected: bare walls, no tables, just an array of chairs in a bleak white room. The only splash of color was provided by the robes of the inmates and monastics; ironically, the hue of their clothing was similar, with the monastics in crimson robes and bold orange drapings, and the inmates in the same shade of orange.

Elias spotted Lucian right away. Vela had described him as tall and handsome, with a penetrating gaze and "a bit of vitiligo"—a condition that affected his skin pigmentation. "Handsome," Elias thought, was an understatement. Lucian had a beautifully sculpted face and large brown eyes that reminded Elias of classical paintings of Jesus. He carried himself with a gentle but confident demeanor, offering quiet greetings and small, welcoming smiles to the visitors, doing the añjali pose with his palms and fingertips pressed together in front of his chest. For a moment, when Elias' eyes met Lucian's, he had the same impression as Vela: Lucian had an X-ray quality to his gaze, as if he could see past Elias' silent thoughts and feelings, perhaps even into his hidden past. The gaze was penetrating, startling, yet inoffensive and almost welcome.

There were other traits, too, that stood out. Lucian's skin was a shade of medium brown, but he had patches of pale flesh on both arms. Across the top of his forehead was another strip of light-colored skin, nearly symmetrical, with little dips and peaks that pointed down toward his face. As Lucian turned to sit, Elias noticed deep scarring along his right arm—the all-consuming scar of a serious burn—and damaged tissue peeking just above his shirt collar.

Elias tried not to stare, but he found it difficult to look away from Lucian's mesmerizing eyes. As the group seated themselves in the chairs, neatly arranged in a circle, Elias hurried to sit where he wouldn't be directly facing Lucian.

Vela started the session with a recap of the last meeting—something about a dharma triangle—and an intention for the coming hour, and then she delved into a visualization meditation. "Think of a particular painful time or incident," she said, "that you would like to make amends for." Vela gave Elias a sudden stern look, and he obediently closed his eyes. "Examine this event with the intent of understanding, not of judging or condemning. Focus on the person you caused the most pain to in this situation. As you breathe in, allow their pain to flow into your heart."

A memory flashed in Elias' mind: standing at the tree line near the abbey, his fangs lurking near the flesh of a small woman, the scents of shampoo and incense mingling with the more vital smell of her blood, and something else—something vulnerable and yearning, as though he could smell her despair. His mind shut off; the image flitted into darkness, and Elias no longer heard Vela's words.

The drone of her voice finally stopped, and Lamia took over. "Remember to practice this meditation on your own, and to include every sentient being in the world," she said.

"It's an exercise in patience and compassion—both toward yourself and others."

Elias' gaze crept back toward Lucian, who sat silent and respectful as one of the other inmates spoke. He seemed absorbed in the man's words.

Vela noticed Elias' lack of attention and gave him another unsmiling look.

"The drama triangle really helped me rethink my habit of blaming other people for my behavior," the inmate said. "I've talked about this in our group therapy sessions, too. I guess it gives me a way to understand it and talk about it. I've been thinking more about how I can be a creator—like, someone who *chooses* what to be. When I get released, I'll be around people who aren't going to accept a kinder version of myself. They're going to think I'm weak—but in prison, I can practice being okay with that. This is a tough place to let new things grow. It's a harsh environment, but I realized, finally, that I'm here for a long journey of self-reflection and change."

Vela was nodding, gazing at the floor rather than at the speaker. After some time, she looked up and addressed the group gently. "Everyone here is on that same journey of self-reflection and change. I have been talking to this young man"—she gestured to Elias—"about why monastics are given new names. Becoming a nun or a monk is about letting go of one's ego; it's about giving oneself over to something greater." Vela brushed a hand close to her robes. "We cut off our hair and we all dress the same. This is our uniform. Prisoners do the same thing; both groups are expected to let go of their personal identities and commit themselves to something greater. In a monastery, it's easy. In prison, the uniform seems like a punishment rather than an opportunity, but we're here to remind you of the opportunity. We offer support once a week, and the rest is up to you. As Rafael said, you must work to become creators in your own lives."

The session ended sooner than Elias expected. Back at the van, he climbed into the front passenger seat, his mind full of suspicions and questions. Vela had hardly sat behind the wheel when he asked: "Do you believe all that stuff the inmates were saying, about wanting to become better people and follow the dharma triangle, or whatever?"

"The *drama* triangle," Vela replied. "That's not a Buddhist thing. It's a sociological model of how abuse can be part of a larger toxic relationship. There's the persecutor and the victim, but there's also a rescuer. It's toxic all around when the victim doesn't find a way to grow out of victimhood, the persecutor fails to self-assess, and the rescuer fails to let the victim develop their own strength and wisdom." She paused. "You can look it up. It might help you understand what we've been saying about you and Leitha."

Elias felt his face morphing into a scowl. He didn't want to discuss Leitha, so he changed track: "Do you believe them, though? I mean, do you think that when they're released, they'll meditate and follow the Buddha, instead of doing whatever they were doing before?"

"It won't be easy once they're released," Vela replied. "Landlords will reject them, so they usually end up living with friends or relatives. That can put them back in the same toxic environment. Most employers that pay a decent wage will also reject them. Even though those men have served their sentence, for the rest of their lives they'll be barred from housing and employment, and they'll be ostracized by people who don't know them. It's another frustration they have to cope with. We try to keep ties with them after their release, so we can give support and vouch for them."

"You just vouch for all of them?" Elias asked.

120

Vera chuckled. "No. No, there have been cases where we couldn't vouch for people."

"Such as?"

"You want to hear an example?" Vela asked.

"Sure."

Vela put the van into drive, slowly edging out of the parking stall. "Well," she said, "among monastics, there are some who have troubled pasts. We're trying to get them more involved in this group, so the attendees can see that it's possible to change. Not only can they walk the path of the Buddha, they can even achieve enlightenment—not in some other lifetime, but in—"

"Yeah, I got it," Elias cut in.

"So, recently, someone suggested that one of our volunteers also join the program. We talked about it, and initially, I said, 'This kid isn't ready to contribute. He's rude, he interrupts people, he refuses to call the bhikshunis by their dharma names—'"

"That sounds like me," Elias said.

The bhikshunis laughed.

"That *is* me. Why am I here, then, if you decided against it?"

"I think it also helps to see someone who is in the process of changing, but who still makes a lot of mistakes," Vela replied.

"We've actually had some pretty close calls," Lamia said. "Last year, one of the convicts in the group—his name was Jim—he expressed a lot of enthusiasm about transforming his life. He gave great talks about changing his karma and following the path of the Buddha, but his speeches seemed a little *too* great, like they were more about convincing us and less about his own commitment. He wanted us to recommend him for a work release program, and we were going to vouch for him, but when the time came, we decided against it. We told him, very gently, that we wanted to wait a little longer, and spend more time with him—and we were surprised by his response. He was *extremely* hostile. He called us names and made threats and everything. He stopped attending the group, and a couple weeks later, a man showed up at the monastery. He said that Jim had offered him money to set fire to the abbey and damage the brake lines on our van. This man wanted to warn us, because he figured Jim would try to hire someone else to do it if he didn't."

"Jesus," Elias breathed. "Aren't you still worried that he'll come after you?"

"I doubt we're at the top of his revenge list," Lamia said. "More importantly, worrying won't do us any good. We'll just keep an eye out and continue our work."

"There have been a couple more like that, who don't like being told 'No,'" Vela added. "They're charming, they're enthusiastic, and they know the right words, but if they feel like you've crossed them, they lash out. Other inmates mess up, too, but the malicious ones are the ones we need to watch out for." She paused and added: "Andrei is like that. He's charming, he's persuasive, and he needs to feel like he's in control. He's riled by the fact that Lucian isn't under his power anymore."

Elias thought of Lucian's beautiful face and enchanting presence. It was no wonder that Andrei was infatuated. "Andrei has spent a lot of time spying on the abbey," Elias said. "We should match him."

"What do you mean?" Vela asked.

"I mean that we should also do more investigating. I've been trying to do it myself, but I can't be at the club all the time. We should enlist more of your volunteers."

"That would put them in danger," Vela replied. "We want to limit the number of people who are targeted by Andrei."

"What about the nuns, then?"

"Nuns at a nightclub would be pretty conspicuous."

She was right, of course. Nevertheless, from the backseat, Lamia said: "I'll go."

Elias turned around. "Will you? When?"

"If you're free tomorrow, let's go in the evening," she said. "You can show me where it is."

Elias expected her to have made the pledge half-heartedly, but the bhikshuni's weathered face was calm and determined, and she looked at Elias with a conspiratorial smile.

"Are you sure?" he asked. "Sneaking around and spying on someone doesn't go against your Buddhist beliefs?"

"Our mandate is to minimize harm," Lamia replied. "I don't intend any harm. I have quite the opposite intention. Let's go there and see what else we can find out about Andrei and his friends. There's something in particular that I want to check."

7

Elias managed to glean some more information about the bhikshunis during the drive. Lamia described most of them as having very "ordinary" vulnerabilities, such as self-doubt and world-weariness, but Ven. Sonam and Ven. Tseten both had criminal records that they were still coming to terms with. "Ordinarily," she said, "we would leave those things in the past, but Andrei has brought them back into focus. It's a good opportunity to re-address them, and to deal with lingering feelings of guilt and judgment."

She and Elias made plans to meet at eight o'clock, after the evening prayers, but Elias arrived at the monastery two hours early. In the kitchen, he helped prepare a light meal for a few of the lay people who had volunteered that day, and for the few bhikshunis who chose to partake. Lamia was among them, along with Ven. Tseten and Ven. Norbu. Elias sidled up to Ven. Tseten in the kitchen, helping her slice tempeh cakes and vegetables.

"I'm thrilled to see some protein in this dish," Elias remarked. "No offense, but most of the nuns look like they need to be treated for malnutrition." He lowered his voice. "Even Lamia is looking a little pale these days. Don't you think so?"

Ven. Tseten smiled, but she withheld comment.

Elias kept up the small talk throughout the meal. Three of the monastery's lay people stayed for the meal and then left.

Elias heartily insisted on doing all of the dishes and cleaning the kitchen, though he simply wanted a more private setting in which to pry into the minds of the nuns. He persuaded Ven. Tseten to join him in the kitchen again, and they washed and dried dishes side by side. She was a petite figure, and dark-skinned, with round spectacles and pale brown eyes, friendly and gentle like the other bhikshunis. She looked up at Elias with a smile and said, "You're so eager to help today."

"I'm trying to get more involved," he replied.

"So I hear. Venerable Dorje warned me that you wanted to pick our brains, and find out what Andrei might try to use against us."

"Um . . . ."

She laughed. "It's all right. I don't mind talking about it. I definitely know what Andrei would go after, where I'm concerned. My parents were con artists. I helped them scam people. They went to prison for a while, and I ended up in juvie."

"Oh," Elias replied, still feeling sheepish.

Ven. Tseten scrubbed the frying pan as she talked, moving in slow, meditative rhythm. "They skimmed credit cards at gas pumps for a long time. When we were arrested, they were running a gift card scam. They would copy bar codes from gift cards and paste fake ones on the card, so when someone bought the cards and activated them, my parents could spend the money themselves." She paused. "*We* copied the bar codes and made fake ones. I keep saying my parents did it, but I actually did most of the work."

"Well," Elias said uncertainly, "you were a kid."

"Yeah. That's what everyone says." Ven. Tseten gave him a wry glance. "I was seventeen, though, and practically an adult. It's true that I didn't want to do those things, but I never stood up to my parents, either."

125

"You shouldn't have to," Elias replied, rather sharply. "I hate it when people blame kids for things that their parents do to them."

"I was lucky that we got caught when we did. If I hadn't had that intervention, I might still be a criminal—and I wouldn't have anyone else to blame."

"Do you feel guilty about it?" Elias asked.

"Well . . . sometimes. We hurt a lot of people. My biggest problem, though, was anger. When I was in juvie, I was always like, 'Why me? Why are my parents criminals? How did I end up in this crappy life?' I didn't really think about how I could move forward—until I met Venerable Dorje and Venerable Norbu. We were at the bus stop, and they were helping me figure out which bus to take, and . . . it turned into something entirely different. The whole bus route conversation was like a metaphor for my life. I thought: 'These people can help me figure out which path to take next.' And they did."

Elias ruminated over the story as he rinsed and dried the dishes. "But you feel like you belong here," he said. "Right?"

"Absolutely."

"I don't feel that way."

The bhikshuni looked at him in surprised puzzlement. "About me?"

"No, no. About myself. I've also done things that could have put me in prison."

"What kind of things?" Ven. Tseten's expression was one of gentle curiosity rather than suspicion, but the question filled Elias with dread.

"The other nuns didn't tell you?" he asked.

"No."

His jaw clenched. Elias wanted to give Ven. Tseten the same honesty she'd gifted to him, but he found himself unable to explain.

"If you don't want to talk about it, that's okay," she assured him.

"It's not that. I'm just not sure you'll understand what I'm talking about." He paused. "Do you know about the creature that made a mess of the prayer room and the garden?"

"The kappa," Ven. Tseten replied.

"Yes. So, you know what it is."

"Kind of."

"You know about . . . monsterization," Elias said.

She peered at him curiously. "Only lately—because of Andrei."

"He's a vampire," Elias said. "Like, a literal vampire."

"So I've heard."

"I used to be like that." Elias kept his gaze on the counter as he spoke. After a moment, he heard the nun chuckle.

"Are you ashamed?" she asked. "In front of *me*?"

"I've done worse things than you have," he replied.

"Are you sure? We ruined lives. We wiped out people's livelihood. I'll never know the extent of the damage I did." She pulled the plug from the sink, watching as the water and suds vanished down the drain. "My parents contact me every once in a while. They want to visit the monastery. I'm terrified that they'll show up someday and cause trouble. They say they've changed, but I know they just want to use me. I can tell by the way they talk that they haven't changed at all." She turned to Elias suddenly, her eyes clear and intense behind the round glasses. "My parents are good at manipulating people," she continued, "but to me, they're absolutely transparent. I don't trust them at all. That has always been hard—but here, at the monastery, I have a family

127

I can rely on. It helps heal the hurt from my past. My parents always saw me as something that could be used. They see everyone that way. In the monastery, when I practice Buddhist ways, I get to see everyone as a precious soul. I've always wanted that, but my parents always told me that other people didn't matter—and that if they got scammed, it was their fault for being gullible."

Elias nodded. "Right." Again, he lowered his eyes. "I used to tell myself that. Andrei knows that about me—that I dismissed normal people as 'weak.' He's trying to make me feel weak and pathetic, so that . . . ." He almost said *so that I'll become a monster again*, but it didn't sound right. "So that I'll lose my way," he finished.

"Oh, yes." Ven. Tseten sighed. "He knows about me, too."

"What do you mean?"

"I ran into him when he was taking a tour of the abbey. He told me that my parents must be very proud of me, and that I'm as good a performer as they are." Ven. Tseten gave Elias a pointed look. "Meaning they're phony, and so am I. He didn't say that outright, but I could tell by the way he looked at me, and by the tone of his voice, that he knew all about them— and about me."

"He doesn't know anything about you," Elias blurted, without thinking. "If he did, he wouldn't waste his breath saying things like that."

Ven. Tseten smiled faintly. "His words didn't make me doubt myself."

"They shouldn't," Elias insisted. "In all the time I've been here, I've never seen you be anything but kind and sincere." He glanced at the clock, remembering the urgency of his mission. "Anyway . . . thanks for being honest with me. You didn't need to tell me all of those things."

She shrugged. "It's nothing."

"No, it's something. You're a good person. Don't ever let Andrei use your past against you."

Ven. Tseten nodded, her eyes betraying a sudden sense of gratitude. "Don't let him use yours, either."

Elias attended the evening meditation, though he usually avoided such events; he found them boring and irrelevant to himself. Wen was there, too, having been specially invited by Elias, who wanted to recruit him to his team of spies. Ana, likewise, had been invited by Wen. When the session concluded, Lamia and the three teenagers climbed into Elias' car and headed for Bull's-Eye.

They parked in the free lot and headed across the bridge— not to save money, Elias insisted, but because he didn't want to arrive too early. "We might see Andrei or his people on the way," he said as he walked, "so keep your eyes peeled. We can look for them while it's still light out, but when we're hanging around the club, we need to take advantage of the dark. If we walk, we should get there when nautical twilight is ending." He pulled the hood of his sweatshirt over his head, hiding his white-blond hair.

Wen looked at him in puzzlement. "Nautical twilight?"

"Yeah. There are names for the different levels of twilight. They're all based on visibility. Civil twilight begins at sunset; you can still see without the aid of artificial light. Nautical twilight begins when the center of the sun is six degrees below the horizon; you can see the major constellations well enough to navigate by them. Astronomical twilight begins at twelve degrees below. At that point, you can still see a little bit of light on the horizon, but you can see more of the night sky, and there's enough darkness that you can lurk without being seen." Elias paused, glancing at Ana as he added: "It's the time when monsters come out. At this time of year, at this latitude, it takes about an hour and forty-five minutes to transition from sunset to true night." He looked Ana up and down, at her brown tweed jacket and thin leggings, and said: "Your legs are going to get cold."

"I'm fine," she replied.

"Next time, wear pants."

"Yes, sir."

They crossed the river bridge and started down the sidewalk, surveying the area as they went. The narrow walkway and the stream of passerby made it hard to walk side by side, so they made most of the trek in attentive silence. True to Elias' prediction, the sky had darkened significantly by the time they reached Bull's-Eye. Ana and Wen went inside, while Lamia and Elias lingered in the alley across the street.

"Do you know where the other exits are?" Lamia asked.

"There's one in the back," Elias replied, "but no one ever uses it. The employees, and Andrei's guests, sometimes use the side door on the left—but they usually just use the front door."

Ana and Wen returned after a while, reporting nothing unusual. "I don't think Andrei is there," she said. "I looked around in the back, but it seemed like the other rooms were empty. There was just some guy back there who told me that I was in a private area."

"What did he look like?" Elias asked.

"Tall, skinny, black hair, lots of acne scars."

"He's probably just one of the employees." Elias sighed quietly. "After tonight, we should take turns doing this. All four of us don't need to be here. Someone should volunteer for tomorrow night."

"I have limited availability," Lamia said.

130

Wen laughed. "I'm amazed you're here at all. Don't you usually go to bed at nine o'clock?"

"Ten."

"Isn't that hard?" Ana asked. "When I stayed at the abbey, it was only for a few days, but I had such a hard time getting up at five o'clock every morning."

"It's not hard if you're in bed at ten. We don't consume caffeine, either, so we have a more restful sleep."

"I want to try it again soon," Ana said. "I'll take a Friday off from work and stay the weekend."

Wen looked at her. Even in the low light, his surprise was obvious. "Do you want to become a bhikshuni?"

Ana looked aghast. "No way!" She turned to Lamia and added quickly: "No offense."

"None taken," Lamia replied mildly.

"I would have to give up too many things," Ana continued. "I love to cook, and I put onions and garlic in almost everything."

"Ah, that's right," Elias said. "That's another challenge. Bhikshunis have a thing against delicious food."

"I take offense to that," Lamia replied.

"So much for reacting like the Buddha. What about you, Wen?" Elias gave Wen a wily look. "You could try living in Vinaya at Shi Miao Xing's monastery."

Wen shook his head. "I actually like the food, but no."

Ana peered at Lamia with genuine curiosity. "Wasn't it hard to give up all of those things? Your own clothes, your own belongings, all kinds of good food . . . ."

"We do eat good food. I never cared for onions. I once had the garlic-soaked fries at Zeke's; I reeked like garlic for two days, and I never ate it again." Lamia smiled wryly. "When I joined the monastery, even before I started making vows, I gained a lot more than I gave up. Clothes, possessions, all

131

those things were a burden that I let go of. The hard part, for me, is . . . feeling like I'm good enough for monastic life. You've heard of 'imposter syndrome'? I feel that sometimes. I feel it *often*."

"That's funny; that's exactly what Nyima said," Elias replied.

"Monastics in general, especially in the U.S., struggle with validation. There isn't a huge Buddhist following here, and the culture is very profit-oriented. We work hard at the abbey—but no matter how hard you work, if you don't generate a profit, you're considered a burden. We depend on a community of lay people to support us, and we often get flak for that. Remember Jim, the man I was telling you about yesterday?"

"The guy from the prison program? Yeah."

"He dug right into that. He said we're a bunch of babbling freeloaders, and he called Venerable Dorje the 'supreme leech.'"

"Ouch," Wen said.

"I don't think I would have a hard time with that," Ana said. "The lay community is happy to support you. They get a lot in return. They get inspiration, peace, happiness, fun, knowledge . . . and a lot more. I think it's just giving up my personal things, and my individual opportunities, that I'm afraid of."

Lamia smiled, looking suddenly nostalgic. "That part was a relief for me."

"Didn't you ever want to have kids," Ana asked, "or a partner?"

Before Lamia could answer, Wen nudged Ana and gestured sharply toward Bull's-Eye. "Speaking of—isn't that a kid? He just came out the side door."

A lone figure moved through the opposite alley, a small figure with skinny, bowed legs. Even before the stranger moved into the glow of a streetlamp, Lamia seemed to recognize it by the sound of its bare feet slapping against the pavement.

"That's no kid." Lamia pushed herself away from the wall and moved to the edge of the shadows. "It's the river monster who tore through the prayer room."

"How do you know?" Wen asked.

Lamia didn't address the question. "Let's follow it," she said.

Quietly, they crossed the street. Elias led the way as they trailed behind the strange creature. Though it tried to stay in the shadows, Elias caught occasional glimpses that intrigued and confused him. The creature did look like a child at first glance, with its short, thin body and clumsy stride, but it had a bald spot on top of its head, a bare circle in the middle of its brown hair. Its skin was a pasty shade of gray-green, and its large feet surpassed the size of its head.

The group followed the creature for a long time, all the way back to the river bridge—often losing sight of it, but able to follow the slapping sound of its feet.

Near the river, the creature left the path and descended towards the water, seeming to become smaller and smaller as it went. Elias stood at the edge of the bridge and watched in the moonlight as the creature's rubbery legs morphed into a sleek, eel-like tail. It leapt into the river, uttering a soft, echoing cry as it disappeared beneath the surface.

"What is that thing?" Elias asked.

"It's a water baby," Lamia said. "A kappa."

"What does it do?"

"It can shapeshift into a human or amphibian form, but it can't survive on land for long. When it takes on a human form, it traps a pool of water in a pocket in its head. That bald spot on its head is just a thin layer of skin that holds the water in. Kappas have to distribute moisture through their bodies, and keep their skin moist, so they can breathe."

"They don't breathe through their mouths?"

"No. Through their skin."

"It seemed sad," Ana said. "Didn't it? Just now, it sounded like it was crying."

"Kappas can be dangerous," Lamia replied, "but they're also easy to overpower. Andrei probably has some kind of control over it. There's a legend that says kappas are intrigued by human courtesies, and that if you show politeness to them, they feel obligated to be polite in return."

"So, what—we just need to be nice to that thing, and it won't attack us?" Elias asked.

"Supposedly," she said, "if you make a deep bow to a water baby, it will bow in return, and that can cause the water to slosh out of its sura—the water pocket. That's how people have either killed the creature or gained its loyalty. If you refill the sura, the kappa becomes obligated to you for saving its life."

"But, what does it *do*?" Elias repeated. "Aside from tear through the abbey and eat all the cucumbers, I mean."

"Well, it also enjoys feasting on human livers—and it has very sharp teeth."

"Ah," Elias said.

"Aside from shapeshifting, it doesn't really have other abilities . . . or appealing qualities. Water babies are known to lurk in toilets as well as rivers."

"Gross," Wen said.

"Wait a minute." Elias narrowed his eyes. "Is that why you didn't want me using the bathroom when that thing showed up at the abbey? You thought it might be hiding in the toilet?"

Lamia didn't answer.

"Why toilets?" Wen asked.

"Well . . . ." Lamia sighed. "It's a long story. Let's get going. Like you said, bhikshunis start their days before sunrise." She started across the bridge, keeping pace beside Elias. He saw a grave look in her eyes as she spoke. "Elias. You told Andrei that you lost the astra in the river, didn't you?"

"Yes." He waited for another question, but Lamia was silent—and he remembered that not only had he mentioned losing the astra, but he had been rather specific: *I very clumsily dropped it in the Mississippi River*. Andrei could easily have deduced that it was dropped from this bridge. Elias felt a sudden pang of alarm. "You don't think . . . ."

Lamia looked at him silently, but with a knowing gaze.

Elias stopped. "He's looking for the astra!"

"Yes, he's likely looking for the astra. Keep walking, Elias. It's late." The bhikshuni waited for him to resume his pace. "I think that's why the kappa suddenly showed up. They're not common here; they're localized to Japan. Andrei probably brought one here just for this purpose."

"But . . . why does he want the astra so badly? Is it just to protect himself?" Elias paused, considering his own question. "It would be better if he just left it in the river."

"He must have a use for it," Lamia said, rather vacantly.

Wen spoke up: "What kind? Is he going to use it on his own people?"

She glanced at him, as if to acknowledge that he had spoken, but she said nothing in reply. Elias met her clouded gaze and saw some hidden idea there—something she would not speak out loud.

8

Elias sat in a prison conference room, gripping the edges of a composition notebook, a flexible pen tucked under his thumb. Lucian sat across from him, placid and unthreatening—yet, something about him made Elias uneasy. It was something in the man's eyes; their warm, inviting energy had too much power, made Elias feel light and giddy. He found himself wanting to look longer and discover the secret behind that energy, but he forced himself to stare at Vela instead.

Vela smoothed out her robes as she sat beside Elias. Lamia and Lucian were gathered close; no table stood between them, allowing them to speak with confidentiality. "Well," she said. "Here we are, just the four of us. Now we can talk."

Elias glanced at the guard who stood near the door, apart from the group but well within hearing range. "There are five of us," he cautioned.

Vela assured him quietly: "Don't worry. He already knows." She turned to Lucian, seemingly unaffected by his gaze as she addressed him: "Lucian, we're very happy to continue supporting you on your path. In confinement, it has been easy—but as we all know, once you are released, you will need some other means of protection from Andrei."

Lucian nodded.

"We already know about your previous relationship with Andrei, and about his possessiveness," Vela said, "but it

136

sounds like there's more to his pursuit of you—his visits to the abbey, his meddling with our volunteers and bhikshunis. . . ."

"There is more," Lucian said. "Andrei is obsessed with power. On the surface, it looks like he's trying to raise an army of monsters and keep them all under his control, but he's not interested in making an army. He's fattening them to be eaten. And he isn't pursuing me because of his feelings, or even because he's possessive. He wants to destroy me just like the others."

"Why?" Vela asked.

Lucian paused, his gentle brown eyes suddenly hesitant and troubled. "Andrei . . . wants to become a wechuge."

"A wechuge," Lamia repeated, raising her eyebrows. "Why on Earth would he want *that*?"

Before Lucian could reply, Elias cut in: "What's a wechuge?"

"It's a creature whose only interest is power," Lucian said. "Traditionally, it's described as someone who gained power and protection through ceremony and vision quests—but they violated that power and became consumed by it. Their insides turn to ice; they take on the appearance of a beast; they drain people of their life force, and then they eat the corpses of their victims."

"They're also hideous," Lamia said. "I've never heard of anyone *wanting* to become a wechuge."

"Andrei was dabbling in mysticism to try to gain more power," Lucian continued, "and he opened himself up to a dark spirit. He thinks he can become a wechuge, but he's actually possessed by one. He won't acknowledge it, but the wechuge is completely in control."

Slowly, Elias opened the notebook on his lap. He wrote a few words: *Andre-possessed by wechooj but doesn't know it. Ravenous. Drains the victim's life force, eats the body.*

"Andrei started collecting certain types of monsters," Lucian continued, "so he can strengthen them, consume them, and absorb their powers. That's what a wechuge does. The spirit inside of him is ravenous, and there's no sating its hunger. It will keep consuming until there's nothing left to conquer—unless someone stops it."

"And how does one stop a wechuge?" Vela asked.

Lucian shrugged. "I don't know. Fire is supposed to work, but as you can see, someone already tried that and failed." He pulled on the collar of his shirt, exposing the expanse of burned flesh along his neck and shoulder.

"What about the monsters he brought to the monastery?" Lamia asked. "There were three of them, two women and a man. Is he grooming them to be eaten?"

"What kind of monsters were they?"

Elias spoke up: "One of the women had a mouth on the back of her head."

"That's Akari," Lucian replied. "She's a futakuchi-onna."

Elias stared at him for a moment. Then he poised the pen above the note paper. "She's . . . what did you say she was?"

"A futakuchi-onna."

"Foota . . . coochie . . . what?"

"Futakuchi-onna," Lucian repeated patiently.

Elias stopped writing. He tapped the pen against the paper. "He's probably not grooming her, right? What's the advantage of having a creepy little mouth on the back of your head?"

"There *is* an advantage," Lucian countered. "Akari can change the composition of her body and grow extra body parts. Did you notice anything unusual about her hair?"

138

Elias remembered the creep of Akari's dark locks toward the plate of dumplings. "I did. She had hair like tentacles. She practically cleared the snack table with them."

"Muscular hydrostats," Lucian said. "Instead of hair, she's growing a system of filaments filled with muscle. Akari is only able to grow a mouth, and tentacles to feed it with, because she has no desire aside from mortal hunger." He paused. "I should give some background, so you understand. Akari has struggled with anorexia since she was young. It has nothing to do with being a futakuchi-onna, but eventually, after she became monsterized, her body grew other appendages that work on their own to feed her and keep her alive. If Andrei gets ahold of that ability, he'll do much more with it than eat your snacks."

"Grow extra body parts . . . and tentacles," Elias murmured, scrawling notes across the page. "What about the lady with the three-foot-long tongue? Brown hair, kind of on the short side?"

"That's probably Maria. Andrei went to the Philippines last year and brought her back with him. She's a manananggal. He wanted—"

"Sorry, a what?"

"A manananggal."

Eilas glanced down at his note sheet. "Manan . . . how do you spell that?"

Lamia took the notebook and pen from him. "Manana-gall," she muttered as she wrote.

"Manananggal," Lucian corrected her.

"Got it. What is it, and how could we go about curing it?"

"Or fighting it," Elias added.

"Maria can disassemble her body and put it together again. Inside the upper half, she grew a pair of monsterized wings and a pair of clawed feet. They're folded up within her human pelvis and back. When she removes the upper half, she gains the ability to fly." Lucian paused. "And her tongue isn't three feet long. It's tucked in layers and coils in a sac that looks like a regular tongue, but when she uses it to attack, it can protract for several yards—and it operates kind of like a hammerhead worm."

"Meaning what?" Vela asked.

"Meaning it can wrap several times around you, dissolve you with acid until you're nothing but a puddle, and suck your remains up through a tube inside of her tongue."

Elias pondered the scenario with quiet horror.

"Okay," Vela said. "Well, we don't want Andrei to have *that* power."

Lucian regarded her with sudden sympathy. "It's unlikely that anyone will cure her," he said gently, "as much as you might want to. If you can prevent her from reuniting with the lower half of her body, it will start to rot. The upper part can't survive long without it. That's probably the kindest thing you can do for her."

"What about the man?" Elias asked. "An Indian-looking guy, kind of zoned out and temperamental, probably in his early twenties."

Lamia answered: "He's a pishacha. We've dealt with his kind before. They're known for leeching human energy and leaving disease and madness in its place."

"There's also a water baby that hangs around Andrei," Elias said. "A kappa, I mean. It seems . . . different than the others, somehow."

"In what way?" Lucian asked.

"Well . . . it didn't seem particularly cruel. It seemed sad, actually—like a lost little kid."

Lucian nodded. "Kappas are like that. This one must be new; it wasn't there when I was around. Andrei probably has some power over it—and he probably *is* grooming it. Kappas have certain . . . ." He hesitated.

"Certain what?" Elias asked. "What turns a person into a kappa?"

Lamia replied: "A kappa was never a person. It's an amphibious creature that learns to imitate humans."

Lucian nodded. "Yes, it can imitate humans—supposedly by eating their shirikodama."

Elias' brow furrowed. "Their what?"

Again, Lucian hesitated. "It's probably just a myth. You know, kappas are also called toilet babies—but we don't need to get into that."

Lamia waved impatiently. "Never mind all that. We know enough about the kappa, Elias. It's harmless to people like you—but I can see why Andrei would want its power."

"Toilet baby power?" Elias asked doubtfully.

"Not that. Consuming someone's soul, shapeshifting and imitating other people."

"What other types of monsters has he been collecting?" Elias asked. "We need to know all of them."

"When I was with him, there was a cauchemar—a nightmare, someone who attacks you in your sleep and drains your energy. There was also a pontianak, a woman with long claws who carves out your organs and sucks your eyes out. There are probably more of them by now."

"Lovely," Lamia murmured.

"The wechuge has a lot of power over Andrei," Lucian continued, "but he's still in there somewhere. The spirit needs to let him have some power so that it can check its own hunger. If Andrei starts devouring his own lips and chewing on his fingers, then it's too late; it means he's gone, and he's become just another corpse for the wechuge to devour." Lucian paused; his voice softened. "At first, when he crafted

141

his plan to consume other monsters, he wanted me to help him. I asked why becoming powerful was so important to him—so important that he would destroy his own friends and live utterly alone. And he just said, 'I *have* to.' With such a desperate sadness in his eyes . . . ." Lucian trailed off, looking distant. "Andrei does his best to seem unaffected by everything, but he's . . . pitiful. I don't know a better way to describe him. He's a sad, scared little man with a fragile ego, trying with all his might to fine-tune himself to seem invulnerable."

The guard spoke up: "Like a lot of the folks you see here. Your time's almost up, so if you have anything else you need to say, say it now."

The unexpected intrusion made Elias jump slightly in his seat. He looked over at the notebook with a troubled frown. "I feel like I'm missing something. This doesn't explain why Andrei keeps coming to the abbey. If he just wants to eat monsters, he could eat the ones he has, and consume their power, and become stronger. Why is he going after you instead? He could just eat the other ones and come after you later."

The bhikshunis exchanged quiet glances. Lucian, too, gave them a knowing look before returning his gaze to Elias. Something brief and dark flashed across his eyes then, a moment of impiety that caused a jab of pain in Elias' own eyes.

"In order to consume a spirit," Lucian said, "Andrei needs to force it out of the body. One way of doing that is to use a basilisk."

"What's a basilisk?" Elias looked questioningly at Lamia. "Isn't that one of the ceremonial knife things that you have back at the monastery?"

Vela answered: "A basilisk isn't a tool. It's a person."

"A monster," Lucian clarified. "A basilisk can kill with its eyes. When it looks at you, it can draw you into a hypnotic state. It fills you with the terror of your own existence, so much that your soul flees from your body. Andrei thinks he can use a basilisk to draw the life force out of his monsters so he can consume them."

"That's what the astra does," Elias mused, looking at Lamia. "That's why he needs the water baby. If he can't find a basilisk, he'll try using the astra instead."

"Andrei *had* a basilisk," Lucian continued, "but he lost it. It's drawing farther and farther away from him." He gave Elias a pointed look. "That's why he started targeting your abbey."

"What does the abbey have to do with . . . ." Elias trailed off as the meaning of Lucian's words suddenly became clear. It was there in Lucian's eyes: the vast darkness that glinted every now and then, the subtle sense of unease that seemed as though it could, at any moment, build to a mortal terror; the contrasting warmth and calmness that, while pleasant, still held too much power. "It's you," Elias said.

"It is," Lucian said softly. He lowered his eyes. "It *was*. I'm not sure what I am now."

The guard interrupted: "Time to clear out. There's a group coming to use this room in a few minutes."

The bhikshunis said quick goodbyes to Lucian and promised to work on "the issue." As Elias followed them back to the parking lot, he muttered: "Andrei sure knows how to pick them. Giant hammerhead worms, soul eaters, people who suck out your eyes. . . ."

"Remember, though, that these are all forms of sickness and imbalance that can be healed," Vela said.

"Sure. Can I ride shotgun again? I get motion sickness if I sit in the back."

In the van, Elias asked for the notebook and perused the notes. As Vela started to drive away, he looked up at her and said: "We need more information than this. And we need to tell the other bhikshunis, and other people who might be affected by it. We should form a committee."

"Lamia and I will discuss it," she replied.

Elias frowned at the scant notes on the kappa. Lamia had written "water baby: astra?" and nothing more. "What's with water babies and toilets?" he asked. "Everyone acts like it's a taboo subject, but if we're trying to be fully informed . . . ."

"Well," Vela said slowly, "water babies are generally harmless, except . . . have you ever heard of a candiru? I went to Peru about fifteen years ago, and I stayed at a place on one of the Amazon tributaries. We were told to stay out of the river because of parasites, and there was one particular parasite everyone was afraid of: the candiru. The locals called it a 'vampire fish' because it feeds on blood."

"So, water babies are vampires," Elias concluded.

"No, that's not why I mentioned it. It's because the candiru has been known to enter a person's . . . *orifices* to drink their blood. As far as I know, it only happened a handful of times, but it was so horrifying that people went to great lengths to prevent it from happening to them. When the locals bathed in the river, they would face downstream and keep their butts covered to prevent the candiru from entering. The fish can even jump out of the water to enter a human."

"So . . . what does that have to do with water babies?" Elias hesitated. "Ew. No way. They hang out in toilets so they can get into your butt? Why?"

"Supposedly, to penetrate through your tissues and eat your liver," Vela replied. "It's their favorite food aside from eggplant and cucumbers."

"Right. Well, at least they have a balanced diet."

144

Vela continued: "Some people believe that our souls reside in a little ball in . . . well, in your butt, and that the kappa is really after our souls."

"The shiri-drama, or whatever?" Elias asked.

"Yes. That's how they learn to mimic humans: by devouring the substance of a person's soul."

Elias let out a small chuckle. "A waste disposal system isn't the best place to keep a life force. No wonder the world is so messed up. Only the anal-retentive people get to keep their souls."

Vela didn't react, but continued her lecture: "The liver is also thought of as the seat of life. It can regrow itself and transform from a part into a whole. If the kappa can appear like a human, it's probably because it slipped into a person and devoured a part of them, and it's using that part to mimic the whole."

"It 'slipped into a person'?" Elias repeated. "Seriously, though, do they really slip in while you're sitting on the can?"

"That part might be myth," Vela replied, "but the traits of the kappa are real enough. A kappa feels empty inside; it desires fulfillment but doesn't know how to achieve it. When it sees other people who have vibrant and happy souls, it envies them, and it tries to obtain that same happiness by consuming those souls." Vela paused and added quietly: "Much like a vampire. I'm sure you understand that habit well enough."

The disgust faded from Elias' face.

Vela glanced at him. "That wasn't a criticism," she said. "I meant that you have a means of compassion and understanding for that kind of pain, so please don't take it personally."

"I'm not," he replied dryly. "I'm just thinking about my newfound fear of toilets." After a long pause, he said slowly, and with emphasis: "It's harmless to *people like you*."

She gave him a puzzled look.

Elias twisted in his seat, facing Lamia. "That's what you said to me when I asked about the kappa: It can be dangerous, but not to people like me . . . because I don't have a happy and vibrant soul. Isn't that what you meant?"

His question didn't faze her. "Yes, that's what I meant," Lamia replied. "You don't have the kind of demeanor that a kappa would take notice of."

"Very few people do," Vela added gently.

"So, who are those very few?" Elias asked her. "Do you have a vibrant soul because you're Thumb Tongue Georgie, or whatever your Buddhist name is?"

Lamia spoke sharply: "She's Venerable Thubten Dorje. There are twelve-year-old boys who come to the monastery with better manners and respect than you have, Elias. If you're so eager to earn our trust, you could start showing some maturity."

Elias settled back into his seat, glowering. He sulked for a minute, and then he pulled out his cell phone and opened a web browser, hoping to find more information to add to the notebook. "I can't find the manana-gall thing," he muttered. "You should have let Lucian tell me how to spell it." He lowered the phone with an exasperated sigh. "I can't look at my phone while we're driving; I'm getting motion sickness." He thrust the phone toward the back seat. "Lamia, can you do it?"

He felt the phone slip from his hand as Lamia grasped it. Elias dug his hands into his jacket pockets, still disgruntled— and after a moment he withdrew the metal padlock. After

146

removing it from the park, he'd carried it with him, its bulk and weight serving as a constant reminder of his promises.

"I found it," Lamia announced. "*Manananggal.* Lucian was right; the upper torso can separate from the lower body. If you sprinkle salt, ashes, or crushed garlic into the lower torso, the creature won't be able to rejoin its lower half, and . . . it says here that the creature will 'perish by sunrise.'"

"What are you reading?" Elias asked. "Is it just somebody's blog, or . . . ."

"It's academic research on mythology."

"We have other resources to call on," Vela said. "We have Buddhist colleagues around the world. If we know where the monster comes from, we can ask those people how to deal with it. I'm not sure if we know anyone in the Philippines, though. We might have to make a new connection there— soon, before Lucian's release date."

"How soon will he be released?"

"In six days."

Elias started. "You have to protect him! Let him stay at the monastery."

Vela glanced at him in surprise.

"We really need to form a committee," Elias insisted. "These monsters that Andrei keeps company with—they're dangerous. *Andrei* is dangerous. He's a hundred times worse than I thought. Lucian should come and stay at the monastery, and everyone else who lives there should know what they're up against."

"Are you that concerned about Lucian?" Vela asked.

Grudgingly, Elias replied: "I'm concerned about Leitha. And . . . Wen, and . . . well, you guys. You nuns, I mean." He looked at the padlock as he spoke, his eyes fixed on the figure of Vishnu. Its face was marred by age, its features hardly visible, yet still evident enough to convey an expression of peace.

"What've you got there?" Vela asked.

"It's . . . something I bought for Aarya. I thought it was a Buddhist thing, but it's Hindu. It has Vishnu and Ganesh on it." Elias ran his thumb over the green patina, tracing the figure of Vishnu.

"Well," she replied, "Buddhism and Hinduism have a lot in common. They both originated in ancient India. They both rest on the idea of reincarnation and the upward evolution of souls toward nirvana, and liberation from the cycle of incarnation. Some Buddhists even adopted Ganesha into their traditions; in Buddhism, he's called Vināyaka. Hinduism, though, teaches that we have individual souls. Buddhism leans toward the idea that the 'self' is an illusion. I chose Buddhism because I believe that my ego is impermanent; there is no 'me.' This life that I have, it's a raindrop making its way back toward a cosmic river. When it gets there, the drop will merge and disappear."

"A cosmic river," Elias repeated. He cast her a wily look. "You used to be a hippie, right? You took a dip in the psychedelic river, and that's what moved you toward Buddhism?"

"Meditation has always been enough for me," Vela replied calmly.

Elias sighed and leaned back in his seat, shifting to make himself comfortable. "Can't you even crack a smile when I'm trying to be funny?"

"Were you?" she asked. "I thought you were just curious."

He peered at her, saw her straight-faced and focused on the road ahead. "You have no sense of humor," he said. "How do you not get bored to death?"

Lamia spoke up from the back seat: "If we did, we would just get reborn."

"It's a common misconception that monastics have no sense of humor," Vela said. "We're actually quite funny."

He stared in bewilderment. "I can't tell if you're serious or not."

"Do you want to hear a Buddhist joke?" she asked. "It applies to you, since you work with computers."

"Well, I work on *a* computer."

"What happens when a computer programmer gets totally absorbed in the program he's working on?"

"I don't know," he said.

"He enters nerdvana."

A short silence ensued. Then, Elias said: "That's the lamest joke I've ever heard."

"I see. Can't you even crack a smile when I'm trying to be funny?"

Vela shot him another deadpan glance from the driver's seat. For just a moment, Elias saw the serious demeanor break. Vela smiled at him, and her eyes bore an amused gleam—but she grabbed a pair of sunglasses from the console and put them on, and the gleam vanished.

9

The quest to master qigong was forgotten. Elias sat at his computer instead, researching monsters and formulating battle plans, describing the strengths and weaknesses of his own companions. Achiravati was a small monastery, still growing its base and doing its best to welcome and support new bhikshunis—but despite its smallness, there were members who Elias didn't really know. His next strategy, he decided, would be to spend time with Venerable Norbu and Venerable Chonyi, and then with some of the lay people.

At the abbey, he once again implored Vela to form a committee. "You should have done that right away," he said, following the bhikshuni to the gathering hall, "as soon as you knew that Andrei was targeting the abbey."

"The other bhikshunis know about Andrei's interest in Lucian and the outreach program," Vela began.

"That's not enough."

Vela stopped and held up a hand. "We've discussed things with the bhikshunis. The problem is that we also have long-term guests who are trying out monastic life. The ones who haven't arrived yet will be asked to come later. As for those who are already here, we're arranging to send them on a retreat—and we're trying to rush it. Things have gotten . . . *interesting* at the abbey."

"How so?" Elias asked. "Did Andrei come back?"

"No, but we had some visitors who were likely sent by him."

"What visitors?"

"Ah . . . ." Vela seemed to struggle for words. "For example, a shapeshifting snake, and . . . a severed head." She paused. "Well, it was *kind of* severed."

Elias stared at her in bewilderment. "A human head?" Vela nodded, and he added: "How was it 'kind of' severed?"

"It had quite a lot of tissue still attached," she said.

He tried not to imagine the spectacle but grimaced anyway. "A head, with no body? How did it get here?"

"It flew."

"O-kay," Elias replied slowly. "A severed head has been flying around the abbey, and . . . what about the snake? You saw it shapeshift?"

"We didn't need to. It got into the kitchen, and we thought it was just a snake at first—but it had eyes and hair like a human. We're lucky our guests didn't see it."

"Ew," Elias breathed. "What did you do with it?"

"I trapped it and brought it to the garden."

Elias gaped. "Of course you did. With all those knives, you could have just chopped its head off—but I suppose you didn't because of your Buddhist mandates. What about the head? I suppose you prayed with it and let it go."

"We have a live trap in case it shows up again," Vela replied. "The head seems to be temporarily detached from the body. If it doesn't reattach soon enough, it will probably die, so there's not much we can do—"

"You could let it die."

"—but we *were* able to do something with the snake. It was a moura: not a human shapeshifter, but a spirit who manifests here from a lower dimension. I sent it back where it came from."

"To another dimension?"

"A moura enters this plane through an enchantment. Andrei must have used the wechuge's powers to bring it here. I removed the enchantment, and the moura shed its skin and disappeared."

"Right," Elias said. "I'm sure that idea gives you some comfort. What did you do, really? Did you bring it outside and kill it?"

She didn't answer, but opened the door to the small prayer room where they had first met. An oriental rug in bold hues cut across the floor, leading to a small table at the back. On the table were a few small instruments, all of sturdy metal that gleamed in the overhead lights: a bell and ringer, a statue of the Buddha, and another instrument covered by thick red fabric. Vela removed the cloth, exposing a metal blade beneath.

She picked up the dagger and extended it toward Elias for closer examination. The ornate handle featured a triad of hideous, sneering faces, joined at the sides and facing different directions, each wearing a crown of skulls. Above them were four ribbed segments that formed a sphere, a shape that Elias recognized as the vajra sphere—a symbol of spiritual protection.

"Who's the demon?" Elias asked.

"That's Vajrakilaya, a symbol of positive transformation. It's no demon."

"It makes transformation look pretty unappealing."

"Change is hard," Vela replied softly. "Habit is easy. That's why we use tools like this one to help people along."

"What's with the skulls?"

"Often, transformation feels like death. To create positive change, your attachment to your former self has to die." She replaced the dagger on the table. "Monsters in general have a reaction to certain types of iron. This phurba is made from meteoric iron, from a substance that has passed through the universe. When it's used by the right practitioner, it can help exorcise demons and cure disease. The blade is the part that destroys demons; the top, with the vajra and the faces of the deity, is used for blessings. It isn't wise to only seek to destroy; we must also preserve and bless." Vela paused for some time, looking at Elias as if to ensure his understanding. "Legend says that a pontianak can be defeated by stabbing the back of its neck with an iron instrument," she continued. "Just as the nape of your neck is particularly vulnerable to wind, it's vulnerable to the influx and outflux of energy. When the phurba strikes a pontianak at the back of the neck, it can destroy the demonic energy and preserve the human soul."

"Just like an astra," Elias said.

"Not quite," she replied. "The phurba is mostly symbolic; it can't be used on its own. In order to use the phurba to expel harmful energy, you must also know how to move qi. It's how I destroyed the moura's enchantment." Vela gazed at Elias, her blue eyes seeming to glow gently in the dim light. "The astra is different because it comes from the astral plane. It needs no symbology, and it needs no qigong master. It works on its own to release harmful energy. That's why it's dangerous. The user can't manage the recipient's qi, and that person's spirit can end up fleeing from the body—the human spirit along with the demon."

"Then . . . ." Elias paused. "If it's so dangerous, why are you encouraging me to make an astra?"

"I've been encouraging you to manage qi," Vela replied. "You must learn that first. When you can move qi in conjunction with the phurba, you and the phurba become like the astra. Only by understanding it in such a way can you begin to create it."

Elias looked down at the table. He let out a quiet sigh. "Learning to manage qi is a long way off for me. I should have spent my time learning about Andrei's monsters, and about practical ways to fight them."

"You couldn't have learned to fight superhuman monsters in such a short time."

"I don't agree. These creatures all have weaknesses that can be used against them."

"Their weaknesses lie in their attachment," Vela said. "Their anger, their hunger, their despair—the root of those things lies in attachment."

"So you say," Elias replied. "But it sounds like Maria's weakness is *de*tachment. Once she detaches from her lower half, I fully plan to dump a pile of ash, salt, and garlic into it so she can't rejoin."

"Learning to manage qi isn't only about going to classes and moving your body. At the monastery, we also encouraged you to make friends. Wen, and even Ana, have moved you. They have the knowledge and skills to help and protect you."

Elias looked at Vela in disbelief. "Ana is going to protect me?"

"Everything here is done with intention and design—from suggesting volunteer tasks, and bringing people together, to the tiniest suggestions planted in their hearts."

"The tiniest suggestions," Elias said. "Is that how you think of it? This has all been about putting little ideas in my head, so I'll become a Buddhist, and, what—help you justify your beliefs, or give money to your cause?"

Vela laughed softly, her eyes crinkling at the corners as she smiled. It was a warm smile, one that gave liveliness to her pale face.

"You're using us," Elias said.

"We're letting you use *us*," Vela replied. "Someday, you'll understand. You'll even do the same for others: showing compassion, helping people release their attachments. You don't see it now, but someday, Elias, you too will become a mahatma—a great soul." She wrapped the blade in the red cloth and replaced the phurba gently on the table. "Plan to come back within the next few days, Elias. We will follow your advice and form a committee. You, of course, will be a part of it. Wen has come into repeated contact with Andrei, and he will be included." Vela paused. "Ana will also have a chance to join."

Elias gave her a cautious, grudging look. "Why Ana?"

"You chose to include her. Her talents are also needed, and likewise, she needs the monastery and the people within it."

Elias knew that he was at fault for involving Ana, but he had been second-guessing his decision. "We're putting her in danger."

Again, Vela smiled. "Are you only worried about Ana?"

Elias lowered his eyes to the table. He gestured to the phurba. "Shouldn't you hang onto that? You'll probably need it soon."

"We have others," Vela replied. "Don't be concerned."

The bhikshuni kept her word. Within the week, she had invited Elias to the first official meeting of those who were aware of Andrei's monsters and willing to help face them. The meeting was held not in the gathering hall, but in a meditation room in the dormitory, a ground-floor space large enough to host a few dozen people. The long table at the front supported a large statue of the Buddha, surrounded by flowers and lit candles. Along the walls, colorful tapestries featured the Buddhist deities—much prettier than the drab corridors and lobby, Elias thought. He realized, with disappointment,

155

that there were no chairs in the room. Instead there were cushions, small and square and flat, and not very cushiony. Elias grabbed one and seated himself beside Wen.

The others sat, too, arranging themselves in a circle of ten. Elias looked around at them: skinny Wen, nice Ana, and a handful of bhikshunis who looked deprived of protein and vitamin D. "Is this everyone?" he asked, not bothering to mask his dismay.

"Yes," Vela replied.

Elias took a breath and muttered: "We're going to get slaughtered."

"Thank you, Elias. We *are* expecting two more. Shi Miao Xing will return soon, and another monk is coming from Indonesia. They should both arrive before Lucian's release." Vela smiled encouragingly at her peers. "It is true that our group is small. As you know, there is strong resistance to the idea of women becoming ordained. Women before us have faced imprisonment, threats, degradation, and much more for seeking ordination. Even here, we must follow extra rules as a 'penance' for some unidentifiable offense. When we discuss equal treatment, we're accused of selfishness and corruption. That's why the work we—"

"Excuse me," Elias cut in. "I don't mean to be rude, but don't you think we should get straight to the point?"

"This *is* the point," Vela replied. "Our work helps others realize that their fear stems from attachment and ego. Not only are we fostering our own growth, we are also fighting against darkness—not just 'out there,' but within our own community."

"Okay," Elias said, "but, more literally, we're fighting creatures that want to impale us and eat our organs, or spray us with acid and reduce us to a puddle, or crawl into our butts and consume our souls." He waved the small stack of papers that he carried in his hand. "I have some notes here on the types of monsters we're fighting. Can we start with that?"

Vela sighed softly. "Creatures that want to eat our organs and consume our souls. It sounds frightening, doesn't it?" Again, she smiled as she looked around the circle. Elias noted the pale hue of her face, how many new age spots had appeared there over the past few months. She was old, Elias thought, old and sedentary and weak. "This is a good moment to remember that our mission is to follow the path of the Buddha," she continued, "and not to be swayed by attachment. As you all know, we've been targeted by a wechuge—a creature whose defining feature is its overpowering sense of attachment, of feeling starved and always wanting more. It might seem intimidating, or different from what we've faced before, but it is only a different form of the same darkness—and we do have means to protect ourselves from it." Vela picked up a bundle of cloth from the floor beside her, withdrawing a phurba from inside of it. This dagger was more ornate than the other, with three spheres instead of one, and so tarnished that Elias couldn't make out the details of Vajrakilaya's face. "Let me ask you this: What kind of weapon do you see here?" Vela asked. "Is its purpose to cause life or death?"

The bhikshunis remained silent. Wen answered: "It looks like a knife—like something that might cause death, but since it's a Buddhist thing, I'm guessing you're going to say that it supports life."

"It's a phurba, an instrument of transformation—of life and death." Vela explained the purpose of the dagger, giving essentially the same summary she'd given Elias, as the phurba was passed around the circle. She explained that cases of monsterization, like possession, were often responsive to such tools, especially those made of iron.

"Usually, in ceremony, the phurba is used on a willing participant," Vela continued. "It exposes our inner demons so that we can understand and overcome them. Thus, even though the phurba pierces and can cause pain, it isn't a tool of aggression. The handle represents the pillar that connects us with a higher purpose. For those who see only fear, the phurba is simply a weapon."

"But . . . aren't we supposed to use this to attack Andrei and his friends?" Ana asked. She held the phurba across her palms, away from her body, as if she was afraid to handle it. Elias looked at the uncertainty in her eyes, at her dainty flower print skirt and thong sandals, and tried to imagine her fighting Andrei and his monsters.

He could only imagine her screaming and perishing.

Vela talked, again, about how the phurba could be "connected" to the body to spur transformation, adding that it could only be used successfully by those who could manage qi. "That means me, Shi Miao Xing, and Venerable Santini—the monk from Indonesia. For the rest of you, the phurba merely serves as a reminder that our mission is not to kill, but to transmute."

Elias tried to refrain from rolling his eyes. "I beg pardon, but Lucian said that there's no point in trying to help these monsters. He said that we should kill Maria by separating her top from her bottom and leaving her to die."

Ana, who had avoided looking at Elias since her arrival, now regarded him with anxious puzzlement. "Her top from her bottom?" she repeated.

Elias began to read from his notes, describing the monsters in Andrei's company, how their weaknesses could be used against them, and how they could be destroyed. "As far as battle terrain goes," he said, "if Lucian is here, they'll come here. It's an advantage for us, because we know the interior of

158

the building—or we *will*, if you'll give us a tour—and we can hide weapons around it as needed."

"The kappa is also familiar with the building," Lamia replied. "Andrei probably knows more about the grounds than we realize."

The conversation continued, with Elias divulging what he knew about Andrei's goons, ending with Lucian and the properties of a basilisk. "Apparently, he's not a basilisk *anymore*," Elias added, "but Andrei either doesn't know that, or he thinks he can change Lucian back." He paused, adding: "He might be able to do that. Andrei tried to change me back into . . . a monster, and he knew which strategies to use. He was close to Lucian, so he probably knows all of Lucian's weaknesses."

Lamia spoke up: "Andrei has also been looking for the astra. He has the kappa searching for it—first at the abbey, and now in the river. If he can't use Lucian to eject the life force from people's bodies, he'll try to use the astra instead."

Ven. Chonyi, the newest addition to the monastery, raised her hand. "What's an astra?"

Ven. Sonam, at the same time, asked: "Why is he looking in the river?"

Elias felt himself redden, but he spoke up and confessed: "I dropped the astra in the river. I took it without permission, to use on Andrei, and . . . it slipped out of my hands."

"An astra is a phurba that is purely functional rather than symbolic," Vela said. "For those with a weak spirit, its force can be powerful enough to cause death. It's probably good that Elias lost it. We were careless with it; we had it in a box under a table. If Elias hadn't dropped it into the river, Andrei would have it by now."

The bhikshuni discussed Lucian's release date, the monks' arrival, and the accommodations for all three men, while

159

Elias pored over his notes to see if he had missed anything. "I'm going to look around the building," he said. "Is that okay?"

Lamia got to her feet. "I'll show you around. Wen and Ana, come with us."

Elias hadn't explored the building much, aside from helping in the kitchen; he'd supposed that it consisted mostly of the nuns' bedrooms, and he was surprised to find only three bedrooms shared among the seven bhikshunis. "The other rooms are for visitors," she said, "and new members. We're a growing community. We're hoping to eventually fill all of the rooms."

Elias stood in the hall, gazing through a bedroom door at the boxspring mattresses on the floor. A single closet was on one side of the room, and the only other objects in the room were a couple of metal bowls and a Buddha wall hanging. "It's very minimal," he said. "That's good. You don't have a bunch of stuff that monsters can hide behind."

Lamia chuckled. "I never thought of it that way, but I suppose you're right."

The next bedroom proved slightly more furnished, with a small table at the far end, and several instruments atop it. "Whose room is this?" Elias asked.

"Venerable Dorje and I sleep here."

"How come you have more stuff? Is it because of status?"

Lamia laughed softly. "No. We usually don't do much in the way of rituals in these rooms, but Venerable Dorje was attacked about a week ago—after her qigong session with Leitha."

"Attacked, how?"

"By a cauchemar," Lamia said. "A nightmare. It tried to paralyze her and deplete her energy. We're actually lucky that it chose her; she was able to fight it off, but it was pretty aggressive."

"A cauchemar," Wen said. "Is that like, the thing that attacks you when you're half asleep, and—"

"She wasn't asleep," Lamia said. "We had just gone to bed, and after a few minutes, I heard her making a sound like she was choking."

Elias made a dismissive sound. "Everyone insists they 'weren't asleep' during sleep paralysis."

"You should put iron around all of the mattresses," Ana suggested, "and shoes with the toes pointing away from the beds."

"What is a shoe supposed to do?" Elias asked.

"Nightmares are supposed to be confused by unexpected things. They end up going in the direction that the shoe is pointing."

"We already have plenty of iron," Lamia said. She gestured to the table, where the bell ringer lay: an elaborate metal rod with four-ribbed spheres on each end. "Venerable Dorje can handle a nightmare. She's kind of like our living vajra; as a qigong master, she focuses on healing and compassion, but healing also necessitates the destruction of ignorance and evil forces." The bhikshuni closed the door and waved the group onward. "That's enough peeking at bhikshunis' bedrooms. Let's go upstairs."

The rooms in the upper level were hardly more furnished than those below. "Our long-term guests are staying in these rooms," Lamia said, gesturing down the hall. "Paul and Tuan, and a few of the women—five guests in total. We put them to work in the garden for now, and we're flying them to a new monastery that opened down south. It's only for a week, so we're hoping that if Andrei is going to mess with us, he'll do it soon."

"He will," Elias said. "If he's possessed by a wechuge, it won't wait." He stopped to inspect one of the wall hangings, this one a metal shield rather than a tapestry. The stamped gold depicted a deity with four faces in a row, its eight arms making various gestures or holding different tools. "What is this supposed to be?" Elias asked.

"That is a Phra Phrom shield," Lamia replied, "sent from Thailand. It symbolizes order, law, and education—the maintenance of chaotic forces through higher intentions and actions."

Elias ran his fingers over the smooth metal. "All of your statues and iron bits seem to represent the same thing."

"They do," the bhikshuni replied, "but people sometimes need to see it in fragments. We all have our particular pieces that we're working on."

They retreated downstairs, silent and reflective. Elias had offered to drive the other teens home; they said their farewells to the bhikshunis and went out into the bright afternoon.

"I'm not depending on transformation to save us," Elias said when the door had closed behind them. "This is war. And I don't have the same view about attachment as the nuns do. I want to keep my life, and I'm going to fight for it however I can. I'm going to start carrying a weapon, and I suggest you do the same—an actual weapon, not some symbolic thing that you can just wave around."

"What kind of weapon?" Wen asked.

Elias paused. "I don't know yet."

He dropped Wen off first, and he instantly regretted his choice of navigation; now, he was alone with Ana. She had seemed less enthusiastic about his company since the staring contest, and he wondered what she had seen in his eyes—if she perhaps saw something that offended her. If she saw something evil. Perhaps she was offended by his brash questioning about her mother. She no longer looked at him with smiling enthusiasm and playful, eager interest.

The idea nagged at Elias until he finally spoke up. "Are you all right?" he asked, feigning compassion. "You're quieter than usual. Are you nervous about what's going to happen?"

"Yes," she said, "but not as nervous as I will be. The reality hasn't set in yet."

"Are you upset with me?" Elias asked, forcing the words out with anxious reluctance. "For asking about your mom, or about our staring contest the other day? You looked upset after that."

"Oh . . . ." Ana sighed. "No, I'm not upset."

"You seemed upset."

"Well . . . I was, a little, but not with you."

Elias glanced at her questioningly.

"Can I be honest?" she asked.

"Sure."

"I've done the four-minute stare with a few people. Everyone else smiled and laughed. But I was sitting there looking at you, and . . . there was not even the slightest speck of amusement, or joy, and I realized that I've never seen you smile. Ever. I've never heard you laugh or express any kind of happiness. And I started thinking about all the times I smiled at you, trying to get you to smile back at me, like my attention would be some sort of magic Band-Aid for your sullenness, and it suddenly struck me as presumptuous. Like, there was obviously something going on that made you never want to smile, and I just ignored it and kept pressing you." She was quiet, waiting, and then asked: "Does that make sense?"

"Sure," Elias said softly.

"I guess I just felt bad for you," she added.

They were quiet for the rest of the ride. Ana turned to him before getting out of the car, kind but seeming to take care not to smile. "Thanks, Elias," she said.

"You're welcome."

She started to depart, and Elias said: "Ana?"

She hesitated, half-turning to look at him.

"You can smile at me. It's okay."

She smiled and left.

As he watched her walk to the house, Elias turned on his stereo and cued up Aarya's "Moody" playlist, hoping it would make him forget the conversation with Ana. The playlists were usually a good distraction; they made him think of Aarya, comforted him, sent him into the depth of his memories.

A Ben Howard song was playing. The words didn't soothe Elias so much as they provoked him; they merely reminded him of his losses. Aarya. Leitha. The song spoke of loss, of waiting, of uncertain ties.

He remembered Leitha grimacing at the idea of being a sister to him. And Aarya—who was he to her? Did she still exist in some form, and would she really wait for him, even if they had to wait through countless lifetimes? He was starting to forget things she had said, but he was sure that she'd promised to wait even if it took until she reached nirvana.

He sighed and shut the music off before backing out of the driveway. The music had done its job, though; he forgot the conversation with Ana and focused instead on Andrei and the upcoming battle. Andrei knew of Elias' loneliness, of his desperation to save Leitha—but despite his confident advances, Elias knew that Andrei was just as desperate and lonely, and just as afraid. It was the fate of any vampire; it was the reason for a vampire's existence. Andrei had his advantages, but his emotional frailty was one of the things Elias could be certain about.

He just wasn't sure how to use it against him. Not yet.

10

Lucian was released on a Tuesday, a bleak and rainy morning that cast the event in a protective haze. Elias had offered to drive him to the monastery, and Lamia and Vela also came to escort him, two gentle but committed guards. They checked in at the prison and drove to the "releases" lot, where Elias parked and sat watching the gate through the distorted spattering of raindrops.

"Wasn't he supposed to be released at eight-thirty?" Elias asked, turning the ignition key enough to check the clock.

"Be patient," Vela replied. "Release times are often 'approximate.'"

"Very approximate," Lamia said. "We'll need patience, but as soon as he comes out, we'll have to rush him. Some new releases like to stand outside for a while, even in the rain, before they close themselves up in a car. We can't dilly-dally here; it's too much of a risk. We need to usher him into the passenger seat and get moving."

Elias' gaze shifted around the near-empty lot. Nearby, a woman and two kids waited in a sedan. A single driver sat behind the wheel of a jeep. None looked suspicious. Still, when the gate finally opened, Elias and the bhikshunis hurried to meet Lucian, just in case someone else arrived to snatch him away.

Two other parolees came out first, accompanied by guards. Lucian emerged then, dressed in a gray sweater and black pants. He was even more handsome, Elias thought, in street clothes, without the harsh orange of the prison uniform tainting the sandy hue of his flesh and the deep brown of his eyes. Something about the softness of the sweater and the stylish cut of his trousers rendered him an elegant tenderness. Wen, he knew, would be instantly infatuated.

At Achiravati Abbey, the bhikshunis helped Lucian get settled. His arrival changed the ambiance of the place; something heavy and hushed settled over the monastery, put everyone on a quiet and watchful alert.

After noon, the bhikshunis met for their pre-lunch talk. Elias tried to maintain his patience as Vela droned on about the amazing elements of creation that helped produce the food, how the people who helped gather and handle the food should be held in gratitude, how the energy provided by the meal should drive its recipients to greater good, and so on. He sat with his foot tapping lightly against the floor as he waited for the meal gong to sound.

A lotus meal had been prepared for Lucian's arrival, and the bhikshunis had also made a tofu and bell pepper stir fry. Another newcomer was at the table: Venerable Santini, the Indonesian monk who had offered his help. He was small, sharp-eyed, and quiet due to his limited knowledge of English. He sat listening intently to the others and offered short, infrequent responses.

When the meal was finished, the group remained at the dining table to discuss their plans. "If Andrei and his people are coming here, I doubt they'll come tonight," Elias said. "Thursday night is the full moon. That's when they'll be at their most powerful. We should brace ourselves in case they come earlier, but they'll most likely take advantage of the moon."

"It's also the best time to use the astra," Lamia said.

Ana's brown eyes had taken on a glint of fear. "Shouldn't we get more people to help us? If it's this dangerous . . . ."

"They *are* powerful," Elias said, "but the full moon can also make them reckless. Latham, for instance. He'll be more aggressive, but if he's like other werewolves, he won't use his best judgment. Werewolves assume that brute force will take down their victims; they don't plan for any other outcome." He looked at Lucian. "Don't you agree?"

"Completely," Lucian replied. He sat with his chin resting on his hand, attentive but tranquil.

"And we *will* have more people," Vela added. "Shi Miao Xing should arrive at the airport any minute now, and we have another monk coming: Venerable Ajahn Chah from Malaysia. That's the reason we're having this discussion. We need to plan—quickly, but thoroughly. Andrei is a strategist. He'll manipulate his team of monsters and use their skills against us. We must be cautious, but we must also keep an eye out for their weaknesses. People with monsterization are often defeated by their own misguided energy."

"Then we should discuss the weaknesses we know of," Lamia said. "Who should we start with? Maria? Akari?"

"I don't think Akari will be there," Elias said. "Akari and Sanjay—I think Andrei just keeps them around because he wants to absorb their mutations, but they don't seem aggressive or . . . *capable* enough to fight." Again, he looked at Lucian for affirmation.

Lucian paused. "I know that Akari and Sanjay can seem pitiful, but they *are* dangerous. Andrei will likely enlist them as pawns—and remember, he's trying to use me to absorb their power, so it's likely that he'll bring them. He'll use people like Latham and Maria as aggressors for sure."

Vela was nodding slowly, musing over his words. "Okay, so we can focus on them. Who else might we be facing?"

168

Wen spoke up: "What about the water baby?"

Elias shuddered.

"Maybe," Lucian said. "Water babies are loyal, and they can be vicious. And this one already has some familiarity with the abbey. Andrei might use it as a guide. Its weakness is its cordiality and its sense of loyalty." He described the vital pool of water that lay beneath a thin sheath of flesh on the kappa's head, and how one could spill the water and then refill it to gain the kappa's loyalty.

"What about this other monster you mentioned—the pontianak?" Lamia asked. "We haven't met her."

"That's Mona," Lucian replied. "She will likely be here, too. She's short and stocky, with long black hair and red eyes. She usually wears the same white dress. You can subdue her by piercing the back of her neck with iron—but it won't last. People usually kill a pontianak by decapitating it."

"We won't consider killing anyone," Vela said. "We have other ways of dispelling the demon and saving the person. What else do we need to know about the pontianak?"

"She's powerful, but her mind is stuck in a state of infancy. You can hear it in her voice; she has a cry like a demon baby. She has the cravings of the basest beast. You need to watch out for her fingernails; they're more like talons. And you don't want to look her in the eye."

"What do you mean by 'red eyes'?" Wen asked. "Like, do they glow, or . . . ."

"Bloodshot," Lucian replied. "They do kind of glow sometimes. When that happens, it's because she's angry. The pontianak hates being looked at. If you stare at her too long, she'll suck out your eyeballs. Then she'll rip open your belly and eat your organs."

"Jesus," Elias breathed.

This time, Ana didn't jokingly correct him. The mood in the room was utterly humorless as the conversation proceeded.

After they had gone through the inventory of monsters and discussed potential vulnerabilities, Elias said: "What about us? We should discuss our own weaknesses. Andrei is going to use them, so . . . we should know what to look out for, and how to help each other."

Vela nodded. "That's not a bad idea. Since you suggested it, why don't we start with you?"

Elias averted his gaze. He felt himself reddening, though he had mentally prepared for this moment. "Well . . . my mom died when I was really young, and I grew up with an abusive stepfather. He isolated me and . . . took advantage of me for years. Andrei knows about that. He tried to use it to get under my skin, and he even threatened to find my stepfather and bring him here." Elias paused and added: "I have a lot of weaknesses. I get angry easily. I lived as a monster for a while, and I'm ashamed of it. I hurt people. I wanted to drain them and ruin them, the same way I felt drained and ruined. Someone ended up dying because of me."

His hands were trembling, he realized. He clutched his knees to steady himself.

"You should discuss your strengths, too," Vela said.

Elias considered that, but he found himself at a loss for ideas. "I don't know what they are. I'm really just here because I want to help my friend Leitha. Andrei has her. That's another weakness."

"Honesty and commitment are strengths," Vela replied. "You're also a good strategist."

Elias looked at her without responding, and she continued: "Ana, will you speak next?"

"Um . . . ." Ana lowered her eyes, looking nervously at the table. "I'm pretty good at Aikido and Tai Chi. My weakness is that I'm afraid. People tell me I'm too nice. I've been beaten up before, and I didn't fight back for a long time because I was afraid of hurting the other person." She looked up, giving Vela an anxious smile. "That's all I can think of."

Ven. Sonam talked briefly about her prison stint and her new outlook on life; Ven. Tseten, sitting beside her, gave a similar speech about her own criminal past.

"It's actually good that Andrei confronted us," Elias said. "He was trying to make us weak, but he also exposed the strategies he's going to use against us. He gave us time to confront those weaknesses and make ourselves stronger. Don't you agree?" He looked at Ven. Norbu. "Did he try to get to you, too?"

"Uh . . . ." she laughed. "I don't know that there's anything he could confront me about. My past is pretty boring. I grew up in the suburbs, I had a great family, I grew up practicing Tai Chi. I actually won two grand champion medals before coming here. I went to college and became a science teacher, and I happened to meet Ven. Thubten Dorje at a restaurant. I was waiting for a table, and she invited me to sit with her group, and now I'm here."

Elias prodded her: "You don't have some sort of self-doubt that he could use against you?"

"Well, I'm like Ana: I don't like hurting other people. I don't know if there's anything else."

"Speaking of food," Vela said, "Venerable Norbu and I are going to clean up. Venerable Chonyi, can you help collect the dishes?"

"I can help, too," Ana offered, but Vela waved her away.

"No, stay here. The rest of you should continue talking. When we're done, we'll do the post-lunch recitations."

171

That's right, Elias thought; *there's going to be more lecturing and chanting.* He considered slipping out of the meeting early, but after the others had finished discussing their potential weaknesses, he found himself absorbed in discussion with Ven. Nyima. She had delved deep into her past, into her potential vulnerabilities, including the ones she had overcome. "It's too bad I can't sit down and have a heart-to-heart with Akari," she said. "I was bulimic for a while in my teens. Fortunately, my mom noticed and took me to a therapist, and I ended up in a support group for kids with eating disorders. I was really embarrassed at first, but it was a good experience. The thing I remember most about that group is this one girl who said 'Whenever I look in the mirror, I just want there to be *less* of me.' That was like an awakening for me. I felt that way, too, but when she said it like that, it made me think about *why* I wanted there to be less of me. It wasn't just about being skinny. I always felt like I was intruding, or speaking out of turn—like other people had the right to take up space, but I didn't. Like everyone else was somehow 'right,' and I was wrong. I had to be noninvasive, and . . . ." She paused. "Inoffensive. I felt like my existence somehow might offend people."

"You still feel that way," Elias remarked.

"I do, sometimes. I beat the bulimia, but not the sense of unworthiness. I think . . . ." She trailed off, suddenly looking aghast. Her gaze had moved past Elias, to the open doorway—but he turned around and saw nothing.

"What's wrong?" he asked.

"Someone was looking in the window, out there in the hall. Except . . . ."

Elias stood up. He went into the hall and moved close to the glass, but he saw nothing outside except lawn and sky.

"It was the head," Ven. Nyima said.

172

"The head?" Elias looked at her in puzzlement, and then he remembered. "The severed head!"

Ana and Wen looked up at him in clueless astonishment.

"There's a severed head flying around the abbey," Elias said. "It's one of Andrei's spies. I'm going to go and look for it. Ven. Nyima, go and get the live trap."

Before anyone could respond, he ran toward the front doors—and then went back to the kitchen, realizing he had no weapon. He startled the nuns by rushing in to grab a knife—but no, a knife didn't feel right, so he took a broom and a couple of potatoes instead. Then he was outside, jogging across the lawn and searching the sky for any sign of a floating head. He spotted it as he turned the corner toward the south side of the abbey: a mass of light brown hair, the face turned away from him, and what looked like a stream of shrunken innards hanging from the cleanly sliced neck. Elias dropped the broom, took careful aim, and hurled one of the potatoes.

His aim was off, but the head happened to fly directly into the potato's path; it veered and dropped toward the ground, the trail of innards piling into the grass. Elias picked up the broom and started forward, but instead of falling, the head stopped a few inches above the ground and turned to look at him. It had the face of a man, narrow and bearded. Its eyes were wide, furious, and fixed on Elias. The mouth opened in an angry snarl; the head darted along the grass toward Elias, dragging its guts behind it.

Elias shouted in fear and swung the broom, knocking the head clear across the lawn. It sailed all the way to the edge of the woods, its innards trailing through the sky like a grotesque streamer.

"Oh my God," said a voice behind him. Elias turned to see Wen standing behind him, staring in the direction of the battered head. "What the hell was that?"

"One of Andrei's monsters," Elias replied.

"What the hell *kind* of monster?" Wen lifted his hands to hold his own head, as if afraid that it, too, might detach and fly away. "It's like . . . the world's most horrific party balloon. Its organs were all shrunken and hanging like a string, but I could see its heart beating." He looked at Elias, who had pulled his cell phone from his pocket. "Who are you calling?"

"No one. I'm looking it up on the internet."

"You're looking up the monster?"

"I looked up 'floating head monster.' Look—there's a drawing of it. It has its own Wikipedia page." Elias moved closer, showing the screen to Wen. "It's a penanggal . . . a nocturnal female spirit, a kind of vampire." He looked up. "That was a dude's head, right?"

"Huh? I guess so."

"And it's the middle of the day. But, look; it says that a person can become a penanggal by doing a cult ritual in a vinegar bath; it shrinks the organs so they can be carried during flight, and again to fit them back into the body."

"*That's* what that smell was," Wen replied. "It smelled like the kitchen on canning day."

They mused over the web page, occasionally glancing up to make sure the thing wasn't returning. "We're at a disadvantage," Wen said, in a voice just above a whisper. "I know you had some idea about us spying on Andrei, but we can't compete with shapeshifting reptiles and flying heads."

Ven. Nyima came with the live trap, followed by Lamia and Ven. Sonam. Vela had been speaking literally about the trap: It was a wire cage with a spring-loaded door, a handle on top, and a guard to prevent the carrier from being bitten.

Ven. Nyima explained that they had intended to catch the head with a fishing net and force it into the cage.

Armed with the broom, Elias led the group to the place where the head had fallen—but as they approached, the thing rose from the grass and fled into the woods.

"Ew," Wen remarked as he watched it go. "Not a wise escape! Its guts will get caught in the tree branches."

Elias let out a disappointed sigh. "It's going to tell Andrei that Lucian is here. We should have caught it and interrogated it."

"Don't worry about that," Lamia replied. "Andrei probably already knows Lucian is here and is just trying to rattle us."

They returned to the abbey, where Vela insisted on finishing the meal ritual. She gave a speech in which she willed that the vitality provided to her would be shared with those in need. The monastics chanted while Elias waited with his head bowed, and then Vela returned to the subject of the starving peoples of the world, those who lacked not only physical but spiritual sustenance.

Her gaze flicked up suddenly, settling on each of the listeners in turn. "That includes Andrei and his companions," she emphasized. "They are all are starving in some way. We think of vampires as creatures who seek blood, but they actually seek that which they do not have: vitality, courage, compassion. They can live on and on without conclusion, stuck in the same place on the karmic cycle. Vampires are strategic in their hunting; they manipulate, they wait, they change strategy if necessary. Many other monsters, though, hunt by instinct rather than logical thought. They fixate on people who exhibit the things they are starved of: happiness, strength, peace. It's true that they'll try to take advantage of our weaknesses, but our strengths are what they hunger for—and in their misguided frenzy, they will try to consume us."

11

The moon on Thursday night was full as promised, an eerily glowing orb in a cloudless night sky, visible long before sunset. Venerable Ajahn Chah, the monk from Malaysia, had arrived. He made rounds among the monastics and their few guests, introducing himself and filling the air with friendly banter before settling down for serious conversation. Shi Miao Xing was there, too, armed with a silver phurba from Henan, China. Elias slipped away while the monastics chatted, beckoning Ana and Wen to join him for a last look around the building.

"I know it's taboo," he said, "but I slipped a bag of garlic into the kitchen. It's in the drawer below the stove, where they keep the pots. Use it on Maria if you need to, but I also brought these." He handed out smaller packets of garlic powder and salt, and added a few long, black tie wraps to the mix.

"What are these for?" Wen asked.

"For when we have to make a citizen's arrest. If anyone breaks in and tries to attack us, we have a right to restrain them. And if we're in mortal danger, we have a right to defend ourselves by any reasonable means." He pulled a folding knife from his left pocket, withdrawing the blade and holding it out for the others to see.

"You're going to stab them?" Ana asked.

"I'll do whatever I need to."

"Well, if you're planning to use that for self-defense, you should have brought a bigger knife. That looks more like a can opener."

"It's big enough," Elias said, "if I stab in the right place." He paused and added: "I don't want to kill anyone. I just want to be able to protect myself."

They conspired for some time in hushed tones before heading for the meditation room, where the others had gathered. On the way, they encountered Lamia in the hall; she was positioned awkwardly, balancing on one foot and hurrying to remove one of her canvas shoes.

Elias spotted a spider scurrying across the floor and up the wall—a large spider, its yellow and black-striped body a full inch across, with yellow palpi visible on the elongated head. The breadth of its yellow and black legs made it at least the size of Elias' palm. "There's a giant spider right next to you," he said, pointing. "It looks poisonous. But I suppose you can't kill it, because—"

Lamia smacked the shoe hard against the wall, crushing the spider. Its guts exploded from beneath the rubber outsole.

The teens looked on in shock. Ana stepped forward to examine the mess on the wall, as if to verify what she'd just seen. "You killed it," she said in astonishment.

"It wasn't alive," Lamia replied mildly.

Ana looked at the bhikshuni in disbelief. "Um, that spider was definitely alive. I saw it crawling up the wall."

"It wasn't a spider," Lamia said. "We had an incident earlier. The spiders came from . . . the incident."

"What incident?" Elias asked sharply.

Lamia explained how, as Venerable Ajahn Chah was on his way to the gardens, he encountered a strange woman outside the front doors. "He greeted her," Lamia said, "and she started to say 'Hi,' but her jaw kept dropping lower and lower, until her mouth was open maybe ten inches, and her 'Hi' turned into a 'Hiiiii*iiiii*.'" Lamia's voice dropped in pitch; her leathery face and wide eyes took on such a disturbing expression that Elias shuddered. "So, at that point, he realized he was facing a monster—and then, spiders started to crawl out of her mouth."

Wen made a sound of quiet revulsion.

"They were all over the monastery. We did a ritual to draw them in and catch them, but every once in a while we find another one. Lucian said that the woman was probably a jorōgumo, a demon who manipulates spiders."

"That's . . . really disgusting," Ana said, her face set in a look of genuine horror.

"That happened to the new guy?" Wen asked. "He seemed very chill just now."

"He was shaken at first," Lamia replied. "Honestly, I thought he would head straight back to the airport—but he's okay now. I think the ritual helped everyone relax. If you see those spiders, feel free to squash them. They're not really spiders."

Elias had pulled out his phone, and now he was frowning at his search results. "They *are* spiders," he said. "They're joro spiders from East Asia." He looked up at Lamia. "You killed a spider."

"They're astral spiders," she insisted.

Elias pointed at the gut-smeared wall. "It looks pretty convincing for an astral projection. You killed a spider. I'm just saying."

Lamia waved the teens onward. "Go and join the others. I'll be there after I clean the wall."

In the meditation room, Vela split everyone into groups to guard different areas. Elias and the other teens were placed with Shi Miao Xing and assigned to guard the southside hall.

178

It was decided that Lucian and Ven. Norbu would spend the first few hours in a small windowless room in the upper middle of the building. If nothing happened, the groups would reassemble and sleep in shifts, with Lucian in the same room but with one of the monks. The monastics debated placing a tapestry of protection over the door, but Elias vehemently argued against it: "You might as well announce that Lucian is in there. Don't put anything there. Make it look just like every other room."

As night began to fall, the group held a final prayer in the meditation room. Lucian and Ven. Norbu made ready to retreat upstairs, but they were stopped by a strange sound—a shrill cry from outside, distant but powerful, a sound like an outraged infant.

"That's the pontianak," Lucian said. "They're here."

"It sounds like it's still far away," Elias replied.

Lucian nodded. "That means she's close."

Vela waved him away urgently. "Hurry! Go upstairs."

He and Ven. Norbu rushed into the upper room and closed the door. The others hurried to their places. Elias and his group were stationed in the back hall, and he had just turned the corner when one of the back windows exploded.

Shards of glass nicked the wall and scattered across the floor. Elias heard more shattering sounds from around the monastery.

He and the others braced themselves but saw no one. Shi Miao Xing moved quietly to the front of the group. Night had hardly fallen; the sky was still set in twilight, and Elias kept staring through the broken window, seeing nothing of note.

A howl cut the air, long and deep, and then undulating and shrill—and terribly close.

Elias swore under his breath, choked and inaudible.

Latham burst through the glassless window. He sailed through the air like a burly anti-hero in an action film—and struck the wall, face first, with a painful thud. He collapsed in momentary torpor, but he slowly got to his feet again. Beside him, a pair of thin arms snaked through the window, followed by a face with cold, familiar eyes.

Elias swore again. "We got the werewolf and the manananggal," he breathed, and grasped the knife in his pocket.

Maria leapt quietly into the hall. She looked at Shi Miao Xing with a chilling fury; then she opened her mouth and shrieked.

Latham lunged at the monk, and Maria followed close behind. In that moment Elias thought only of running. He could not fight these monsters; his only certainty was that his friends would fall in front of him, and he would flee in terror.

He stood helpless as Shi Miao Xing fought arm in arm with the werewolf, barely avoiding the beast's sharp teeth and strong nails. Maria, too, was using her claws. She slashed at Ana's face but missed; she ripped a thangka from the wall and tried to bash Wen's head with the wooden rod at the bottom. They fought her off, and somehow they ended up exchanging monsters with Shi Miao Xing; Latham suddenly went after Ana, and Maria faced the monk with a throaty hiss. Ana deftly threw off the werewolf; he lunged and sailed past her, crashing against the wall and floor in a stumbling fury.

The manananggal opened her mouth. Her monstrous tongue unfurled in a stream of dark pink muscle, twining around the monk, staining his robes with slime. As the tip of her tongue pointed at the monk, Elias suddenly remembered the knife in his hand. He opened the blade and slashed at the tongue, finding it tough and unyielding—but Maria screeched

180

and withdrew. The tongue snapped back into her mouth, and she turned to Elias with eyes that gleamed hate.

A moment later, the tongue enveloped him like an impossibly long worm. Elias wheezed as its grip crushed the air from his lungs. Shi Miao Xing came to his aid, moving Maria's qi with quiet gestures, closing in with the silver phurba. Irritated, she released Elias and whirled around to face the monk.

A crater formed in the wall where Ana and Wen had managed to heave the werewolf into it. Shi Miao Xing had a moment of indecision; then he hurried to Latham's side, pressing his knee against the dazed werewolf's back and the silver phurba against the back of his neck.

He began to chant.

Maria screeched and fled through the window. The werewolf snarled and heaved, trying to throw off the monk, but Wen and Ana helped to pin him, and the werewolf's strength seemed suddenly depleted. He snarled and writhed uselessly as Shi Miao Xing moved his left hand in slow, liquid movements, the silver phurba still pressed firmly against the werewolf's neck with the other. The muscles began to relax, and the snarl became a low, irritated rumble.

From other parts of the building there came only one other sound of conflict: a voice filled with hate, one that boomed and croaked like a demon, uttering profanities and complaints and threats.

The other sounds were softer, more reassuring: the sounds of chanting and prayers.

"I think they're handling it," Shi Miao Xing said quietly, without looking up from his work. "Let's keep watch on this hall for now."

A crash sounded directly overhead. Elias listened to the sound of glass cascading onto the floor and said: "It's Maria.

She probably separated from her lower half so she could fly." He tried to embolden himself, embarrassed by his spate of paralyzing fear. "I'll find a way to distract her. Ana and Wen, take the garlic and salt outside. See if you can find the rest of her body."

Wen called after him, but Elias hurried up the corner staircase alone, knife brandished. As he neared the top, he hesitated, shuddering briefly at the recollection of Maria's freakish tongue.

He ascended to the second floor and found the hallways empty. One of the back windows had shattered, and countless shards of glass gleamed there in the moonlight. Darkness had finally fallen, and it was deepening quickly, the light of the moon becoming a ghastly white that pierced through the dark. Elias wished that they had left the upstairs lights on; they had unwittingly given an advantage to the creatures of the night.

Elias forced himself onward, quietly creeping across the back hallway, only wanting this battle to be over.

On the hall table was a small statue of the Buddha. Elias picked it up, ready to hurl it at Maria at first sight. He would force her into defense, and then he would stab.

Elias tried to move silently, but glass crunched under his shoes. Maria must have heard him coming—yet, when he found her just around the far corner, her legs bent and ready to spring, she seemed startled to see him.

Her hesitation probably saved Elias' life. He was momentarily immobilized again, struck dumb by the sight of Maria's transformation, fully illuminated in the moonlight. She stood on two long, thin, bird-like legs, scaly and gray, the thick toes graced with steely talons. At her hips, two fleshy wings were folded horizontally, bulging there like two badly made leather purses.

The manananggal overcame her surprise. She opened her mouth and began to screech—a shrill sound that was cut short when Elias hurled the Buddha statue at her face.

She staggered back, and Elias lunged at her, meaning to stab the knife into her throat, or at least to cut her tongue if she unleashed it again. He wasn't fast enough; Maria saw him coming. She hissed and, with a surprisingly strong blow, knocked him backwards.

The knife clattered to the floor. Elias got to his feet, starting toward the knife. Something—a small, black, flitting figure—blocked his way, brushing against his face and causing him to duck. He straightened up, and the figure was gone. There was only Maria, her mouth opening, about to launch another attack.

Elias fled.

He raced around the corner and into the bathroom, slamming the door and locking it. He pushed his weight against it, expecting Maria to come crashing into the other side, but the hall was strangely quiet. The sound of his own ragged breath filled his ears—and then he heard another small sound, a single splash that he took no account of. He was in a bathroom with cheap plumbing. The sound of water presented no threat.

He heard it again, a splash, and then the smack of water droplets hitting the floor. An alarm bell began to ring in Elias' mind, some warning that tried to break through his fixation on the deadly manananggal that lurked outside.

And then he remembered.

Elias whipped around, pressing his back flat against the door. He reached for the wall switch and flicked on the light.

Bold fluorescence filled the room. Elias blinked, but in that first flood of light he had already seen the thing he dreaded. Across the small bathroom was the toilet, occupied by a strange creature with sleek green skin. A small head, rounded but flat on top, peeked out of the porcelain bowl. Two tiny webbed hands gripped the front of the seat. A pair of yellow eyes stared from the face, and below them, a long, flat nose descended, coming to a point over the wide mouth. Shiny bits of white and yellow peeked from between the rubbery lips: two long rows of small, sharp teeth.

The creature didn't move. Elias realized he had stopped breathing; he exhaled slowly, and then he took in an equally careful breath. "Hey, little guy," he said softly. "Just stay over there, okay? I'm, like . . . not your type. I don't have anything you would want." Elias made a slow half-turn, raising his hand toward the door lock.

The kappa stared at him, its eyes large and round, but human-like. Its lips began to part.

"I'm really not appetizing at all," Elias insisted. "Ask anyone. Just look at my eyes, and you'll—"

The mouth opened wide, revealing a frightening array of teeth. A threatening hiss rose from the creature's throat.

Elias screamed.

He threw open the door, tripping over the bottom corner in a panicked rush. Sprawled on the floor, Elias twisted around to brace himself against the kappa, instinctively covering his butt with one hand.

The kappa had emerged from the toilet. Its sleek tail stood on the floor like a boneless leg, and Elias watched as it split in two; the ends thickened and flattened against the floor, forming a pair of feet.

The creature took a step forward.

As Elias scrambled to stand, he was aware of someone standing beside him. Before he could run, the kappa was suddenly knocked backwards, striking the hard porcelain of the toilet bowl; water splashed from the top of its head, and as

184

the creature fell sideways onto the floor, the remaining drops of water spilled out onto the tiles.

Shi Miao Xing stood there, his arms stretched toward the threshold of the restroom, palms out. He lowered his arms as Wen helped Elias to his feet. "It's the kappa," Wen said. "It lost its water. Doesn't that mean . . . ."

Wen hurried into the bathroom. He turned on the faucet and cupped his hands, catching the stream of water and then kneeling beside the injured kappa. Gently, he said: "Can you sit up? I brought you some more water." He glanced back at his companions. "Elias, can you help? I think it's hurt."

"No thanks," Elias breathed.

Shi Miao Xing helped the kappa to sit upright while Elias watched the hall. When the reservoir in the kappa's crown was full, Wen stepped back and looked down at the creature uncertainly. "Um . . . you don't need to obey Andrei anymore, okay? Just go home."

The kappa sat on the floor, caught in an unfinished transformation, with scrawny legs that looked more like two smooth green eels attached to malformed feet. It looked up at Wen with its large yellow eyes, exhausted and silent.

"It looks sad," Wen said. "Doesn't it?"

"Let's go," Elias replied. "Maria's still out here somewhere, and . . . ." A prickle of alarm ran up his spine. "Where's Ana?"

"Downstairs. We tied Latham with zip ties, so—"

Elias turned and raced down the staircase, back to the hallway where Maria had first burst through the window. The shattered window had been pulled open, the bits of glass brushed from its frame. Elias peered out across the yard. Seeing nothing unusual, he crawled through the window and looked again. Moonlight illuminated the spread of green grass and the woods and gardens beyond. Elias caught sight of a dark figure moving near the tree line, and he made a slow jog in that direction, only speeding up when he recognized Ana's orange sports shirt.

"Ana!" he called, his voice hardly above a whisper.

She heard him and turned, holding her hands out in front of her.

"What are you doing?" he asked—and then he saw the thing on the ground, the pair of legs whose pale flesh gleamed in the moonlight, and the hips covered only by a pair of thin nylon shorts. It looked like the bottom half of a mannequin—except that it smelled like flesh and blood, like an open wound in need of treatment, only slightly masked by the pungency of garlic and the sharp smell of salt. Elias stepped around it and saw that the hip area opened to a mass of red flesh, smeared now with clumps of white powder.

"I put the garlic and salt in it," Ana whispered, staring at her hands. Elias moved to stand beside her, and he realized that her hands, too, carried the smell of open flesh.

"Wipe your hands on the grass," he said.

She did so, several times, trying to wipe away the residue and the stench. When she stood, her hands were shaking; she still held them away from her body, staring at them in quiet horror.

Gently, Elias grasped her hands in his. "It's okay," he said. "You did a good job. Let's go back inside."

They quickened their pace as a screech tore through the air, followed by other sounds of calamity within the monastery. They crawled back through the window, and in the hall they stopped short. Ven. Tseten and Ven. Santini stood near the corner staircase; a strange figure was pressed flat against the wall beside them. Its arms were spread at its sides, as if pinned there, its massive hands bony and studded with large veins—and when it whipped its head around to face

Elias, he caught a glimpse of a man's face, its eyes desperate and agonized.

The image only lasted a moment. Elias blinked, and suddenly the face was no longer that of a man. He recognized the close-cropped hair and round cheeks, the dark skin and long-lashed brown eyes. Where there had been a pair of jeans and a man's button-down shirt, the figure now wore a sparkly crop top and cut-off shorts.

"Elias!" it cried, its eyes full of fear. "Help me! They're trying to kill me!"

It was a good impression of Leitha, Elias thought. If he hadn't seen the transformation, he might have believed in it.

The monastics seemed unfazed by the show. They stood by side, Ven. Santini in his bold orange robe and Ven. Tseten in a crimson robe with a yellow wrap. They chanted quietly, heads bowed, hands held palm-out as the creature pleaded for Elias' help: "Elias, please! They're burning me!"

As Elias stood watching, the face suddenly distorted. Its cheekbones sharpened; the eyes darkened, and the mouth widened and sneered. "Yes, Elias, help her!" it barked, its voice deep and grating. "Oh, but you *can't*, can you? Helpless weakling!" The thing laughed, its dark eyes staring at Elias with mocking delight, the boom of its laughter seeming to shake the hall. "You can scream like a child at a harmless little salamander; you can run away and fall over your own feet; you can get beat up and tossed around night after night!" It laughed again. "Is it fun to be ridiculous? Will you cower and cry when we feast on your wimpling friends?"

Elias heard the strategy behind the creature's words, yet he also heard reason. He felt himself frozen to the spot, thinking rationally, yet overcome by fear—and he recalled the calming, powerful presence that Andre had instilled in him, still lingering somewhere in his psyche, moving through his body with the flow of his blood. That power—he had forgotten it! Such a force could not be diminished by a petty demon. It could bend a demon to his will . . . if Elias allowed it.

The creature's thick tongue lolled from its mouth, circling slowly over the lips. "The first of your wimpling friends was delicious," the creature growled, and chuckled deeply. "Don't you want to know how the rest will taste?"

Elias stared into the creature's mocking eyes. He could tear out those eyes, if he chose. He would not even need to become a monster to do so. All he needed was that confidence, that sense of power, something to replace the fear and revulsion that rooted him to the spot. He had heard of vampires that could grow a great set of jaws, like a monstrous wolf, and chomp a person's head off in one bite. Greater vampires than him had the power to shapeshift, to fly, to whisper suggestions that the hearer was helpless against.

Ana put a hand on his arm. "Elias."

He jerked away from her, suddenly offended by her scent—that of garlic and rotting flesh. Maria's lower half must have already started to deteriorate, likely spurred to ruin by the garlic and salt, a toxic combination for demonic forms.

"Get away," Elias said. "You stink." He tried to cover his nose, but the smell had defiled his own hands as well.

The demon-thing laughed, once again wearing Leitha's face. It smiled at him and said: "All humans stink."

"Elias," Ana said again. "Stop looking at it." She grasped his wrist, gently, but Elias tore away as though he'd been burned. He reached into his pocket, meaning to grab his knife, but he found the pocket empty. Elias reached into the other, ready to open the blade and lunge for the demon, to cut out its eyes and prove his own power—but his fingers closed around Aarya's lock, and he hesitated.

A growl sounded in the demon's throat. The illusion of Leitha disappeared, once again replaced by sharp features and a large mouth. The deep rumbling became a cry of rage, and the demon lunged at Elias, breaking away from its seeming imprisonment against the wall.

Instinctively, Elias defended himself. The heavy padlock was still grasped in his hand, and he swung it wildly toward the creature's face. The demon flinched, jerking its head back. The brass padlock smashed down on its chest.

The creature stopped. It drew in a wheezing gasp, its eyes and mouth open wide, its breath putrid as it exhaled into Elias' face. Elias choked on the stench and stumbled backwards.

The demon thudded to the floor, its mouth still open, its eyes wide but unseeing. The chanting stopped. Ven. Tseten approached the motionless figure with slow caution.

"Is it dead?" Elias asked.

"Not really," she replied.

"What is it?"

"It's a rakshasa, a kind of demon." The bhikshuni knelt beside the creature. "It shows up at ceremonies to disrupt prayers and prevent healing. We have certain mantras specifically to deal with this demon." She gazed down at the creature, her expression one of compassion rather than disdain. "Supposedly, it's a creature that lived at the end of the golden age. It was born into peace, but when it experienced violence and trauma, it coped by becoming cruel. Rakshasas believe that by perpetuating cruelty, they're in control of it and won't become victim to it. They see love and compassion as weakness."

Ven. Santini came to stand beside the fallen demon. He resumed chanting, his voice soft but determined. Elias

189

watched as he knelt beside the creature and withdrew the phurba.

"In Buddhist legend," Ven. Tseten continued, "a similar demon tried to antagonize the Buddha, but it ended up becoming his follower. Keep it in mind. We're not here to destroy souls, but to teach them."

"It tried to make me into a vampire," Elias said.

The bhikshuni gave him a sympathetic glance. "It's all right. It got to me, too. It must have known my weaknesses, because it called me a fraud and a criminal who only pretends to deserve forgiveness—and despite my training, I felt like a criminal."

A crash sounded from the upper floor, followed by Wen's voice calling for Shi Miao Xing.

Ana and Elias exchanged glances. They hurried past the fallen demon and clambered up the stairs.

At the top, they found the hall empty, but the sounds of struggle led them to an open door with artificial light streaming through. Elias motioned for Ana to stay back, but as he approached the doorway, a figure burst through it: Wen, his skinny form crashing against the opposite wall. He let out a grunt and sank to the floor.

Inside, Shi Miao Xing was in battle with Maria. Elias saw a flurry of movement between them, and then he realized that Maria had his knife. She slashed at the monk again and again, but he expertly dodged the blade—and then the manananggal opened her mouth, releasing the monstrous tongue.

Elias reacted without thought. He grabbed the only weapon at hand: the Phra Phrom shield that hung on the wall. A moment later he was rushing toward Maria, shield raised, ready to smash the brass shield into her skull. Instead, he found himself face to face with the end of the manananggal's tongue. The tip opened into a circular cavity, aimed and ready

190

to douse him with a stream of deadly acid. Elias thrust the shield in front of it. The stream made a hissing sound as it made contact with the metal; Maria seemed to cry out in pain, and the tongue retracted—and then Elias was hacking away with the edge of the shield, trying to sever the worm-like projectile that held Shi Miao Xing in its grasp.

Maria screeched and released her grip; the tongue unwound and retracted into her mouth. She looked at Elias with unbound rage, and her arm shot toward him in a wide arc as she slashed at him with his own knife.

Elias leapt back, feeling the sting of the blade in his forearm. He tried to brace himself for another attack, but Maria once again retreated, racing across the room and leaping through the window.

Shi Miao Xing stood for a while near the opening, looking out into the night. Then he quietly moved back toward the hall. "Let's go downstairs and help the others," he said.

On the first floor, they followed the soft sounds of chanting into one of the bedrooms. The monastics had lit candles around the room, and the details of the space were illuminated by a mix of flame and celestial light. A man sat in the middle of the floor—or something like a man, a thin figure wearing only a rag around its waist, its gray flesh hanging from bony shoulders like a soiled sheet. Its two thin hands rested in front of its large belly, and the eyes were closed, the face weary but restful. Ven. Ajahn Chah sat facing the creature, quietly reciting a mantra. The monk's bold orange robe was wrapped in a way that left his shoulder exposed, and something about the candlelight against the brown hue of his skin made him look like a living statue, a Buddha figure of bronze or gold. One hand rested in his lap, and the other was lifted with the index finger touching the thumb, the symbol of the dharma wheel.

The two bald-headed figures, facing each other in nearly the same pose, almost seemed two versions of the same man, one emaciated and one replete.

Vela, too, chanted quietly nearby, in unison with the monk. Their soft incantations, and the gentle flickering of candlelight, bathed the room in an unexpected serenity—a mood contrasted only by the sight of the futakuchi-onna.

Ven. Nyima stood facing the doorway, eyes closed, arms at her sides. Like Sanjay, her face was set with a placid expression, but Elias' breath caught when he realized that she was bound from head to toe in an array of thin black tentacles. Akari stood just behind her, her hair like a dozen long, slender leeches imprisoning the bhikshuni in a taut embrace.

Elias started toward her, but Shi Miao Xing put a hand on his shoulder and whispered: "Watch."

Vela's hands moved in simple, fluid gestures. She stood close on one side of Akari, then moved to the other side, pausing there to sweep her hands up and down in slow movements. The bhikshuni made two fists near her hips, motioning as though she was putting on a belt. Elias watched as she transitioned into a striking movement, a slow-motion punch that stopped just short of Akari's torso. After a couple of repetitions, the bhikshuni paused with her arm drawn back—and then she punched hard, again stopping just short of contact.

Around the room, flames flickered; several candles were extinguished, leaving the front of the room in partial darkness. The tentacles released their hold, dropping like limp black noodles. Vela caught Akari as she fell to the floor.

Ven. Nyima opened her eyes. She turned to help Vela, and in the low light, Elias saw something on the back of her bald head—something dark and oval, like a bad tattoo. The flesh below it was smeared with a dark trail that had dripped down and stained the nun's sanghati, the yellow cloth she wore over her robe. Something about the sight created a sharp, tingling sensation in Elias' mouth. He recognized, then, the rich, coppery scent of blood, and he realized that the jagged oval was a set of teeth marks.

"It *bit* her," he whispered.

Akari lay on the floor, her head resting on Vela's lap. Vela looked up and said to Ven. Nyima: "Bring some water."

Something about the sight offended Elias: Vela cradling the monster and asking its bleeding victim to take care of it.

"They have it under control," Shi Miao Xing said quietly. "Let's find the others."

Elias followed him toward the front entrance, but he repeated: "It bit her."

The monk nodded. "Yes, I saw."

Wen asked: "Is she going to be okay? It's not, like, a zombie bite, where she'll get infected?"

Shi Miao Xing smiled. "No, there is no infection."

The conversation halted as they reached the front lobby. Once again, they were faced with an unexpected sight. Sanjay, the man who'd disrupted the Chenrezig session, was lying on his back in the middle of the floor. Nothing about him appeared monstrous. He wore gray pants and a blue button-down shirt, and he lay with a cushion tucked under his head, as relaxed as if he had just decided to take a nap.

"Is it really this easy?" Ana asked. "You just say some mantras, and the demons sit down and start meditating?"

"No," Shi Miao Xing replied. "It's not easy."

Lamia sat beside Sanjay, while Ven. Sonam and Ven. Chonyi stood watchfully at either side of the room. Ven. Chonyi looked questioningly at Shi Miao Xing. "Have you seen Andrei?"

The monk shook his head. "No, but the futakuchi-onna and a preta have been subdued, and the werewolf is unconscious in one of the guest rooms. The manananggal was here, too, but we lost track of it."

"And the kappa," Wen added. "It was in the bathroom upstairs. Shi Miao Xing spilled its water, and I refilled it. I told it to go home."

"What about you? Is everyone all right?"

"Elias is hurt," Wen said.

Elias examined the slash along his forearm. He was both pleased and disturbed to see it in an advanced stage of healing. The bleeding had stopped, and the wound had drawn closed and scabbed over. *Too fast*, Elias thought; *it's healing too fast*. The exchange with the rakshasa, when he had felt the beginnings of monsterization—that had caused it. Even the smallest step toward being a vampire gave him the power of rapid healing. *And it's not over. I salivated at the scent of blood. I can feel Andrei's presence churning inside of me.* And perhaps, for the time being, that small strain of vampirism was protecting him. He could use it without succumbing to it. "I'm fine," he said. "It's just a small cut."

"I'm going to sit with the werewolf," Shi Miao Xing said. "I'll do some work before it wakes up—but it would also be wise to look for the manananggal."

"And Andrei," Elias added, gazing at Sanjay's slumbering form. Ana's comment weighed on him; it had been far too easy to subdue these monsters. It seemed that the werewolf and manananggal were the only ones who had put up a real fight. If Andrei wanted Lucian so badly, why had he chosen such pitiful creatures to breach the monastery? He must have some other plan—or perhaps this *was* the plan. While the monastics were occupied with caring for these fallen monsters, Andrei could roam the building unnoticed.

It was a shame, Elias thought, that he couldn't get into Andrei's head, the way Andrei could get into everyone else's psyche. That ability seemed not unreachable to him. By getting into Elias' mind, Andrei had left the residue of that power. Perhaps Elias could tap into it, could use it just a little, just enough to seek out the vampire, and then—

Sanjay abruptly sat up. His gaze fixed on Elias. The man's demeanor was no longer restful; the face bore a look of horror, and the flesh succumbed to a smattering of sores that opened and festered before Elias' eyes. Sanjay's mouth opened wide, emitting a long, screeching belch. A blast of foul breath hit Elias' face, and he winced, trying to shield himself with his arms.

Sanjay began to chant, a deep and piercing sound that reverberated through Elias' body. Elias lowered his arms and looked again, and in Sanjay's rotting face he saw insects crawling, parasites embedding themselves in the open wounds, spindly worms circling the eyeballs.

He gagged.

As Elias covered his mouth, the residue of garlic and salt once again sickened him. He stooped over with his hands on his knees, avoiding looking at the pishacha—but his own hands, too, had begun to rot. His flesh was discolored with red and black sores. Tiny worms and bugs moved beneath his skin, looking for places to deposit their eggs and multiply.

No, Elias thought. *This can't happen. I can't be infested so easily.*

He looked up, desperately staring at the pishacha, as if for help. Sanjay's face had returned to its peaceful state; the rot had subsided, the wounds vanished, the horror replaced by indifference. The sickness had been transferred to Elias; he was now the infested one, had succumbed to the pishacha's attack without even a fight.

If he had still been a vampire, he knew, this could not have happened to him—*but I chose to be a human, just a weak and stupid human. . . .*

Wen was saying his name, asking if he was all right, but Elias deliberately turned away from him. His gaze fell on Ana, who stood looking at him with concern. Elias suddenly hated that look. Of what use was her concern? What power did it have? Resentment filled his being, disdain and disgust toward every feeble, gullible creature like Ana, toward everyone who had weakened him with promises of strength through compassion and righteousness. Ana had been foolish to show up here. She was healthy, supple, but naïve and easy to overpower. Her weakness granted that she didn't deserve such health. Elias would take it from her, would use her vitality to shed his own sickness. Ana, the weak one, could have that sickness instead. He would drink her blood and chew her vibrant flesh, and leave holes in which to deposit his parasites.

Vela stepped between the two of them, thrusting a burst of energy toward the pishacha. Sanjay fell backwards from the force of the blow, and Elias also felt as though he had been struck. He blinked, steadied himself, and drew in a shuddering gasp. He looked down to see the disease gone from his hands, his skin intact and healthy.

When he looked up, Vela was kneeling beside the fallen man. She lifted his head and placed the iron phurba beneath it, holding it in place with one hand while the other moved above Sanjay's face and chest.

"Are you all right?" Ana asked.

Elias looked uneasily at her, flushing with guilt at the recollection of his own thoughts. "Yeah," he said, ducking his head.

Shi Miao Xing started for the stairs. Elias began to follow, but Vela looked up and commanded him in a sharp tone: "Elias, stay here."

He lingered there uncertainly while Vela continued her work. Ven. Sonam and Ven. Chonyi joined the others, so that only Lamia and Vela remained with Elias and the pishacha.

At last Vela stood up and went to Elias. "Hold still," she said. "Close your eyes."

He did as she said. At first he heard nothing, felt nothing. Vela stood by him silently, but after some time he felt some movement within him, as though some force was being shifted from one place to another in his body. Then, a cold sting as the tip of the phurba blade pressed into the back of his neck.

"Ow," he said.

"You can handle it," the bhikshuni replied. "It hurts worse than being possessed."

"Was I possessed?"

She chuckled. "Do you think you weren't?"

Elias waited quietly for her to finish. When she told him to open his eyes, he found himself unable to take a step. He reached for the door frame as his legs began to give out.

"Sit," Vela said. "You might feel off balance for a while."

"What did you do?"

"I helped you."

After some quiet conversation, the bhikshunis decided to move Sanjay, Akari, and the preta into the Tara room. Akari and the preta, seemingly dazed and helpless, were able to walk with assistance, but Sanjay was another matter. Elias helped Vela, Nyima, and Lamia grab him by the limbs and carry him spread-eagled down the hall.

They decided that Latham, the werewolf, was better left alone for the time being.

Vela and Lamia moved around the room, lighting the votive candles that had been placed on the tables and wall sconces. When all were lit, Vela turned off the overhead lights and knelt behind the preta, who was sitting upright in a meditative position. Elias was again struck by its form: the large belly protruding from the emaciated body, the sagging flesh, the slender neck and tiny, wrinkled mouth. The bhikshuni was mostly silent. Occasionally she whispered and moved her hands, her palm hovering just a few inches behind the creature's flesh. Vela's face was shadowed, but her blue eyes seemed ethereally lit—and when she looked up at Elias, there was something bold and frightening about her gaze.

He looked away, toward the yellow warmth of the flames. "Aren't you afraid of knocking over the candles?" he asked, making an effort to keep his voice steady. "Maybe it was different down here, but we had a pretty vicious fight with Maria and Latham."

"We have extinguishers," Vela replied.

"Are candles that important?"

"Well," Vela said, "technically, they're a symbol of the fire that burns away attachment—but I use them because they create a relaxing ambiance. These things are important, too." She smiled, and the piercing quality of her gaze seemed to soften.

Elias shook his head, mildly bewildered. How could she be so relaxed with a vampire and a flying hammerhead worm on the loose?

Ana entered the room quietly. Vela beckoned her, and as Ana knelt beside her, the bhikshuni whispered something Elias couldn't hear. Ana nodded. A long silence filled the room, and then Vela began to chant.

Elias listened in fascination. The nuns were chanting in monotone, and Ana sang the same words, but with a more

198

melodic inflection. The preta sat with its eyes closed, occasionally letting out a sharp moan, its face contorting as if it was in pain—and then the countenance would relax again, easing into placid relief.

Ven. Nyima came to stand beside Elias. "Come closer," she whispered.

Elias looked at the strange, quiet spectacle in front of him and shook his head. "No thanks."

The bhikshuni smiled.

"What is that thing?" Elias asked.

"A preta. A hungry ghost." She leaned close to Elias and urged him again. "We're giving it the tools to move past its hunger."

"What are they singing?"

"The Tara verses. Do you want to help?"

"Me?" Elias looked at her in astonishment. "I don't know any verses."

"You don't need to know them. I'll show you what to do."

"What if . . . ." Elias looked uncertainly at the preta.

"Are you afraid of it?" Ven. Nyima asked.

"No. What if I infect it?"

The bhikshuni beckoned him. "Come here."

She guided Elias to a spot just behind the creature's right shoulder and bade him place his hand there. Gingerly, Elias laid his palm against the creature's rubbery flesh, his fingers resting against the bony curve of its shoulder.

"Just wish it well," Ven. Nyima said quietly.

Ana, beside him, continued singing the verses in her way, bold yet gentle, soothing and yet somehow melancholic, so that Elias felt his eyes tearing up. He lowered his gaze, not knowing why he suddenly felt overcome with emotion. He tried to focus on the preta's well-being, but he found himself thinking of his own melancholy, his own struggles and sadness, his own need for reassurance and hope. He was pulled from his self-reflection, though, when he felt the preta's rubbery flesh dry up like sandpaper and crumble beneath his fingers. Elias jerked his hand away, certain that his touch had caused the injury—but he looked at Ven. Nyima, and she smiled reassuringly. "Don't worry," she said. "It's just getting ready to be reborn."

Elias watched as the figure collapsed in front of him. It fell to a shapeless heap on the floor, disintegrating into smaller and smaller grains until nothing was left but a thin layer of dust. Ana and the bhikshunis sang the last few verses, and the group sat for a while in silence, gazing at the spot where the preta had passed on from its ghostly form.

12

The others searched the building from back to front and back again, blocking the windows as they went. Elias heard them pounding nails into the wooden frames, covering them with rugs and whatever else could provide a barrier until the glass could be replaced. Ven. Nyima and Ven. Chonyi quietly checked on Lucian and Ven. Norbu. They returned and reported in hushed voices. Lucian was fine; he and the bhikshuni were meditating.

Eventually, most of the group gathered in the Tara room, having searched both levels and finding no monsters except one.

"The kappa is still in the bathroom," Wen said. "I told it to go home, but it's just sitting there."

Lamia spoke up: "I doubt that it has a home here. Andrei probably brought the kappa from Japan."

"Oh," Wen replied. "I just assumed it lived in the river." He paused, frowning. "So, what should we do? Just let it hang out in the toilet?"

"Let's refrain from using that bathroom for now," Vela said. "We need to take care of these two first, and Latham. Then we'll decide what to do about the kappa."

The group had a solemn discussion about how to proceed, with plans made to call for police and paramedics, and to ensure that the intruders received follow-up care. It was decided that the monastics should do some work on Latham before making the call.

The werewolf didn't appreciate the attention. Elias sat on the floor of the Tara room with his knees drawn up to his chest, anxiously hugging his knees as he listened to Latham's screams and howls, and to the outraged thudding of his body against the wall. Wen and Ana sat beside him. Now that the trouble had passed, and the three had time to reflect on the horrors they'd just witnessed, they huddled close together like a trio of frightened children.

"Andrei might still show up tonight," Wen said. "We'll have to guard the windows. He'll be able to come in quietly—maybe in a few hours, when everyone's asleep. We should still plan to sleep in shifts."

Elias was also pondering how Andrei might next approach the monastery. The drama of the evening began to slip away, and as Elias eased out of survival mode and back into a clarity of thought, some memory nagged at the edge of his consciousness—something about the upstairs room, about his encounter with Maria and the dark, flitting figure that had nearly struck him as it sailed past.

"He's already here," Elias said.

Ana and Wen looked at him in quiet perplexity.

Slowly, Elias loosened his arms from around his legs. "He's been here the whole time. I forgot that Andrei can shapeshift. I saw a bat come in earlier, through the upstairs window, but I didn't even have time to think about it. Did you look in the rafters? Andrei and Maria can both fly."

"We looked there," Ana said. "There aren't that many rafters. There are just a few beams in the meditation room."

Elias' urgency rose as he recalled the events of the past hour—the exchange with the rakshasa and the allure of Andrei's presence; his own quiet yearning for a dark and baneful power; his overpowering disgust at the idea of being human. "He's definitely here," Elias said, getting to his feet. "This whole time, I've felt him. He's been trying to get into my head."

He hurried toward the front stairs, and in the hallway a small movement caught his attention—some small, flitting, colorful thing scurrying along the wall. Elias stopped in a moment of caution, and then he recognized it: a black and yellow joro spider. He was about to jump over it when a thin stream shot from the spider's torso. *Venom!* Elias thought, but he quickly realized that the creature had ejected a strand of silk onto the opposite wall. It shot another, and another, speedily blocking the path with sticky strands.

Elias started to reach out, but he was afraid to touch the webbing. It might ensnare him; it might burn. One never knew with monsters.

"Lamia!" he shouted.

She had already followed him out to the hall, along with the other teens and a few bhikshunis. As soon as she saw the web, though, she was gone, retreating to the kitchen. Elias tried to run the other way, toward the back stairs, but he found the way being blocked by yet another spider.

"They're everywhere!" he cried.

Lamia came back with a plastic spray bottle. She aimed and sprayed the web, and Elias was astonished to see that it immediately dissolved. "Nothing a little bleach and water can't solve," Lamia said calmly.

Elias began to slip off his shoe, but he stopped in shock when he realized that the spider was no longer merely the size of his palm. It was expanding, mutating, its torso surpassing the size of a small rodent, its legs stretching across the floor.

"It's growing!" he said. A thick strand of silk shot across his foot, adhering it firmly to the floor.

Lamia gave him a pointed look. "I told you it wasn't a spider."

"Lamia! Do something."

She slipped off her canvas shoe and brought it down hard on the spider. Elias flinched as the creature's guts burst from its body with a sickening sound, a subtle crunching overpowered by a loud, wet burst. The legs curled inward, detaching from the ruined body and scattering across the floor.

"God," Elias breathed, looking at the guts strewn across the hall and on the bhikshuni's robes. Lamia calmly sprayed the webbing around his foot—and then Elias remembered Lucian, and he ran.

He made it to the room where Lucian and Ven. Norbu were sitting in animated conversation. Elias slipped into the room and closed the door behind him, and the two fell silent, looking at him with curious expectation.

"Andrei is somewhere in the building," Elias said quietly. "He knows you're in here."

Lucian, sitting on a cushion with his back against the wall, straightened up. "How do you know?"

"Can Andrei shapeshift?" Without waiting for an answer, Elias continued: "I've felt him, trying to get into my head—and if he can shapeshift, I'm pretty sure I saw him. Maria broke one of the upstairs windows, and a bat came in. I haven't seen it since. I haven't seen Maria, either. Only Akari, Sanjay, Latham, the kappa, and the preta are accounted for." He paused. "The preta is dead. And the joro thing just sent its spiders after us."

"What about the pontianak?" Lucian asked.

Elias tried to recall Lucian's description of the pontianak. He remembered something about a woman with red eyes and long claws—and then the plaster above his head shattered, falling in chunks to the floor, and Elias looked up to see the ceiling pierced and broken by a set of long talons, thick and curved and black like the claws of a giant eagle. Behind them, glowing in the shadows, was a pair of anguished and malevolent red eyes.

The pontianak's pale face moved closer to the opening. It opened its mouth and screeched, an almost human sound, like that of a demonic infant. Elias felt the creature's breath on his face, saw the throat vibrating with the force of the cry, but the sound seemed strangely far away.

"Don't look at it!" Lucian shouted, springing to his feet.

Elias forced himself to lower his head. His eyes already ached after meeting the pontianak's gaze, seeming to throb violently in the sockets; he closed them and pressed his hand hard against his eyelids, as if to keep his eyeballs intact. He gagged on the stench of the creature: an artificial floral scent, like a cheap air freshener, followed by the stink of rotting meat.

He heard sounds of chaos: cracking, thudding, grunting, shouting, voices shrill with desperation and fury. When Elias opened his eyes, Ven. Norbu was sprawled on the floor, her nose dripping a slow stream of red onto the floor, her hand and upper arm bleeding from long gashes. Her eyes were closed, her face set in an expression of pain.

Andrei stood in the middle of the room, looking calm and fashionable in a long black jacket and tall boots. He didn't acknowledge Elias, but stood looking at Lucian, who crouched near the fallen bhikshuni. The pontianak had also dropped into the room. It stood with its back against the door, its head mercifully bowed—and behind it, several yellow and black spiders crawled.

Elias barely noticed them. His attention was fixed on Maria, who stood beside the pontianak on her bird-like legs.

205

He hadn't gotten a thorough look at those legs, but now, with the action at a standstill, he noticed with quiet horror the three front toes ending in steely gray sickle-shaped claws, and the short toe in the back that supported a much longer claw—one that looked like an oversized straight razor rather than part of the foot. She smiled with cruel delight as the joro spiders shot their silky strands across the door and doorknob. Elias heard a commotion in the hall, a rattling and a loud thumping against the door—but it was already too late. The door was stuck fast, glued in place by the accumulating webs.

Elias didn't move. A slow, creeping helplessness filled him. He inched closer to Ven Norbu and slipped his hand under her head, noting with some relief the signs of life: the chest rising and falling, the pulse steadily beating. While Elias silently vowed to protect her, he willed with all his might that she would wake up and become the protector. Ven. Norbu was supposedly skilled in martial arts and had the means to fight against monsters.

The pounding on the door didn't stop. The monastics threw their bodies against it in rhythmic intervals, desperate but futile.

"Let's all calm down," Andrei said. Though he was slightly out of breath, his voice was smooth and steady, his demeanor one of assured tranquility. He let out a long sigh. "So much drama," he said, "over such a simple visit. Lucian and I are old friends—and he is also acquainted with Maria. How could we miss his release?" The vampire went to Maria and put an arm around her small shoulders, gently guiding her so that she stood facing Lucian. "The custom, on such an occasion, is to treat the returning citizen to a meal."

Lucian's gaze remained fixed on the fallen bhikshuni.

Quietly, Andrei continued: "I never thought that when we reunited, it would be like this. You, sitting in a place like this .

. . stripped of your power . . . communing with a weak and pitiful woman." The vampire's eyes flashed with sudden resentment. "And with that cold indifference, even refusing to look at me. Are you afraid to look?" Andrei lowered his head, peering at Lucian, trying to meet his gaze. "You could never harm me with those eyes. You know that, don't you?"

Lucian didn't move.

"Will you really give up what we had?" Andrei asked, his voice smooth and soft as velvet. "Give it up for this—this cistern of pontificating women and lifeless routines?"

The pounding on the door had paused, but now it resumed, louder this time, a hard and persistent bludgeoning.

"You're mistaken about me, Lucian," the vampire continued. "Those pitiful creatures downstairs, from our little circle of acquaintances—I didn't bring them here to harvest their power. They are useful for one purpose only: to distract those tiresome monastics, who are so easily blinded by their self-indulgent pity for others. My biggest desire is for *you*."

Still, Lucian didn't respond. Andrei stood upright. He turned to Elias, his dark eyes lit with ingenuine warmth. "And you, Elias *Hellström*, what is your desire? I can see in your eyes that you feel overpowered. How uncomfortable must it be." The vampire smiled, as if in sympathy. "You've been thinking about what I can do," he said softly. "What *you* could do, if you allowed yourself. What would help you in this situation? Persuasion? Shapeshifting? Or perhaps something even more other-worldly?"

Elias didn't reply, and Andrei continued: "I do aim for greater power, but even now, I have talents that you haven't imagined. I have seen your mind; I know what you desire most. And I could give it to you easily." He paused and added with emphasis: "I could teach you to take it for yourself."

He held out a hand, palm out, toward Elias. For just a moment, Elias focused on that hand, on the lines of the palm and the thin, pale fingers—and then he realized that the room had changed. The back wall had vanished, and in its place was a haze of swirling white cloud amid shards of blue, as if the monastery had been transported into the sky. A figure lingered in the center of that cloud, a humanesque outline, vague and undefined.

"You can take such a power for yourself," Andrei said, "by becoming *more* than a vampire."

The outline began to take on details: long hair. The cut of a baggy T-shirt and jeans. A face—feminine, with fierce eyes and a mouth set in solemn determination.

Aarya.

The face contorted into a look of fear. The eyes shone with desperation; shadows fell across her body like tarred stripes as columns of gleaming white rose and descended, gigantic shining fangs that closed in front of her like the bars of a prison. Aarya's mouth moved in a muffled cry: *Elias! Help me!*

Andrei waved his hand in a quick, jerking motion. The portal closed; the image of Aarya vanished.

Andrei's eyes were on Lucian, now. "By joining to a more powerful spirit, I have learned to open dimensions, channel power . . . and revive the dead." His dark, cold gaze flicked back to Elias.

"That wasn't Aarya," Elias said defiantly.

Andrei shrugged. "One too weak to accept power is apt to deny its authenticity. I have no need of you, Elias. Remember that I did extend my generosity to you." He smiled, cold and unaffectionate. "I *can* open such portals, but the effort tires me." His gaze slithered toward Ven. Norbu. "I am rather in

208

need of refreshment. Ah . . . so weak a life force, this ridiculous nun, but still delicious, I am sure."

Elias pulled Ven. Norbu closer, and Andrei laughed. "Don't waste your energy. You can't protect her any more than you could protect Leitha. She's dead, by the way. Didn't choose her company carefully enough."

"You're a liar," Elias said. He knew that Andrei was just trying to enrage him; yet the comment rattled him, plagued him with a needle of doubt.

"So you say. It is inconsequential to me." Andrei lifted his chin and looked around the room. "Well," he breathed. "This turned out so perfectly. Here we are, the true beasts of power, with all of the weaklings shut out from us. Well, *almost* all of them." He nudged Ven. Norbu's shin with the toe of his shoe. "Elias prefers helplessness, and this one . . . well, she isn't really present, is she?"

Lucian's voice pierced the room: "Leave."

"Here we have a basilisk, a vampire"—Andrei's gaze settled triumphantly on Elias—"a manananggal, and a pontianak, and whatever I am. What am I, Lucian? Look at me and decide." As he spoke, Andrei gently guided Maria to stand in front of him. He peered at Lucian over the top of her head. "We are destined for this power," Andrei continued softly, "no matter how much you deny it." He looked at Elias, his pupils dilating, becoming twin pools of alluring darkness. "No matter how much *any* of you try to deny it."

You won't get me, Elias thought, steeling himself. *I won't let you. I won't. . . .*

Yet, the scent of the bhikshuni's blood took on a sudden sharpness. Elias felt his senses tingling, his mouth aching. He glanced down at Ven. Norbu, at the way her head tilted back under his grasp, her throat exposed. There was something sensual about the curve of her neck—about the delicate trails of her veins, the mingled vitality and vulnerability in the scent of her lifeblood.

He closed his eyes. Then he rested the bhikshuni's head on his leg, freeing his hand to grip the padlock that weighed down his pocket.

When he looked up again, the persistent pounding on the door had cracked the wood. A splintered bulge was forming near the pontianak's head.

Andrei grinned mockingly at Elias. "Are you tempted? I'm terribly sorry, but I already promised the nun to someone else." He tightened his grip on Maria's shoulders, lowered his head to speak in her ear. "Isn't that what I promised? A feast on the flesh and blood of one who claims to be pure? As we all know—" Again he flashed a smile at Elias, smug and cruelly delighted "—that kind of blood is the most delicious."

"Don't you dare," Elias said. He looked around the room for something to fight with, but there were only the tools of the monastic: the phurba, the vajra and bell, a few useless candles. Elias felt a heated frustration—no, anger—at the lack of weapons. No knife, no shield, just his bare fists and fingernails and teeth, whatever he could use in a desperate move to protect himself and the bhikshuni. The phurba was his best bet, he decided. The blade, though not sufficiently sharp, could produce massive damage with a hard enough thrust into soft tissue. If he needed to, he would put it through Maria's eye.

"Oh, I dare." Andrei gestured to the widening hole in the door. "Your friends, I'm afraid, are rushing us, and there is no point in delaying the inevitable. Don't you agree, Lucian? You must have known, during all of your meaningless little prayers and your docile therapy sessions, that there is only one possible outcome for us. You can reclaim your power, or you can stay helpless and watch your nun friend be devoured—her, and then the other weaklings." Andrei lowered his voice, speaking quietly in the mananangal's ear, but his words were clear and bold in the interval between the pounding: "Have at her, Maria."

Again, chaos erupted. Maria opened her mouth; the monstrous tongue shot forth, and Elias tried to grab it, reaching for the tip. It twisted from his grasp again and again. The banging stopped, and Elias glimpsed a skinny arm—Wen's arm—reaching through the door, groping toward the webs.

"Wen, don't!" Elias shouted. Maria lifted one of her deadly talons and tried to slash at him; he shoved his foot against her shin, and she struggled for balance.

"Lucian!" Elias shouted, hoping for some help.

Lucian didn't respond. He sat quietly staring at the pontianak. The creature stood unmoving, returning Lucian's gaze, her bloodshot eyes seeming to glow with a subtle red light.

Elias caught hold of Maria's tongue. It thrashed in his grasp, and he called again for Lucian, but the only reply he received was Andrei's chuckle.

"That's it," the vampire said. "Use your power, Lucian. Your *true* power." Wen reached through the door again, and Andrei paused to whack his arm with the iron bell, causing a quick retreat. Calmly, the vampire set the bell down and placed a hand on the pontianak's shoulder. "It is a pitiful creature, isn't it?" he asked, his voice an enchanting velveteen murmur. "If there is any being who should be in the path of your power, surely it's this one." He shook the pontianak's shoulder gently. "Such miserable creatures shouldn't exist, and they succumb easily. They are as easy to kill as they are to manipulate. You could destroy this one with a glance—and I *know* you want to."

Elias held fast to the manananggal's tongue as he looked up, fearful of what he might see—but Lucian's face was tranquil, his eyes clear.

Maria gave up trying to attack with her feet. With her long claws she slashed at Elias, and as he ducked out of her reach, he lost his grip on the monstrous tongue. He managed to catch it again, and before Maria could launch another attack, he took the tongue between his teeth and bit down hard.

The manananggal shrieked. Maria threw herself at Elias, and as they struggled, Elias was dimly aware of a hissing sound emanating from the pontianak, quiet but harsh, like a snake slithering across sandpaper.

"That's it," Andrei said again.

Elias grabbed Maria and tossed her aside, sending her small figure hurtling across the room. Andrei looked down as she crashed against his legs, and when he looked up again, his face became fraught with surprise, and then with panic. "Lucian!" he said sharply.

Lucian's eyes were red and raw. Sad, but still calm, with no sign of the basilisk that still lurked somewhere inside him—but something else was wrong was wrong with those eyes. Bright red drops of blood appeared in the corners.

And then the pontianak rushed forward, arm outstretched. It caught Lucian's face in its clawed hands and pressed its mouth against his eye. A loud, wet sucking filled the room as the creature suctioned Lucian's eyeball from its socket.

"Stop!" Andrei screeched. He stumbled over Maria as he rushed toward the pontianak. He caught himself and pulled on the creature's arms, then on its head. "Stop! *Stop*, you wretched—"

Lucian, too, gripped the pontianak's head, his fingers embedded in the dark hair. He screamed in agony, but Elias realized that he wasn't pushing the creature away. He was pulling, fighting against Andrei—but his hands shook with pain; his grip loosened; Andrei and the pontianak tumbled to the ground. Lucian's face was contorted in agony, smeared with blood. As he brought his hand up to cover his eye, Elias glimpsed the ravaged flesh and empty socket.

"Lucian," Elias breathed, momentarily forgetting the unconscious bhikshuni. He began to stand—and then an outraged Maria was lashing at him again, shrieking as the damaged tongue unfurled from her mouth. She tried to launch a stream of acid, but she flinched as it leaked into her wounds, sizzling there on the flesh.

Andrei stared at Lucian's bleeding face, his eyes glassy with desperation and outrage.

Lucian tilted his head up. He opened his remaining eye, focusing dimly on the pontianak even as he gasped and choked on his pain.

He didn't look long. Andrei made a strange, growling sound deep in his throat. His mouth opened, exposing the white curve of his fangs. It opened wider, his head tilting back, still releasing that strange growl, and Elias thought for a moment that he was simply overcome by rage.

But the mouth opened wider, the jaws extending outward, the teeth and gums protruding. Something savagely animal shone in Andrei's eyes, something unreasoning and out of control.

Elias' breath caught. He remembered, then, the legends— the vampires who could not only bite the neck, but who could completely sever the head from the body in one bite.

Wildly, he cried: *"Don't!"*

Ven. Norbu was momentarily forgotten. Elias let her head thump against the floor as he leapt to his feet; he grabbed Andrei by the throat, forcing his jaws away from the pontianak.

Andrei snarled. Elias caught another glimpse of his eyes, ice-cold and outraged and completely inhuman. The impossibly large mouth opened again, pushing closer, and Elias felt the fatal heat of the vampire's breath on his throat— and then Lucian spoke.

"Andrei," Lucian said, shaken but resolute. "I'll come with you."

A dim light of recognition appeared in the vampire's eyes. He released Elias. The mouth relaxed; the massive jaws began to recede.

For some seconds, all was quiet. The pounding ceased. Elias looked toward the door and saw Maria looking on with greedy interest, and Vela peering grimly through the hole in the door.

The banging resumed. The bhikshunis were using a statue of the Buddha as a battering ram. The plywood door was coming apart, the hole nearly large enough for a small adult to breach—but not quite large enough, not yet. The spiders were retreating through that hole, presumably to attack the monastics—but Elias heard each of them meet its end beneath Lamia's shoe.

"I'll come with you," Lucian repeated, "if you leave them alone."

Andrei's eyes were lit with a semblance of reason. He turned to his former lover.

He found himself face to face with a basilisk.

Lucian no longer bore the gentle beauty that Elias had so admired. There was something sinister in it now—not just in his face, but in his voice when he spoke. "Because you absolutely insist," he said, "I will do as you wish."

Elias heard poison in that voice: a mix of exhilaration and loathing.

214

A basilisk, he recalled, was known for having a venomous voice, for leaving a trail of poison in its path. It was particularly associated with the venom of a snake, and was even said to have the same effect. The neurotoxins in snake venom could induce both paralysis and relief from pain; they released dopamine and granted feelings of pleasure and motivation. Such venom was addictive because, even as it attacked the muscles and withheld blood from the limbs, and as it suspended the user in half-sleep, it also trapped the user in a temporary state of bliss. The aftermath, though, was depression, chronic exhaustion, and the craving for another hit. In severe cases, a bite necessitated amputation or resulted in disfigurement.

All of these details raced through Elias' mind as Andrei perished in Lucian's grasp. Lucian didn't need touch him; he merely looked at Andrei, his eyes all rancor and death. The pale diadem on his forehead glowed with a dark hue, and his face no longer seemed his own, but was inhumanly sharp, angular, and luminescent gray. Andrei's soul, it seemed, was ejected from his body, the meager luminescence of his being escaping and leaving behind a vulnerable husk. Maria looked on, immobilized with horror, and even the pontianak flinched as the vampire dried up like a prune under Lucian's stare. His hands turned blue, and then they withered into little gray lumps, and his arms did the same. The fashionable clothes slipped to the floor, no longer supported by Andrei's frame. His body imploded and took shape around another, hidden form: that of the wechuge.

The monster's guise seemed to suddenly erupt from Andrei's form. Its head and shoulders were studded with what looked like antlers and spiky fur, but Elias quickly recognized the protrusions as shards of frost and ice. For just a moment he saw the creature's face—a gaping, ravenous mouth, large eyes so empty and cold that they made Maria's gaze seem human in comparison. Elias' breath caught as he looked into those eyes. He felt the creature's barrenness, the starved and emotionless void in which it existed—and then the gaping mouth shrieked, desolate and soul-piercing.

The wechuge, too, was powerless against the basilisk. The icy façade cracked, falling piece by piece to the floor, until all that remained was a distorted sheath of seemingly mummified flesh. It clung tightly around Andrei's bones until nothing was left but a withered, misshapen skeleton—and then the bones shattered, just as easily as if they had been made of the thinnest glass. The room filled with a stench like burnt hair and mothballs, and the corpse shrank into an undefined heap.

The heap crashed to the floor.

Elias forced himself out of his horrified stupor. He rushed to the door, positioning himself between Lucian and the group in the hall. "Don't look!" he shouted at them. "Lamia, give me the bleach."

She passed the plastic bottle through the hole, and Elias began to spray the thickly laid strands. "Don't look in here," he said again, hearing the trembling in his own voice. "When I get the door open, I'll bring Venerable Norbu out—but don't look!"

Please! he begged silently, willing Lucian to refrain from attacking him, though he anticipated being torn to shreds at any moment. *Please! Remember me; remember yourself. Don't kill us!*

He sprayed the webs until none were left, then dropped the bottle with a loud thud and cracked the door open.

Lucian had been waiting for that moment. No sooner had Elias started to open the door than Lucian shoved past him, his head ducked low, his fatal gaze fixed safely on the floor. He fled past the crowd in a stumbling run.

Maria, too, looked out at the monastics and emitted a fiery screech. She raced past them, claws slashing as she went. A set of fresh wounds opened in Lamia's arm, and then in Ven. Santini's chest.

Elias turned and looked at the near-empty room. The pontianak was cowering in a corner, seemingly stunned. A hideous gray shell was all that remained of Andrei, shrunken and misshapen, with his clothes and the black tourmaline necklace scattered around it. The implosion had completely shattered the vampire's skeleton and crushed it inward. The only recognizable elements were the fangs, now scattered uselessly on the floor.

"Venerable Norbu needs help," Elias said. He went on trembling legs to where the bhikshuni lay. Tried to lift her. "Help," he said, weakly—and then Shi Miao Xing was there, taking the bhikshuni in his arms.

The following moments would later be nothing more than a blur in Elias' mind. He was in shock, he supposed. All he remembered from the next few minutes was that Lamia and Wen led him to the meditation room and helped him sit down. Lamia babbled, tried to comfort him, and then commended him for protecting the pontianak. "They're working on her now," Lamia assured him. "They'll help her. It was good of you to keep her safe. Now, she'll have a better start in her next life, and maybe a better future in this one."

Elias replied dully: "I don't give a damn about the pontianak or her next life. I saved her to help *us*. You can explain a few intruders to the cops, and you can even explain having to stab someone in self-defense, but how would you explain someone getting decapitated in the monastery? How do you explain decapitation by a giant set of jaws? I did that to keep *us* out of trouble." He paused, and asked: "How are you going to explain Andrei? His body . . . it doesn't even look like a corpse. It looks like a mummified cocoon."

"We won't need to explain it," Lamia replied. "There's nothing left of it now but a pile of wet ash. Venerable Dorje swept it into a container. We'll bury it tomorrow."

"Where's Venerable Norbu? Is she still unconscious?"

"She's awake. Ana and Venerable Dorje took her to the hospital."

Elias started to respond, but he stopped as a sound reached his ears: an anguished, outraged screech from somewhere outside. "More monsters," he said.

Shi Miao Xing and Wen went to investigate, and soon, Wen returned alone. He explained in quiet awe: "We found the jorōgumo. Shi Miao Xing and Venerable Santini are handling it."

"Are they?" Elias asked. "Then, why is it still screeching?"

"That's Maria. She can't put her body back together, and . . . she's *pissed.*"

Elias was overcome by a morbid curiosity—or perhaps he just wanted to assure himself that Maria was no longer a threat. He ventured out onto the moonlit grounds, toward the woods, where Ana had found the manananggal's lower half. He followed the frustrated shrieks until, in the stark moonlight, he saw Maria fumbling away from the slow advances of Shi Miao Xing. He followed her at a distance, merely observing as she dragged her doll-like lower half through the woods. Every few paces she snapped her head around to glare at the monk, grunting and screeching; then, with a final burst of strength, she lifted herself into flight and vanished beyond the treetops, still dragging her useless lower half.

Shi Miao Xing turned to Elias. Gently, he said: "There's nothing we can do for that one. Not at the moment." He beckoned Elias and started back toward the abbey.

13

"Is it going to die?" Elias asked.

He and Lamia stood on the riverbank, watching as the kappa trudged silently toward the water. The sound of its footsteps was drowned out by the rushing waters, turbulent after a rainstorm; black currents swirled and collided, forming large crests that gleamed white in the moonlight. Lamia shivered in the cool night air and wrapped her sanghati more snugly around her shoulders.

The kappa seemed unaffected by the cool night air. Elias supposed it was unaccustomed to warmth. He watched as the creature plunged into the current without the slightest hesitation. *I should do the same*, Elias thought. *Jump in, and quit worrying about being swept away.*

Wen, realizing that the kappa couldn't just "go home," decided to take advantage of its sense of obligation: He commanded it to scour the riverbed once again for the astra.

Elias had offered to drive the creature back to the river for the search. As he watched the lonely figure disappear into the dark waters, though, he regretted the decision.

"If Venerable Dorje uses the phurba on it, yes, it's going to die," Lamia said. "The phurba will evaporate a kappa. It isn't human. It's a manifestation of a demonic spirit. It will die and return to the cosmic wheel, to be reborn in some other form." She flashed a sympathetic smile at Elias. "That's my belief, anyway."

"That doesn't seem fair," Elias murmured. "It doesn't seem demonic. It just seems sad."

"Did it just seem 'sad' when you encountered it in the bathroom?" Lamia asked.

Elias recalled his horror at the creature's glaring yellow eyes and frightening teeth. "Point taken." He felt suddenly cold; he shoved his hands into his pockets and turned away from the churning water. "Let's go."

They headed for the parking lot, passing several noisy twenty-somethings who were headed out for a night of fun—probably for Bull's-Eye, based on the faux leather "Forbidden Friday" attire that peeked from their jackets. Elias wondered if the club was still operating, or if the absence of Andrei and co. had left it in suspension.

"Energy doesn't actually die," Lamia continued in a reassuring tone. "The kappa will become something else, something not demonic—but like everyone else, it will always be susceptible to demons."

Elias thought of the kappa's slouched, weary-looking posture as it crossed the riverbank. "We're not making it less susceptible by keeping it under our command. It needs to be shown compassion."

"I agree."

"Let this be the last time we give it an order," Elias said. "If the kappa has been looking all these days and nights for the astra and hasn't found it, it's probably well hidden."

"Don't you want to recover it? Leitha might still be in danger."

Elias gave the bhikshuni a knowing look. Lamia was probably just testing him. "It's better off in the river," he replied.

They drove to the abbey in silence. Lamia seemed deep in thought, and Elias also had serious matters on his mind.

When they reached the monastery, Elias put the car in park and said, "Can you stay a few minutes? I need to talk about something."

"Sure. What is it?"

Elias didn't respond right away. His chest suddenly ached, and his eyes filled with tears. Lamia waited patiently while he composed himself.

"There's . . . something I found out," Elias said.

"What is it?"

"I've been thinking for a while about looking up my stepdad on social media." Tears spilled over Elias' eyelids. "And, this morning, I finally looked. There's this place . . . it's a performing arts camp for kids. They teach kids how to be circus performers—tightrope walking, aerial maneuvers, gymnastics, stuff like that. And that bastard is a volunteer there. He's an assistant coach and does stage support."

Lamia nodded. Moonlight streamed through the windshield, illuminating the bhikshuni's eyes; Elias saw understanding and compassion there, shining and gentle in the rough, weathered face.

"I've been thinking about what I should do. Like, do I send them an anonymous warning, and tell them what kind of person he is? There's this number I can call to report people like him, and I've been thinking I should call them first, to ask for advice. But . . . ." Elias blinked away another set of tears. "I'm really scared." His voice shook as he said the words.

"I know," Lamia said.

"I'm really, really scared. I'm going to need help."

"I know, Elias. We'll do whatever we can."

Elias reached into the center console and pulled out a handful of tissues. He wiped the tears from his face and neck. "I'm just going to call and ask questions at first," he said, "until I feel like I'm brave enough to talk about what happened. I actually tried calling today, but my hand shook so much when I picked up the phone. I got sick to my stomach, and I couldn't do it."

"Come here as often as you need to," Lamia said. "You can come to prayer, if you want, but we won't pressure you to do that. Just come if you need a friend. You can call them from here if you want. I'll sit with you."

Elias nodded. His eyes blurred again, and blinking didn't clear them. Lamia's moonlit face was distorted, and her eyes invisible, but Elias felt the sudden press of her hand around his own.

He bowed his head, sniffling, and felt himself begin to shake—and then the bhikshuni's arms were around him. "You'll be okay, Elias," Lamia said. "We'll always be here for you, and we'll support you."

Elias sobbed quietly into her shoulder. She held him until his trembling ceased, and then she released him with a quiet sigh. "I never thought I would be out past curfew," she said, "lurking in the shadows with my arms around a man."

Elias laughed and wiped his eyes. "You're not really hiding. The moon is putting a spotlight right on you. Anyone who looks out the window will see you breaking your vows."

She chuckled. "I'm not breaking any vows. I'm like you; I'm ready to take another step forward. I'm taking my vows more seriously than ever." Lamia smiled, her radiant eyes once again visible in the moonlight. "Formalities exist for a good reason, but if I need to ignore a formality to show true compassion, then it's the right thing to do." She squeezed Elias' hand again. "Will you be okay to drive?"

Elias nodded. "Yeah."

"I meant what I said. Come over or call us any time—whenever you need us."

Elias spent the next few days struggling to catch up with his work. His time at the abbey had set him back, but he managed to focus long enough to meet the week's deadlines. On the third day he made a short phone call to the This Is Not An Excuse hotline. He asked a few general questions and then hung up. It seemed a good first step.

He was considering calling again when Wen texted him: *I'm going to the river. If the kappa comes up, and no astra, what should I do?*

Elias texted him back: *Don't go yet. Wait for me.*

A couple of hours later they were gathered with Ana, Vela, Shi Miao Xing, and the kappa in one of the abbey's meditation rooms.

Wen gave the kappa a cushion to sit on, and he held one of its rubbery hands as it made itself comfortable. Elias was glad he wasn't the one who had filled the kappa's water reservoir; he'd endured two car rides with it, and though he pitied the creature, its quiet presence in the backseat made him uneasy. It was only when he looked directly at it, and saw its child-like form and melancholy eyes, that his unease dissipated.

The kappa's yellow eyes suddenly flicked to Elias, its gaze fixing on him, and Elias resisted the urge to look away. He didn't want the creature's last moments to be laced with revulsion and fear.

Quietly, Vela began to chant. She knelt behind the kappa, holding the phurba close to its neck, moving it down the creature's spine and up again. The kappa's eyes closed. It sat still, its body upright but relaxed, the face set in a neutral expression, as if in sleep. At length, Vela held the blade against the creature's neck, at the place where the spine joined the skull—and the figure vanished, as if it had been a mere projection that was suddenly switched off. Nothing

224

remained of the creature except for a fine layer of gray dust that settled on the cushion and floor.

Wen moved closer, examining the cushion. "It's gone," he said softly. "I feel kind of bad. I know that thing was dangerous, but whenever it was with me, it just seemed like a sad little kid."

"It isn't sad anymore," Vela replied. "If you feel bad about it, just remember the look of peace on its face as it transformed."

The bhikshuni swept up the little bit of dust that was left. She collected it in a dustpan, to be buried behind the garden.

Vela walked beside Elias as the group headed outside. "Have you heard from Leitha?" she asked.

"No," Elias said. "Bull's-Eye is closed, and I checked the places she used to hang out at, but I haven't run into her. I suppose Lucian hasn't made contact, either."

"No. It's possible that he's still a basilisk. Lucian must have been in a tremendous amount of pain; it may be one reason he transformed. A basilisk is insensitive to its own pain."

"He became a basilisk to save me," Elias said. "Without being monsterized, he couldn't have fought against those three. They would have torn us to pieces." He paused. "Even if he isn't a basilisk, though, he probably feels ashamed. It seems like a lot of monastics feel like they're not good enough to be at a monastery. Lucian probably feels the same way—like he doesn't deserve to be here, or to be protected by you."

"There's no such thing as being good enough," Vela said. "Following the path is a consistent choice, and you can make that choice regardless of your past. Lucian knows that, but it's true that he struggles with forgiving himself."

Wen spoke up: "For what? I mean, what did he do?"

225

"He was arrested for drug possession," Vela replied, "but he confessed to us that he helped Andrei run a drug and prostitution ring. He had enough guilt because of that, but I'm sure there were other things he did, things related to his monsterization."

"It would be pretty tough to get past that," Wen said, "and then to cause trouble for the monastery on top of it. We had a whole mahatmas-versus-monsters battle because of him."

"When you're farther along this path," Vela said, "you'll realize that there is no real distinction between mahatmas and monsters. They're the same person, making different choices—but both can change. A mahatma is not invulnerable to ruin, and a monster can always transform into something greater."

"But there are only a few people considered worthy of being called mahatma," Elias replied. "That's a pretty clear distinction."

"What I mean is that we are all on the path to becoming a mahatma: someone who is great-souled, someone who has made a long-lasting effort to conquer the darknesses in their soul. It takes time, but if you look at the end of all journeys, you will find the same result—even though it may take a thousand lifetimes for some."

"That sounds exhausting," Ana said. "I want to do it in one or two lifetimes." She paused. "At least two. Maybe three or four. This lifetime is too soon."

They reached the garden, and Vela used a small garden shovel to bury the little bit of dust. The wind had blown some of it away and scattered it across the lawn, but Shi Miao Xing said that it was appropriate, as ashes were often scattered rather than buried.

"What's next?" Ana asked. "The windows have been fixed, the monsters have been taken care of . . . ."

"The website needs updating, we need lunch prep and a menu for next week, we need to find another volunteer videographer, and Shi Miao Xing needs that ride to the airport," Vela said. "There's plenty to be done."

Ana cast a mournful look at the monk. "You're going to be missed. Thanks for kicking butt and saving our lives."

The monk laughed.

"This is a really sad moment," Ana insisted. "We just buried someone, and our group is breaking up. Venerable Santini and Venerable Ajahn Chah are gone, Lamia is in Taiwan, Wen is going to China for a month, and now Shi Miao Xing is leaving."

"We have five other guests who are returning," Vela reminded her.

"Yes, but they weren't part of *this*." Ana gestured to the little patch of disturbed soil. "I feel like we should have a reunion next year, or something."

"That's attachment," Vela said. "We should be open to whatever opportunity comes next."

"It's gratitude," Ana countered. "We should at least make a commitment—that if there's ever another problem with monsters, or something else that needs to be kept secret, we'll show up and fight together."

Shi Miao Xing chuckled. "Venerable Dorje and I have already made that commitment."

"We haven't, though." Ana turned to Elias and Wen. "The three of us should make a pact."

"I'm in," Wen said.

"We have to make an actual pact." Ana stuck her hand out, holding it palm-down toward Wen. "Elias, come here. Put your hand on ours."

"I don't think that's necessary," Elias replied.

"Come on, Elias." Wen placed his hand on Ana's. "Don't be such a snowflake. Touching someone's hand won't kill you."

Elias scowled, but he moved closer, placing his hand above Wen's.

"Elias, just put your hand on his hand," Ana said. "Like he said, touching his hand won't kill you. Let's make a pact: that if we're needed again, we'll show up. From now on, we're . . . Dharma Friends."

"I'll show up, but I'll pass on the Dharma Friends thing," Elias said. "Dharma Friends is the name of the prison outreach newsletter—the one that goes to criminals."

"So what? You told me you committed crimes, so don't be judgy."

Elias' eyes narrowed. He glowered at Ana as best he could, but she smiled and placed her free hand on his. She pressed down, and then pushed upward with her lower hand. "Dharma Friends forever! Too late, Elias; you're one of us now."

He shuddered and withdrew. "That's so cheesy. Let's get going. We have to get Shi Miao Xing to the airport."

"I have plenty of time," the monk replied, but Elias started away down the hill.

He heard the thump of Ana's clog sandals as she hurried to catch up with him. She walked beside him for a few paces, and then said: "You're not really mad, are you?"

"I'm just cringing," Elias replied. "Deeply and thoroughly cringing."

Ana glanced back at the others. In a low voice, she said: "I hope you don't mind me talking about it, but Lamia told me that you're thinking of reporting your stepdad."

"Of course she did. Bhikshunis talk about modesty and respect, but they're the world's biggest gossips."

"She wanted to make sure you have support. She knows I've been through the same thing, so . . . ."

"Don't tell anyone else," Elias said. "I don't want other people to know. It's okay if you know, because . . . I kind of trust you."

Ana gave him a doubtful look. "Do you? Since when?"

"Since I spent four minutes staring into your eyes." Elias looked at her, direct and solemn, and then broke his gaze away. "You seem okay, and Wen is okay, but I don't trust other people."

"But, Elias, that's the abuser's tool," Ana said. "They try to make you feel ashamed and afraid because that's what keeps you quiet, and that's how they don't get caught. If someone abused you, you should be able tell everyone: 'That person is abusive. They need to be held accountable, and they need to be stopped.'"

"It doesn't matter what you say when people prefer not to believe you," Elias retorted. "People choose not to believe because they don't want to be accountable."

"You still have the right to speak," Ana said. "I didn't want other people to know either, for a while. I just wanted to fix things with my mom, and then she convinced me that if I spoke up, people would think I was a crazy liar, and that I was an ungrateful child who would stab my own mother in the back—but that's what made me realize I needed to speak out. I knew that she was projecting shame onto me so that I would keep my mouth shut."

"That's not the same," Elias said. "I was abused differently than you."

"But he's using the same tactic. It's his shame, not yours. He's projecting it onto you to protect himself."

"It doesn't matter. We live in a culture where people are fascinated by other people's pain; it's just a source of gossip and morbid entertainment for them. I've been looking at this website that talks about reporting abusers, and it claims that even if you're an adult, your identity will be protected by the news media—but I know that's not true. Reporters will refrain from mentioning your name, but they're not interested in protecting victims of abuse. They're interested in divulging the most details to gain the largest readership and make the most money. There was a kid at my school who reported an adult man for molestation, and the news media never mentioned his name, but they described everything that came out during the court trial: his age, the neighborhood he lived in, his routine, his relationship to the perp, and specific details about what happened. After all of that information came out, *everyone* in that town knew who the victim was. This was in middle school, and other kids were not kind to him. They bullied him so badly that his family packed up and moved away. Adults aren't any different. They love to judge, question, and stomp all over the victim."

Ana considered that in doleful silence. "Well, you're not wrong," she said at last, "but I don't think most people are entertained by stories of abuse. I think most people are genuinely repelled."

"They're not repelled. People also seem to love mysteries that revolve around women and kids being molested or murdered—or both. Look at our popular TV mysteries and novels, and you'll find plenty of those stories."

"Maybe they just want to read the part where the perp gets caught, or they want to know how to handle it if it ever happens to them—or to someone they care about."

"It's a nice thought," Elias said. "I don't buy it."

Shi Miao Xing retreated back to the abbey for his meager bit of luggage, and the others waited in the front courtyard.

Ana and Wen practiced tai chi in the middle of the court, while Vela and Elias sat beside the Buddha statue, watching.

"When is Lamia coming back?" Elias asked.

"In a month. She has to go through another series of trainings before the actual ordination."

"Do you think she's ready for it?"

"Yes, she's more than ready. I think that watching Venerable Tseten and Venerable Sonam has helped her. They've both committed crimes, but neither they nor Lamia have committed offenses that could prevent them from becoming ordained bhikshunis. They served their sentences, paid their debts, and gave back to society through volunteer work. I think Lamia needed to see people who hurt others in the past, but who overcame their pasts and obtained ordination." Vela gave Elias a humorless look and added: "When she returns, you'll have to call her by her dharma name."

Elias sighed. "Can I call her by the shorthand name? Ven. Whatever?"

"That is also appropriate," Vela replied. "You should also start calling me properly."

"Your name is hard to pronounce. Besides, Aarya always called you Vela. I blame her."

"Aarya met me years ago, when I was running my qigong practice. And she was stubborn. She told me that if she was ordained, she wouldn't want to change her name, and that Aarya Khurana would be just as good a bhikshuni as anyone else. She even called the Dalai Lama by his birth name, Lhamo." Vela laughed. "She didn't want to become a bhikshuni, though. She had other plans."

"I know," Elias said softly.

"What about *your* plans, Elias? Are you still practicing qigong?"

231

"I've been doing tai chi," he replied, "and it's just as boring. I'll keep at it—but it's not because I want to make another astra. I'll try to do what you said: learn to manage qi, so I can become the astra." Elias paused. "Maybe in thirty or forty years, or in my next life, I'll get there."

"It's easy to judge the arts harshly when you don't understand them yet," Vela said. "It's especially tough in this culture, where people want instant results."

"I agree. I totally misjudged qigong—and you, too. I used to call you the 'potato nun' because . . . well, you barely eat any protein, and—"

"What?"

"—you're kind of pasty and pale, like potatoes," he finished.

"Ah," she said. "I *look* like a potato."

"No offense."

"As you can see, I am outraged."

"My point was," Elias continued, "that you don't seem particularly strong, and you go around giving all these speeches about peace and non-aggressive conflict resolution, but I've found out that you're actually a badass."

"So you say."

"You can kick ass when you need to," he added.

"I didn't, though," Vela replied. "Neither literally nor figuratively."

He looked sidelong at her. "Venerable Georgia?"

"Dorje," she corrected him.

"Venerable Dorje. You're a badass. Just accept it."

She looked at him wryly, but she smiled.

They sat watching Wen and Ana. Wen had deep bruising on his wrist from the vajra, and he and a few of the monastics had needed stitches—but the pain was subsiding; the wounds were healing; Venerable Norbu and the other monastics were expected to make a full recovery. Wen was smiling and chatting away, the sun gleaming on his black hair as it peeked from behind a cloud and doused the court in sunbeams.

"I overheard you talking to Ana," the bhikshuni said suddenly.

"Of course you did. And now you'll go and tell all of the other nuns what we said."

"No, not this time. You can bring it up with us when you need to. I just think it's good that you're talking to Ana." She smiled as Ana and Wen, who were trying to mirror each other's movements, broke down into laughter. "I let her become involved for both your sakes," she added.

"What do you mean?"

"You both need friends. For your part . . . ." The bhikshuni paused. "Ana and Wen are good people. They're kind, they're brave, and they seem fun. And perhaps most importantly, they're open and honest. People who are willing to be vulnerable can help crack other people open."

Elias considered that, trying to overcome his grudging sense of self-righteousness. "Do I need to be cracked open?"

"Everyone does, to some extent."

She's evading my question, Elias thought. "But what about Ana and Wen? They're kind, they're honest, they'll be a good influence on me. Right? So, what do I have to offer them? Or am I just a recipient of their charity?"

Ven. Dorje looked at him, her eyes full of compassion—the kind of compassion that conveyed reverence rather than pity. "You will offer the same," she said. "Kindness. Bravery. And don't look at me like that—like you can't offer those things. Whatever you think you lack, I've already seen it in you. You must be willing to bring it into the light, instead of keeping it hidden." She kept her gaze on him, her eyes seeming to glow with the conviction of her words. "You will be a great person, Elias. You need to forgive yourself and move on."

Shi Miao Xing came, then, with his "luggage": a small cloth bag containing his passport, an extra set of robes, a bowl, and a few toiletries. As the group headed for Elias' car, he joked about baggage fees and getting through customs, and about the time he was detained after "stupidly" trying to bring a safety razor on the plane. Shi Miao Xing mimicked his interactions with customs officials whose language he couldn't speak, pointing to his band head and rubbing his bare chin, saying: "It's for haircut! Shaving! No hair allowed! My hair, it grows too fast! I need razor!" By the time he got into the backseat, he had the group laughing; the somber mood of only minutes ago was lifted.

Aarya's "Kinda happy" playlist came on as Elias started the car. He had cued it up for the kappa, hoping to bring some joy into its last minutes. An Amber Run song was in mid-play now, an a cappella piece that sounded like it had been recorded in a chapel; it was about love, the kind of song Elias usually bristled at, but there was something sacred in its sound—and something melancholy. When Elias had first heard it, he thought it belonged on the "Moody" playlist. He could feel Aarya nudging him in that song, speaking to him through the words. The song spoke of using someone as inspiration, of positive growth despite sorrowful loss.

Elias heard his own plea in those words: *Aarya, I won't lose sight of you. I've kept my promise. I've come so much farther than I thought I could . . . but I miss you. I miss you so much.*

Elias hesitated with his hand over the gear shift. He looked in the rearview mirror, at the image of Shi Miao Xing and Wen laughing in the backseat. The monk was still talking about razors: "We try to reject plastic because we don't want to harm the earth, but plastic disposable razors are one of our favorite donations. We get so excited when we see them, because we can shave without bleeding all over our robes."

The song continued, celebrating the finding of love in near and unexpected places. Elias tuned out, then, not wanting the others to see him getting emotional—but Ana, beside him in the passenger seat, must have noticed it. She suddenly stopped laughing and stared at Elias with a mixture of delight and surprise.

For the first time ever, she had seen him smile.

Author's Note

This novel explores many Buddhist concepts, but I don't claim to be any kind of expert on Buddhism. I relied on numerous conversations, lectures, and writings by Buddhist monastics to create this story—including Dharma Friends, which is the name of a newsletter created for people who are incarcerated. The website *No More Excuses* is loosely based on the website *This Is Not An Excuse*, an actual website for people who are thinking about reporting abuse, or who simply need someone to talk to.

If you enjoyed this novel, please consider leaving a review somewhere online, such as Goodreads or any online bookseller. Indie books have very few opportunities for exposure. Reader reviews are our main way of signaling to the public whether our stories are worth reading, so if this book made any impression on you, please let others know.

I dedicated this story to Robert Fusaro Sensei, my Shotokan karate teacher of many years (first at college, then at the dojo). He was welcoming, profoundly skilled, and dedicated to his art, and he practiced a kindness and generosity that seemed rare at the time of our meeting. He was often deeply perceptive and could often tell when something was wrong; he was bold and insistent in his teachings, but he also had a quiet way of pulling people aside and encouraging them to share their troubles. When I was the one going through a tough time, he sensed it immediately. He listened, took me seriously, and offered help. I dedicated this book to him because I often thought of him while writing about the martial arts aspects—particularly about the compassion and strength of the practitioners, and the ultimate goal of the art. Fusaro Sensei has served as one of my role models; his way of balancing strength and compassion is something I strive for.

I'll end with a quote from Gichin Funakoshi (the founder of Shotokan Karate) that was displayed at our dojo, one very relevant to this story:

"The ultimate aim of the art of karate lies not in victory or defeat, but in the perfection of the characters of its participants."